LOVE
STAR

LOVE
STAR

a novel

Andri Snær Magnason
Translated from the Icelandic by Victoria Cribb

Seven Stories Press
New York

Seven Stories Press
140 Watts Street
New York, NY 10013
www.sevenstories.com

College professors may order examination copies of Seven Stories Press titles for a free six-month trial period. To order, visit http://www.sevenstories.com/ textbook or send a fax on school letterhead to (212) 226-1411.

Book design by Jesse Heuer

Library of Congress Cataloging-in-Publication Data
Andri Snær Magnason, 1973-
  [Lovestar. English]
  Lovestar : a novel / Andri Snær Magnason ; translated from the Icelandic by Victoria Cribb. -- 1st English-language ed.
    p. cm.
  ISBN 978-1-60980-426-8 (pbk.) -- ISBN 1-60980-426-0
  I. Cribb, Victoria. II. Title.
  PT7511.A49L6813 2012
  839'.6934--dc23

                                        2012028468

Printed in the United States

9 8 7 6 5 4 3 2 1

SEED

A seed becomes a tree becomes a forest green as a carpet.
An egg becomes a bird becomes birds fill the sky like clouds.
An egg becomes a bump becomes a man becomes mankind, manufactures cars, writes books, builds houses, lays carpets, plants forests, and paints pictures of clouds and birds.
In the beginning all this must have been contained in the egg and the seed.
Forest. Birds. Mankind.
A human egg is not heavy but the first egg held the kernel of all that later came to be:
love, joy, hate, grief, art, science, hope.
In the beginning there was nothing but a seed.
Everything grew from that seed.

Man could create everything but life.
It was scientifically proven.
Man could kill life and destroy life and change life,
he could cultivate life, multiply life, kindle life from life,
but he could not create life, still less a seed.
So there is nothing more precious than a seed.
A man sat in a jet as it soared over the Atlantic at
*   three times the speed of sound.*
He had found a seed.
It rested in his hand.
If anything happened to the seed all hope would be lost.
Of course he didn't know that all hope was lost any-
*   way.*
He would be dead within four hours.

ARCTIC TERN / STERNA PARADISAEA

WHEN THE ARCTIC TERNS FAILED TO FIND THEIR WAY HOME ONE spring, appearing instead like a storm cloud over the center of Paris and pecking at the heads of pedestrians, many people thought the world was coming to an end, and that this would be the first in a long series of calamities. They stockpiled canned food and hoarded water, and waited for a plague of locusts, droughts, floods, or earthquakes, but nothing happened, at least not in Paris. The aggressive terns overran public parks and traffic islands, but the locals soon grew used to them and old men were able to sit on benches in peace as long as they carried a bag of sardines to placate the birds.

The terns no longer flew from pole to pole. Summer nights in the Arctic were screech-free and peck-free; summer nights in the Antarctic likewise. The birds' innate sense of direction had become confused, and some instinct informed them that their global position was correct, that they were undoubtedly on the right spot north of the Arctic Circle. The city must have sprung up while they were away down south. The older terns were irritable and disorientated but the first generation of birds in the city knew nothing other than traffic noise and human crowds. The terns soon became one of the typical Parisian sights. Tourists could buy postcards with pictures of a tern-white Eiffel Tower and street vendors tried to press people into buying bags full of guppy fish to feed them. This didn't bother the terns, and as no predator was directly dependent on them it didn't significantly upset the balance of nature either.

A few seasons later, Chicago filled up with bees as if it were covered with honey, though in reality there was barely a tree or flower to be found. On weather satellite pictures a black depression seemed to cling low over the city, a gray swirl twisting anticlockwise around a black epicenter. The bees buzzed and droned and stung and drove the citizens mad. The only answer was to poison them: planes specially designed to extinguish forest fires flew back and forth, dusting the city with insecticide. Yet the bees continued to be drawn there and so the poisoning continued until the last citizens finally abandoned the place.

Eventually the streets were covered with a one-foot-thick layer of fallen bees carrying seeds and pollen on their feet. Flowers sprang up in every nook and cranny, putting down roots among the dead bees. Vegetation climbed the walls of the skyscrapers and spread over the sidewalks. The largest glass buildings turned into greenhouses, hot and damp, full of reptiles, insects, and tropical plants sprawling unchecked from their pots, while other buildings resembled huge beehives full of honey, which oozed down the walls and between the floors. Bears got wind of the city from as far away as Alaska. They licked the buildings, birds fluttered from flower to flower, and the poor took their life in their hands and ventured into the city in search of valuables and honey.

In the center of Chicago a golden pond of honey formed, which trickled along the streets, over squares, and dripped into the drains, absorbing every imaginable scent and substance that crossed its path. Those in search of unusual sensations tried spreading it on bread and found that the world and time itself turned as golden, viscous, and sweet as honey.

Shortly after the bees lost their bearings around Chicago, monarch butterflies began to behave oddly as well. Each year, for as long as people could remember, the butterflies flew in enormous swarms across the United States to Mexico where they would hibernate for the winter. The hibernation forest would turn red with monarchs as they clustered on every trunk, branch, and leaf. But one autumn the monarch butterflies flew in the complete opposite direction. Instead of heading south to their wintering grounds, they flew north. People tried to redirect them with giant fans and nets; they were trapped from helicopters and taken to the butterfly forest by force. But some instinct was telling them to fly north and that's what they did the moment they were released. They set a course for the North Pole and swarmed around it until they froze in the air and fell to earth like giant snowflakes. They continued to flutter north until the ice cap around the pole was red with monarchs. Polar bears, wandering around in the camouflage they had evolved over 10,000 years, could now easily be spotted from miles away. When the white blobs moved over the butterfly-patterned carpet of snow, the seals yawned and slid unhurriedly through holes in the ice. The polar bears almost died of starvation; they didn't have 10,000 years to turn orange. But eventually they learned to roll in the butterflies when their pelts were wet, and if enough monarchs froze to them they became invisible again. Their tracks remained white but the seals weren't smart enough to beware of white tracks with sharp teeth approaching at speed.

People soon began to suspect the reason for all this: the world was so saturated with waves, messages, transmissions, and electric fields that animals were reading all sorts of gibberish from the air. When four jumbo jets crash-landed the same day exactly five miles from their intended destination, people began to seek a substitute for these waves in earnest. A monarch butterfly weighing ten grams could travel one thousand miles without the help of a satellite. An Arctic skua could fly year after year from its nest on Melrakkasletta in north Iceland to its favorite rock east of Cape Town in South Africa by instinct alone. Creatures with brains the size of a nut, seed, or piece of fluff could do this, yet humans with their heavy heads would have needed eighteen satellites, a receiver, radar, maps, compasses, a transmitter, twenty years' training, and an atmosphere so thick with waves that it had almost ceased to be transparent.

No one could prove that the waves were harmful to humans, but people were ready to believe it and that was enough—the rest was mere detail. The world was radioactive. Everyone who got ill, with anything from leukemia to a cold, blamed the waves. "Put on a hat!" mothers would tell their children. "It'll protect you from the waves. Otherwise your hair will be electrified and steal your life force!" "Put on your gloves, son! Bare fingers are like lightning rods that attract waves." "Keep a stone in your left pocket and a small bottle of water in your right. That'll balance the flow of energy."

Legal proceedings were initiated weekly against the world's most popular radio and television stations for the most unrelated problems blamed on wave pollution. Fanatical members of radical protest groups blew up microwave transmitters and broadcasting towers, but these incidents were generally hushed up by the media to prevent an epidemic. It was mainly newspapers that covered such stories, as their sales increased in direct correlation to the number of towers blown up.

Scientists shook their heads over the public's stupidity, academics refused to take the field of study seriously, and doctors continued to insist that waves had no proven effect on the human body. In an old hangar at Reykjavik airport, however, a small international group of ornithologists, molecular biologists, aerodynamicists, and biochemists had gathered to dabble in waves. Day and night they worked, dissecting and examining terns, pigeons, bees, salmon, and monarch butterflies. They were driven by the unshakable belief that it was possible to unlock the secrets that lay behind the navigation instinct. The organization was called LoveStar, as was the head of the company himself. No reasons were given for the name and people soon gave up expecting a sensible explanation.*

The LoveStar research department's motto was simple: "Everything has substance. The complex exists, the strange exists, the incomprehensible exists, the unexplained and imaginary exist, but the supernatural does not exist, though nothing is ruled out." In the laboratory, scientists pondered questions such as how a shoal of fish could spin round on the spot as if they had a single body, without it being possible to detect a message passing between them. Or how a flock of birds could fly in perfect unison, as if controlled by one mind.

Measuring equipment was developed that could detect signals so weak as to be at levels formerly considered supernatural. This is where the firm's strength lay, and it wasn't long before the LoveStar experts were on the trail. They discovered how to transmit sounds, images, and messages between human beings using birdwaves that were weak, harmless, and could be picked up by devices as light as a butterfly's brain. They had found an unexpected and fabulous virgin territory for science, one that would eventually free mankind from cords and render copper wires, fiber-optic cables, satellites, and microwave transmitters obsolete. The discoveries of LoveStar's Bird and Butterfly Division transformed the world in a matter of a few years. The "cordless man" arose, freer than a monarch butterfly and with a keener sense of direction than a skua.

---

* When the satellite companies went bankrupt, the firm's name soon made sense. LoveStar paid some Chinese astronauts to tie a bunch of satellites together and make them twinkle over Mt. Hraundrangi in the Oxnadalur valley in northern Iceland. This was a literary reference to a romantic poem called "Journey's End" by Iceland's beloved nineteenth-century poet, Jonas Hallgrimsson, in which the poet described a star of love shining over the lava spire. Hence the name: LoveStar.

Forty years after mankind was freed from cords, the LoveStar headquarters had long since moved out of the old hangar at Reykjavik airport. It was now located in the excavated mountains and lava spires of the LoveStar theme park in Oxnadalur valley, which the corporation owned.

On the surface, plovers scurried, a vixen barked, a raven croaked, and a shepherd herded his sheep. Smoke curled from a turf-roofed farm and a bearded farmer would recite verses when he was in the mood. The landscape looked exactly as it had for the last thousand years, but the surface was only a shell, and once in a while, people were shown an unexpected glimpse of the world that lay beneath. Sometimes a rock would open and a blue-clad woman spread out a white cloth to dry. Sometimes steam rose from the hayfield as if a hot spring boiled below.

If the shepherd had disobeyed his father's orders and climbed the rocky hillside behind the farm, passed over the heathery slopes and flowery dells, scaled the sheer crags, screes, and rock falls to lie down flat on the mountain peak and gaze upon the world beyond with his own eyes, he would never have been the same again. The other side of the mountain was a 2,300-foot-high perpendicular wall of shining glass, as if someone had sliced off half of the mountain along the length of its ridge. Vehicles waited in ranks at the bottom of the neighboring Hörgárdalur valley, while tens of thousands of people streamed like ants in and out of the giant main entrance with its 2,200-foot-high ceiling. Sometimes clouds formed up in the dome where seabirds, who slipped in through the air-conditioning ducts, soared silently in rings like white angels. The lobby could hold one hundred thousand people at a time and the whole structure was made of polished stone and glass.

The mountainside from the Oxnadalur river up to the spire of Hraundrangi (now rechristened LavaRock) was a heathery shell over the most stupendous labyrinth ever built by man: chamber after chamber, vault after vault, gallery after gallery, with no danger of claustrophobia because of the stupendous view. The galleries and restaurant looked out over the unspoilt, romantic Oxnadalur valley through carefully camouflaged windows built into the cliffs, while those who had a view through the glass wall over Hörgárdalur valley could watch black airships floating by.

Three or four air vessels, each the size of a steamship, hung over the nearby Myrkárjökull glacier at any one time, lowering freezer containers marked "LoveDeath" into cold stores underneath the ice. Blinding flashes rose from the peaks at regular intervals as launchpads catapulted rockets into space, bright as comets. The clouds billowing behind them were mirrored in the glass wall, on which a giant star was painted with golden letters: LoveStar.

No one was permitted to walk on the unspoilt surface of the Oxnadalur valley apart from the inhabitants of the protected farms and LoveStar himself. On fine days he could be seen strolling through the valley dressed in a white suit with a hat and brown cane. He was generally accompanied by a black dog, an old dog that LoveStar had owned five times before. When LoveStar walked around the valley, the protected inhabitants of the farms pretended not to see him, though their children watched him walk into the rocky crag and thought he must be God.

When this story took place, LoveStar was sitting aboard his plane on his way north to Oxnadalur. In his hand was a seed. The scheduled landing time was in four hours and fifteen minutes. He had only three hours and fifty minutes left to live.

A CORDLESS
MODERN MAN

THE CORDLESS MODERN WORLD HAD AS LITTLE AS POSSIBLE TO DO with cords and cables — not that they were called cords or cables anymore. They were known as chains, and gadgets were known as weights or burdens. People looked at the chains and burdens of the past and thanked their lucky stars. In the old days, people said, we were wire-slaves chained to the office chair, far from birdsong and sunshine. But things had changed. When men in suits talked to themselves out in the street and reeled off figures, no one took them for lunatics: they were probably doing business with some unseen client. The man who sat in rapt concentration on a riverbank might be an engineer designing a bridge. When a sunbathing woman piped up out of the blue that she wanted to buy a two-ton cod quota, bystanders wouldn't automatically assume this was addressed to them, and when a teenager made strange humming noises on the bus, nodding his head to and fro, he was probably listening to an invisible radio. The man who breathed rapidly or got an erection at an inappropriate time and place probably had his visual nerve connected to some hard-core material or was listening to a sex line. (There was no limit to the filth that flooded through the connected minds of some people, but of course it was impossible to ban them from filling their heads with obscenity and violence. You might as well ban thinking.) If someone stood beside you and asked: "What time is it?" and you answered right away: "It's half past nine," the person would respond, even though there was no one else in sight: "Thanks, but I wasn't talking to you."

Indridi Haraldsson was a cordless modern man, so the average person could not tell if he was going mad or not. When he spoke to himself in public there might be someone on the other end of the line. When he laughed and laughed it might be for the same reason, or he might be listening to a comedy station, or he could have a funny video playing on the lens. In fact it was impossible to tell what was going on in his head but there was no reason why it should be anything abnormal.

If he ran down the street shouting: "The end of the world is here! The end of the world is here!" most people assumed he was taking part in a radio station competition for a prize of free hamburgers. When he rode naked up and down the shopping center escalator seven times in a row people assumed something similar. It was difficult to tell what prize he was competing for because he was naked and people could only guess his target group from his hairstyle, age, and physical build. Indridi was twenty-one, thin, and pale-skinned, with fair, dishevelled hair, so he was definitely not the target audience of a radio station that advertised bodybuilding, sports cars, highlights, and solariums. He had no tattoos or piercings, so he wasn't the target of the station that played rock and punk and advertised raw beer, unfiltered moonshine, and high tar cigarettes. He was naked and unkempt and definitely didn't belong to any of the more sober target groups. Maybe he was a performance artist. Artists were always busy performing. Perhaps the escalator scene was worth three points on the College of Art's performance art course. Or he could, of course, be in an isolated minority target group. There were plenty of them around, but generally an attempt was made to direct people into a popular area where they could be reached more economically.

If Indridi suddenly barked at someone: "IIIIICE-COLD COKE! IIICCCCCE-COLD COKE!!!" for ten seconds without his eyes or body seeming to match his words, the reason for this behaviour was simple: the advertisements being transmitted to him were directly connected to his speech center. People assumed he must be an ad howler. He was probably broke enough to fall outside most target groups, so it wasn't worth sending him personal advertisements. But it was possible to send ads through him to others by using his mouth as a loudspeaker. Those who walked past howlers could expect an announcement like:

"IIIIIICE-COLD COKE!"

This was more effective than conventional reminders on ad hoardings or the radio. So when Indridi met a man on his way to the parking lot, he howled:

"FASTEN YOUR SEAT BELT! SLOW DOWN!"

The man had been arrested for speeding without a seat belt. As a punishment he was made to listen to and pay for two thousand edifying reminders from ad howlers. That was probably the best thing about the new technology. It could be used to improve society.

"LOVE THY NEIGHBOR!" howled a shady-looking man at half-hourly intervals. A rehabilitated murderer, people would correctly assume, giving him a wide berth. Prisoners could be released early if they howled for charities or religious groups.

Howlers were not all broke. Many were simply scrounging for discounts or perks, and some only became howlers for the first three months of the year while they paid for the latest upgrade of the cordless operating system. Those who didn't get their system upgraded could have problems with their business or communication. Cordless home appliances and auto door-openers only recognized the latest system, and the same applied to the latest car models, so they wouldn't automatically slow down if someone with the old system crossed the road.

If Indridi came across a group of teenagers he might yell: "GROOVY SHOES! YOU WERE UNBELIEVABLY COOL TO BUY SUCH GROOVY SHOES!"

Getting someone to buy a product first and then arranging for them to be praised afterward was a revolutionary new strategy. It was believed to strengthen behavior patterns and bring things into fashion earlier.

The announcements were sometimes absurd, sometimes just one word, slogan, or phrase, unconnected to anything else. In that case it was probably part of a longer campaign, a so-called teaser campaign that encouraged people to think long and hard. On the way down the high street you might meet an old woman who said out of the blue: "Smoothness!"

Further down you might meet a teenager who said: "Smartness!"

And even if you veered round sharply and headed up the next street, you would hear whispered from a basement window: "Reliability!"

Finally somebody would come racing down a side street on a bike shouting:

"FOOOORD! FORD!"

These campaigns always hit their marks; there was no way of escaping them. Everything was measured to within half an inch and the announcement was perfectly tailored to the recipient's target group, which was categorized down to their most minor eccentricity. The howler system was efficient, simple, and convenient, and ordinary citizens could order a howler for a small fee if they needed a reminder.

"You have a meeting with the minister at three o'clock and don't forget your wedding anniversary!"

Those who had recently moved to the city liked to order a howler or two to greet them on the street or strike up a conversation.

"Hello, Gudmund, what lovely warm weather we're having!"

This made the big city seem less cold and unfriendly. Uprooted farmers who wanted to wake up to a rooster call could get their neighbors to crow at 6:00 AM if they were lucky enough to live near a howler.

"Cock-a-doodle-do! Time to wake up!"

Many entrepreneurs felt it essential to receive a confidence boost first thing in the morning:

"You're the best!" said the Chinese cleaning woman.

"No one can stop you, Magnus!" said the shifty caretaker.

"You're looking good!" said the taxi driver. "Today's a day to win!"

Passersby were prepared for anything, so no one paid any attention when Indridi sat in a café and wept. He cried his eyes out in a corner, but few people thought to ask him what was wrong. It was probably Greek tragedy week with his target group. Or he could be an advertising trap.

"Why are you crying?"

"I want a Honda so much, they're such great cars, and there's an amazing offer this week."

Advertising traps or AdTraps went further than howlers; they hired out not only people's speech centers but also their primitive biological and emotional reflexes. The method was still technologically imperfect so sometimes traps couldn't stop laughing or crying for days on end.

Many people let themselves be persuaded to become traps, as it paid as much as ten conventional speech-center ads and was generally more effective, especially if people were made to do something funny like wet themselves, cry in public, or say to a woman with a howling baby:

"Now would have been a good time to have 100 percent absorbent Pampers!"

When the cordless, connected modern man emerged on the scene with his lens and invisible earpieces, most borders were broken down. For example, it was never possible to know where a company's parameters really lay. If Indridi met an old school friend in public, he could never tell whether the school friend was actually "serving" him. After some small talk (which, on reflection, did begin with the words: "Hi, Indridi, can I help you?") the conversation generally ended the same way:

"It's clouding over," said Indridi, "better get going."

"Oh, that doesn't bother me, I've got an excellent umbrella. Can I offer you an excellent umbrella like this?"

"No thanks. There might be a thunderstorm. Don't want to be hit by lightning."

"Oh, I've got such a great insurance policy with LoveLife. I got the umbrella as a freebie when I bought this great insurance policy with LoveLife."

It was clear that the old school friend was a secret host and his conversation was slanted toward his goal of selling an umbrella or insurance. The offer was like a drain, and every single conversation was doomed to be sucked down that drain, regardless of what was originally being discussed.

Family:

"How's your mother?"

"She's fine, she's got such great life insurance with LoveLife . . ."

Art:

"What did you think of Jonas Hallgrimsson's poem?"

"I wonder what sort of life insurance they had in the nineteenth century. LoveLife hadn't been founded then . . ."

Sports:
"Good game yesterday."
"Yes, poor Gisli—torn ligament—I wonder if he's covered for that. I'll look him up at LoveLife. You're insured with them, aren't you?"

It was difficult to distinguish a secret host from anyone else, so people didn't always know whom it was safe to believe and trust. A host could be anyone, even a member of one's own inner circle. Unlike traps and howlers, secret hosts advertised on their own initiative. A good secret host was careful not to give himself away and alternated products regularly. Some sold nothing directly; they merely advertised by creating the right mood or image.

"I recommend this *film*, you should go and see this *film*, it's supposed to be a really good *film*. I'd go right now."

Secret hosts sometimes worked as spies and sent reports to iSTAR (the LoveStar Mood Division's Image, Marketing, and Publicity Department). Only a handful of managers worked in the iSTAR office; the rest were cordless modern people, scattered around the globe, drawing their information from a database on Svalbard.

iSTAR had no problem collecting basic information about culture consumption, television viewing, radio listening, food bills, musical tastes, daily journeys, main interests, and opinions, but more detailed information could come in handy. Hosts and spies twisted their conversations around to the company's interests, while iSTAR experts got to be a fly on the wall. A discussion among a group of friends about love, death, God, or friendship could abruptly take a U-turn when the spy asked out of the blue: "Did you think the politician's tie was tasteful? What about his opinions? Do you sympathize with them? What about the last major international conflict? Do you remember how many civilians were killed? Would you put up with a greater loss of human life if you listened to more pop news? The president has a cute little cat called Molly. Do you find him more likeable now? What about the disabled? Are they fun? Would you take a cut in your standard of living in order to provide them with more services? What do you really think of Madonna?"

Indridi was on his way home that day, but no one said to him encouragingly: "Hello, Indridi! You're looking good today!" as he couldn't afford such luxuries. On the way up through Rofabaer he began to sing "Yesterday." All the howlers in town were singing "Yesterday" at that moment; it was part of a publicity campaign for an international song initiative the following week. The song echoed round the town, but it was hard to tell who was singing voluntarily and who wasn't. It wasn't considered cool to be a howler, so many people pretended to be singing voluntarily by doing their best to look as if they were loving it. To most people, Indridi appeared a living, light-hearted advertisement. Their lenses showed the notes pouring from his head along with the lyrics, which hovered cheerfully in the air, and a message from the sponsor:

"Sing and be happy! International song week starts on Monday!"

When the song was over, Indridi had to fight back tears. Something unbelievably important had been struggling to emerge from his mind, but he had lost the thread when "Yesterday" began. His life was going to the dogs and everything was upside-down; only a few weeks before life had been as sweet as a strawberry, love as golden as honey, but now he wasn't sure that his love would be waiting for him when he got home.

INDRIDI WASN'T
USED TO CRYING

INDRIDI WASN'T USED TO CRYING. HE HAD NEVER REALLY HAD ANY
reason to cry. His life had gone smoothly and almost without a
hitch since his rebirth. Most people agreed that he was a good
boy, but it was virtually the only thing they could find to say
about him.

"Indridi, he's a good guy," said his friends.

Indridi was a fine, honest, promising kid who had received a
good upbringing with decent parents in a tasteful house in the
suburbs. He was lucky to be alive and owed it to the fact that
he was born at a time of ethical uncertainty. When Indridi was
born it was, for example, permissible to keep two frozen tubes
containing spare copies of each child. If you had a child and lost
it, you could resurrect it by having the same child born again
using special "doctors" who undertook the "rescue procedures"
(Chinese women, fertilized abroad, brought over in the eighth

month of their pregnancy). Ninety-seven percent of parents who lost a child got over the loss within two years if they resorted to a spare, while those who had a different child recovered late or never. Those who resorted to a spare had, technically speaking, not lost a child; their child had had a narrow escape. Research showed that the long-term effect for the parents was similar to that of relatives of people who lost their memory. In reality the spares merely lost their memory and their lives were delayed by a few years.

But like all new technology, rebirth was inevitably overused and the rules were interpreted loosely by both individuals and businesses. The existence of spares made some people irresponsible, and Indridi's parents would probably have taken more care the first time he was born if it hadn't been for the spare copies held by the insurance company.

Indridi had not always been a good boy. He was a spare copy of the Indridi who had been born five years earlier. Of course, he had no memory of that period of his life, but his family showed him photos and home movies so he felt as if he remembered various things. The first time he was born he quickly became the most nightmarish child anyone had ever known. Not only was he naughty, he was also cheeky and foulmouthed from the first stages of language acquisition. His first word caught on film was "cunt." Indridi was a liar, aggressive, easily influenced, and an intolerable crybaby to boot. He was diagnosed as completely amoral, egocentric, and incapable of empathy. He seemed incapable of "empathizing with emotional parties in his environment," to quote the insurance company advisor's report following his four-year-old test. His mother had addiction problems at the time and was incapable of looking after children, while his father worked from dawn to dusk in the loading bays at LoveDeath. When he came home, more often than not stinking of "money" and wanting to "cuddle," his mother had to knock back doubles to dull her sense of smell. On top of that they were inexperienced in bringing up children and at the insurance company's five-year-old test their parenting was judged a complete failure. The specialist compared the results to a computer model projected on the wall behind him.

"As you can see, it would take a major statistical miracle to save this specimen from bad company, drinking, smoking, vandalism, and drugs, and it would not surprise anyone if he took to crime at a very early age. Has he stolen anything from you?"

His parents thought.

"He often takes biscuits without asking," said his mother.

"And once he took a cuddly kangaroo out of a toy shop and set off the alarm," said his father. "But that was a year and a half ago."

The child-development specialist continued, "All the findings indicate a downward trajectory. You can see that here in 3-D."

"Cool 3-D," said his father.

"It's new," said the specialist smugly. He pressed a button and one of the bars in the bar chart began to move, grew hands and feet, danced back and forth across the screen, then took a pie chart and smashed it in the face of a fearsome-looking Venn diagram.

Mother and father laughed. "That was funny."

"That big ugly bar chart is your boy," said the child specialist sternly, and their laughter was abruptly silenced.

"Now I get it," said the father. His target group was not mathematically inclined so the chart had to be lively and amusing for him to understand it. "Yes, now I get it," he said again, to emphasize his words.

"What can we do?" asked the mother.

"You must understand that there is no way we can insure individuals of this type; the premiums would cost you both your annual wages. I'm talking here about the damage he will in all probability cause others. As far as he himself is concerned, he would be 100 percent liable for his own damages, with no health insurance."

"That could become expensive," said the father. Drug rehabilitation for a youngster who was not insured could cost as much as a family home.

"Are you sure he'll be that bad?" asked the mother.

"I could show you examples all day. Nearly every prisoner in the city jail got better marks in his five-year-old test than your boy."

"But we're working on him," said his father. "We're finally taking a vacation together, and I'm quitting LoveDeath this summer and starting a job at iSTAR. We're getting ourselves sorted out. Can't we just have a review this time and then see how his six-year-old test goes?"

"As you can see, not a single child has reached adulthood unscathed when burdened by statistics like these. By six he could already be causing untold and irreparable damage."

Once this would have been counted as a final, statistical death sentence for Indridi because the research results did not lie. They were based on the most stringent assessments, psychiatric personality tests, and astrological charts. But Indridi had had the great luck to be born at a time of uncertainty when no one knew any longer exactly how to define an individual. Individuals must make their own definition of the individual, said individualists, and so the matter was settled. The insurance company offered Indridi's parents a unique opportunity to learn from experience and "rewind."

"We can offer you the opportunity to rewind around five years and then you can make an effort from the outset to protect the individual from lifelong unhappiness. Wouldn't it be better to rewind now and ensure one hundred years of happiness rather than get stuck with ninety-five years of misery? In reality he'll gain five extra years. Wouldn't you want to add five years to your own life if you were offered the chance?"

Indridi's mother was a bit doubtful, but it was the same lecture she had heard from most of her friends. She'd lost count of all the old ladies who had taken umbrage at Indridi's bad language and snapped: "Why hasn't this child been rewound and taught some manners?"

"Are there no other options in this situation?" she asked. "We really wanted to get the upbringing over and done with before our fiftieth birthdays. We've been paying installments on a world cruise."

The specialist leaned over the table with a grave expression. "People have sued insurance companies abroad because this opportunity was not exploited. A man in England was sent to prison when his son murdered an old woman. During the investigation it emerged that he had been repeatedly offered the chance of rewinding the boy but had been too stubborn. So it was actually his fault."

"When could we 'rewind'?" asked the father.

"According to the definition of the individual that you have selected and the spare copies that were filed at the time, your boy could get a new life in ten months' time, as soon as the end of October. Of course, the premiums will go down immediately as a result, which will weigh against the cost of the procedure."

On the wall the dancing bar chart was now replaced by a flashing sign:

> 10,000 points a year! 10,000 points a year!
> + 15% discount on car insurance!
> Only for the next five minutes!
> Choose now!

Mother and father looked at one another while the clock on the wall counted down. The ideology suited cordless modern people, and they had been brought up with the concept since childhood. It was like wiping a hard disk, or starting a computer game with three lives so that when things went wrong you could always start over.

"As soon as this autumn, yes," said his father, looking through the glass wall to where Indridi was chewing the head off a Barbie doll.

"But then he wouldn't have the same birthday, would he?" said his mother. "His birthday's in February. Won't it be difficult for him to adjust to the change?"

The advisor demonstrated to them how Indridi would get on better under a different star sign. His faults in Aquarius would turn out to be positive advantages in Scorpio. His aggression would emerge as determination and perseverance instead of erupting at regular intervals as an outlet for repressed rage and introverted feelings. As a result, instead of being quick-tempered, irritable, and impatient, he would be hypersensitive and painstaking under a star sign that suited his genetic makeup.

"He's got his father's temper, but that's not seen as a disadvantage in your family unless the star sign conflicts. In his case it's like oil and . . ."

"Fire?" said his father in consternation.

"FIRE!" yelled his mother. Indridi stood in the middle of the room behind the glass wall, the doll in flames.

"How did he get hold of a lighter?"

His father stamped on the remains of the Barbie doll and the melted plastic stuck to the soles of his shoes.

"INDRIDI, REALLY!" yelled his mother, chasing him round the room. "DO AS YOU'RE TOLD, INDRIDI! COME HERE AT ONCE!"

"This autumn?" asked the advisor, looking at the clock. He had got up and was now standing in the rays of the projector, "10,000 points" flashing on his forehead. The countdown had reached twenty-nine seconds.

"This autumn!" shouted the father as he pursued Indridi down the corridor.

The wait for autumn proved hard. Especially during weekends when Indridi wasn't at school. Finally the day of his "rewinding" came, and the advisor greeted them with a smile. Indridi was wet-combed and dressed in his Sunday best with a blue bowtie.

"Where am I going, Mom?" he asked.

"You're going through that door," she said, pointing to a black door, "then you'll come back out of that white one, and it'll be your birthday and we'll give you a present."

"Goody," said Indridi, "thanks, Mom," and kissed her on the cheek before being led by the advisor through the black door.

Before his mother could utter a word, there was a sound of joyful singing from behind her. A nurse and the advisor carried Indridi out through the white door. His face was red and rumpled and his body covered in white birth fat. He was bawling.

"He weighs nine pounds and four ounces!" said the nurse with a tender smile. "Congratulations. Hopefully he'll get on better now."

"Oh, he's so tiny," said his mother, her eyes filling with tears.

She took him in her arms and Indridi soon stopped crying when his mouth was plugged with a bottle.

"Here are his clothes," said the advisor, passing them his folded Sunday best.

"Where's the blue bowtie?" asked his father, glancing around, but the insurance advisor pretended not to hear him.

"This is a fine boy! He'll soon grow into his clothes again."

For whatever reason, Indridi's upbringing succeeded much better this time around. His mother went into rehab and his father started as a service rep at iSTAR and so no longer stank of his job. Indridi received extra special care, attention, and rewards for being well behaved and good. He was made to watch film clips showing that he had once been naughty and bad and what would happen if he didn't learn from the experience.

"That's what you were like on your last fourth birthday," said his parents and showed him a home movie in which he was bashing his little cousin over the head with a plastic sword. "You must be good now."

"Otherwise we'll have to start you all over again, Indridi son," said his father. "We'll get there even if it takes twenty years for you to become a good, well-behaved ten year old!"

Indridi was determined to do well and feared nothing more than the third test tube, which was waiting to take his place. He never felt truly secure, never felt he did well enough, and always wanted to do better (thanks to his Scorpio star sign). He was in perpetual competition with Indridi number three, who could no doubt outdo him in anything he turned his hand to. His parents were a great support to him and from them he received precisely the amount of love and warmth that research demonstrated was necessary for children. His father was proud of his son but never completely satisfied and so encouraged competition with number three.

"Amazing," his father might comment from behind the morning paper, "if you had been born today we could have used these exciting new theories. Look! They result in a 30 percent increase in reading speed, 9 percent greater emotional maturity, and 18 percent improved concentration. Look how exciting the school syllabus for eight-year-olds is nowadays! The kids stay in school till seven in the evening."

He continued reading, but Indridi lost his appetite and went straight up to his room. Just a few weeks later he had achieved a 30 percent increase in his reading speed and an 18 percent improvement in concentration.

Indridi longed for nothing more than his sixteenth birthday, because then it would be impossible to rewind him again.

"It's too late to improve oneself after the age of sixteen! There's no turning back, remember, my dear boy," said his father, patting him on the shoulder in a fatherly way.

Indridi achieved stunning results in his end-of-school exams. He was near the top of the class with an average grade of 9.3 out of 10. He had friends, had been active on the social scene, and played sports, but as he helped his parents prepare for his graduation party he still wasn't sure of himself and couldn't stop himself asking: "What happens now?"

"You have your future ahead of you, Indridi dear," said his mother in nasal tones. Her new nose was still under wraps. She'd had it grown especially for his graduation as her old nose had long gone out of fashion. The new nose was supposed to be beautifully curved with neat, round nostrils. She was blonde, in keeping with the summer fashion, and brown eyed because it was Wednesday. Indridi coughed.

"Yes but, what'll happen to Me number three?"

His mother and father smiled teasingly and looked at one another.

"Indridi, we meant to tell you a long time ago."

"The law was changed shortly after you were born," said his mother. "The individual was redefined in the old way."

"It's no longer legal to rewind. It hasn't been for fifteen years."

"Then where is Me number three?"

His mother laughed and his father slapped his thigh.

"He was disposed of when the rules were changed and the insurance company's rebirth department closed down!"

"But he was a good model for you," said his father.

"Which is why we were advised not to tell you."

"Yes, he acted as a motivator and so became part of you. Just as number one served as a warning of the dark side that you didn't want to become, number three was the perfect model, the goal you could never achieve."

"Without him you'd never have turned out so well."

"HAS ME NUMBER THREE BEEN THROWN AWAY?"

Indridi looked disbelievingly at his parents, who smiled and carried on kneading the dough for his marzipan cake.

"Don't look at us like that. You wouldn't have been so successful without constant motivation from number three."

"We can't be forever using fairies or bogeyman to get children to do better, can we now?" asked his father, searching for something on the table. "Pass me the icing sugar, love."

Indridi tore open the freezer door and snatched out a frozen green tube.

"What's this then? Isn't this Me number three?"

His father roared with laughter. "No! That's a green popsicle."

"An Ice Breaker," added his mother.

Indridi's mother and father got up and began to break-dance around the kitchen while the world spun before Indridi's eyes. He had never really quarrelled with his parents. Now he felt as if he should have screamed and raged, but his upbringing had been so successful that he could do neither. He was simply not made that way, and when it came down to it he felt his life had been perfectly okay. His future lay ahead. His parents continued break-dancing and he could do nothing about it. He burst out laughing and joined in.

"We were only teasing," said his mother.

"You really fooled me," said Indridi, break-dancing.

Indridi lay awake that night. All his life he had been so petrified of number three that he hadn't even rebelled as a teenager. He had often crept into the kitchen in the dead of night and felt tempted to defrost number three but had always chickened out at the last moment.

He had never had a reason to be a difficult teenager as such. Relations were generally harmonious in his home; he was allowed to stay out as late as his friends, and he had everything he wanted given to him on a plate. All doors were open to him. But now all the neglected possibilities ran through his mind. "I should have gone abroad as an exchange student, I should have sailed to South America with LoveDeath, I should have tried going to sea and getting into fights at port, I should have kissed Gugga when she offered me the chance, I should have thought about the future and finished high school quicker by studying during the summers, but then of course I'd have had to give up South America and the trawlers and Gugga . . ."

He felt confused; there were so many possibilities that his head was ready to explode. He connected himself to REGRET and asked: "What would have happened if I'd sailed to South America with LoveDeath instead of attending my senior year of school?"

The answer came straight back: "You would have died."

"Good," said Indridi, and a weight was lifted from him. "I'm glad I didn't go on a cruise with LoveDeath."

"Do you want to know more?"

"No, thanks. It's a good thing I finished high school. Otherwise I'd have died."

REGRET enabled people to put their past in order and get to grips with new circumstances. The world followed certain laws. If a stone was dropped from a height of fifteen feet it was possible to work out the speed at which it would land, so it was also possible to work out what would have happened if Indridi's 160 pounds had turned right and not left at a given moment in the past, the domino effect it would have had on everything else in the world, what would have happened afterward, and so on. REGRET could work it out. It was LoveStar's brainchild. People needed only to call REGRET or send an email and the world was worked out in advance and the answer came right back. The remarkable thing about REGRET was that it didn't matter how often people asked: What would have happened if . . . ? The answer was almost always along these lines: You would have died.

Death was the best of a bad bunch. Other possibilities included disablement and, in some cases, the end of the world, and it was all scientifically proven. In this way REGRET helped people come to terms with life, the world, and their fate.

For Indridi REGRET fulfilled the role of dreams and nightmares. He found the thought of life hanging on such a narrow thread absolutely terrifying, but there was no point in brooding on it too much as life didn't come with an instruction book indicating which steps led to fortune or ruin. Indridi sometimes ordered in-depth information about the gory deaths that one small sideways step would have caused him:

"I see that your right arm would have been located at: [N64°05.536' W21°55.321']. The front left wheel of the bus would have been on that exact same spot at the same instant. Forty fractions of a second later your head would have been under the rear left wheel of the bus and four seconds later I can see part of you, probably the guts, wrapped round the front wheel of a Peugeot 205GR. Would you like an artistic or pictorial transcript or will an oral account be sufficient?"

"It's okay. I'm satisfied. I'm glad."

"Do you still have regrets?"

"No, I have no regrets."

"Good. That'll be 1,300 points."

REGRET was intended to bring the world closer to happiness. Unhappiness was nourished by regret on the one hand and fear of the future on the other. The more the choice of possibilities multiplied, the more complicated and difficult life became. People lived in one world, but beside that world there were a million other worlds that could have been. People could regret countless life-paths that they could have taken in the past.

Every single neglected opportunity was a burden on the present. But that's not the whole story. In the future there were millions of new possible choices and millions resulting from each of those millions. Finally, when one choice was chosen over another, something rather remarkable occurred: everything that was not chosen was converted into regret. As a result, people were forever crushed in the present, under the weight of the future, on top of the pressure of the past, and things did not get any better. The choices multiplied and regret increased in direct correlation until people could not move and became tangled in an invisible web. At this point REGRET came to the rescue and set the past in order. According to REGRET, every single decision people made was the ONLY CORRECT decision. Every single sidestep would have led to death or the end of the world. Every single person had been in mortal danger and only just escaped by making the ONLY CORRECT decision. So people had a duty to be happy. They had survived against all the odds.

Five years later Indridi was still a very good boy, and he was glad he had never rebelled or got into any other stupid messes. He didn't need REGRET to tell him that. Otherwise he'd never have met Sigrid when he went out to celebrate his graduation at the dance in his old high school. She had just started the same summer job as him, in the gardening department of LoveDeath's energy section, but he hadn't yet had a chance to talk to her. He had seen this beautiful girl pulling up chickweed on the other side of the Ellida river. She wore a white sleeveless top and orange waterproof trousers and wore her hair in two plaits. Next, she was standing on the landing of the old high school with her girlfriend. She smiled and their eyes met and from that moment on they were always together.

Sigrid was beautiful, good, and fun, and she was still like that more than five years later. Their relationship might've been going to the dogs but Indridi was still head over heels in love with her, though he no longer knew whether his love was returned. "Yesterday" echoed in his head. He walked with heavy steps up the stairs to their apartment, a knot in his stomach, opened the door to the second floor and called:

"Sigrid, honey. Are you home?"

He closed his eyes, fought against tears and wished fiercely and in earnest that life could be like it was before. When love was red as a strawberry and life was as sweet and golden as honey.

"Sigrid? Are you home?"

LEMON SUN

LOVESTAR SAT ALONE IN HIS JET, SOARING SOUNDLESSLY OVER the Atlantic. The scheduled landing time was in three hours and fifty minutes at the LoveStar headquarters in Oxnadalur. He didn't dare move because in his hand he held a tiny seed. An hour ago the seed had been green and seemed to quiver but now the quivering was fainter. He thought the seed looked gray, though the grayness might have been caused by the lighting in the plane.

There was a knot in his stomach. LoveStar had had a greater influence on the world than any other man in history. Everything he touched had turned to gold, but in his hand he held a seed that seemed only to be turning gray. He didn't know what it contained, but it was sure to be more powerful than an atom bomb.

Though everything had gone according to plan, LoveStar didn't know what would happen next. As a rule he'd had ideas for the next twenty years, but now he was quite empty. In fact he had been empty for some time, having developed a sufficiently strong immune system to ward off stupid ideas.

It was a long time since he had slept the whole night through. He invariably jerked awake, feeling as if someone were whispering in his ear. As if someone were sitting on his chest, almost suffocating him. He didn't dare sleep with the light off any longer. He was distracted at board meetings, lost the thread, was oblivious to questions, and couldn't come up with any answers when asked. He often sat alone at night, waiting for news of the search. Generally he sat at a glass table drawing, writing, or doing calculations. There was nothing he could do but wait. In the days before he boarded the plane, he'd sat in his office with a white sheet of paper in front of him, calculating:

> For God, every day is like 1,000 years
> every hour 41.67 years
> every minute 0.69 years or 251 days
> every second 0.012 years, which is 4.2 days
> a moment is a day.
> The speed of light is 186,000 miles per second, so light travels 186,000 miles in 4.2 days, according to God's sense of time.
>
> The speed of light from God's perspective is therefore around 0.5 miles a second or 1,845 miles an hour. That's three times faster than the top speed of an empty jumbo jet.
>
> For 1,000 years in Your sight are like a day.

He looked up, listened, then continued his calculations: "I'm 71 years old. I've lived 25,992 days. For someone who perceives each passing day as 1,000 years I am almost 26 million years old. Humans sleep for three centuries. When they wake up in the morning they take five days to open their eyes. I don't need to sleep for three centuries; just now I slept for a third of a moment. That's eight hours in God-time. It's half-past two. I haven't closed my eyes for 100 years."

Putting down his pen, he got up and looked in the mirror. He closed his eyes and opened them. He used to do this sometimes when he was small. By opening his eyes quickly he tried to see what he looked like with his eyes shut. He closed his eyes and opened them. His palms were sweating and his hands shook. The maid came in and drew white curtains across the windows. She was carrying a round plate on which there was a slice of bread spread with honey.

"Chicago?" asked LoveStar.

The maid nodded.

LoveStar looked at the bread. A round slice of bread spread with golden honey. Sun on a white plate. LoveStar took a bite out of the sun; it looked like a waning moon and his tremors vanished. Two bites, and he chewed slowly until the world and time turned golden and viscous. He looked back in the mirror and saw himself sitting with closed eyes chewing the golden honey.

"I can see myself dreaming."

When he saw himself open his eyes in the mirror it was night again. He'd managed to leapfrog a whole twenty-four hours. His thoughts were still viscous when he sat down and continued writing.

"Every day is like a thousand years and a moment equals a day. God can stroke a bird in flight or pluck flies out of the air. Even if he goes to Africa and comes back after a whole God-year, little will have changed because barely two minutes will have elapsed in the world of men. A fragment of a second equals an hour and in an hour a fly will have buzzed half a long-drawn-out buzz, a taxi driver's diesel engine will have turned two revs. The noise of the engine is a heavy drawn-out purr. The driver says something on his walkie-talkie but he who perceives each day as a thousand years would take a whole week to listen to the sentence. For a whole hour nothing has been heard but a long drawn-out [ä].

"In three hundred years' time the sun will crawl above the eastern mountains and its light will take about five seconds to flood over the whole city. Like lemon concentrate pouring from a round spout, the light will flood from the sun, covering the city like resin, and, coated in this, people will move so slowly that it will take them a whole year to brush their teeth. But perhaps the light is more like honey because when it oozes under your eyelids, you wake up and murmur, 'Mmmm honey . . .'"

The old cord-phone on the desk rang, disturbing further calculations. It emitted a shrill tone and LoveStar twitched at every ring. He looked at the phone for a good while before picking up the receiver.

"Hello."

It was the leader of the search party.

"The search was successful," he said solemnly. "We've found the spot. It all ends in one place."

"What did you find there?" asked LoveStar.

"We don't know," said the search leader, "but we've found the spot."

"What did you find there?" asked LoveStar in a tremulous voice. "WHAT DID YOU FIND? WHERE DOES IT ALL END?"

The search leader was silent.

"Answer me!" LoveStar looked at his shaking hand.

"No one dares to look. No one dares to go anywhere near the place."

"Damn it . . ." said LoveStar and looked around. He suddenly felt there was someone listening. "What are you going to do?" he whispered.

"I don't know," answered the search leader. "I simply do not know."

"What about you?"

"I'm not going anywhere near it. I've got a wife and children at home. You can fire me, sir, but I don't dare go anywhere near."

LoveStar slammed down the receiver.

He went himself.

He found a seed.

Which is why he was sitting in a plane with a seed in the palm of his hand and an infinitely heavy sensation in his chest. His heart was like a broken egg. The shell jabbed into his spine, diaphragm, and lungs, making it difficult to breathe. His suffering would soon be at an end. The honey sun would never again flood under his eyelids. He only had three hours and thirty-three minutes left to live.

HONEY

WHEN INDRIDI AND SIGRID'S LIFE WAS SWEET AS HONEY, THEY woke in the morning sunshine as if glued together with it. Not intoxicating Chicago honey but pure, golden, sugary royal honey. Palm clasped to palm, bodies pressed together, and legs so entwined that it was hard to see which foot belonged to which body.

"Honey," murmured Indridi and removed his tongue from Sigrid's mouth to say good morning, but she pouted and sucked his tongue back between her lips, hugging him closer and clamping her thighs around him. They lay like this for a good half hour, and although he was inside her, they weren't exactly having sex. It was more an extension of their embrace, a question of maximum unity and surface contact. The feeling that they were not only one soul but also one and the same body.

Although they found it almost impossible to tear themselves apart, they crawled together into the living room, more like an eight-footed spider than a cartwheel on its spokes, and when their mouths parted at last she let fall a word. Just one tiny word and then the dam burst because the word precipitated a chain reaction in their brains. The words flowed in and out of them like a cycle. Biologists would have said that they were nourished by the word-synthesis that streamed through them, round and round. They lay on the floor for a good while, talking and giggling and fooling around because together they were as complete and true as a circle.

They were not nourished by words alone but also by silence. When they fell silent the silence was so rich and the feeling so resonant with meaning and understanding that when one of them broke it with a word or sentence it was frequently to add to what the other had just been thinking.

Of course, Indridi and Sigrid had to work like other people and after they made love on the kitchen floor while they were waiting for the kettle to boil, Indridi managed to use the last of his strength to free himself from the honey-glue and Sigrid slipped into a jumper and panties. With a combined effort they were able to get dressed and part their lips long enough to eat breakfast, though without completely ceasing to touch. Then they gazed long and deep into one another's eyes to say a reluctant: "Bye, see you at lunchtime."

But love had not had its final word. They left the house together and Indridi stood on the street corner, staring after Sigrid as she walked backward along the pavement toward the geriatric unit down the road. Indridi used hand signals to let her know if she was steering into flowerbeds or bushes. When she reached the junction she stopped and blew Indridi a kiss before taking the big step: out of sight. It was as if a cloud had covered the sun. Their hearts beat lonely and forlorn in their dark rib-casings and they missed each other so inexpressibly much that they just had to ring:

"Where are you?" asked Indridi.

"I'm here around the corner."

"Do you miss me?"

"Yes, I miss you."

"Shall we take a peep?"

"Yes, let's peep one more time."

They retraced their steps, peeped around the corner, and waved to one another. Sometimes they couldn't stop themselves from running back together and letting a few beautiful words flow from lips into ears where they turned into a thrilling, tingling electric current that undulated like the Northern Lights over the dark surface of their brains. Indridi held her around the waist and they gazed into each other's eyes.

"I missed you," he said.

"It's so hard to part," said Sigrid, looking apprehensively at the geriatric unit down the road.

"See you at lunchtime," said Indridi.

"Bye," said Sigrid. After the good-byes they stood speechless for ten more minutes, neither able to take the first step, until at last they said "one, two, go" and ran straight to work without looking over their shoulders; they were both late.

At lunchtime Indridi and Sigrid would sometimes cycle down to the harbor and sit in a café on the docks. Above them towered the Statue of Liberty, a one-thousand-foot-tall statue of Leif Eriksson straddling the harbor entrance with moles under his stone feet. It was LoveStar who donated the giant Viking hero to the nation, the largest statue of liberty in the world, which bore a suspicious resemblance to LoveStar himself. The statue stared out at the restless sea, eternal flames of liberty burning in his eyes to guide the snow-white cruise ships as they sailed to land like capelin-laden trawlers. When the gangway was extended, a thousand impatient, love-craving customers poured from the ship and hastened as fast as they could go north to the ever-green Oxnadalur valley where sheep bleated, foxes yapped, love was proven, and LOVESTAR twinkled behind its cloud.

On fine days trucks would stream back down south with piles of lovers cuddled up in soft hay, then dockworkers would strap the couples into harnesses and they'd dangle over the harbor like eight-footed horses before being lowered into the ship's hold. Indridi and Sigrid had half an hour to word-synthesize. In their eyes glowed happiness itself, bright as LOVESTAR.

Indridi and Sigrid's love had grown in the five or so years that they had been together, and their love was not just a little seed in their hearts but had put down roots and tentacles all over their bodies, right into the extremities of their limbs, making their fingertips as sensitive as clitorises. When Indridi and Sigrid held hands they stroked their middle fingers together, causing a strangely thrilling sensation to spread through their bodies and calling forth a mysterious smile upon their lips.

Many people regarded Indridi and Sigrid's love as an obstacle;

Sigrid's mother went so far as to call it a handicap. Indridi and Sigrid had, for example, both given up being cordless modern employees. They had made many attempts to enjoy the free, flexible working hours—at home, at the summer house, or on a romantic beach—but it never worked out in the long run. If no one insisted that they be at a given place at a given time, they got nothing done and were tempted to steal a kiss or caress, which ended often enough with them lying cuddled up and satiated in bed.

So Sigrid gave up her career as a cordless construction engineer and got a job at a geriatric unit where she tended to old people before they were sent north to LoveDeath. Her mother, who had grander ambitions for her daughter, regarded the job as beneath her dignity and talents.

"Did Indridi push you into this meat processing?"

"Don't call it meat processing, Mom."

"But you're not a *free* person!"

"Freedom doesn't suit us, Mom," said Sigrid, smirking at the thought. "We don't get anything done."

"Does Indridi have to be glued to you the whole time?"

"It's me too, Mom," said Sigrid. "He's not the only one who wants to stick together."

Indridi had sacrificed his career as a cordless web designer and got a job tending and cultivating the grounds around the Puffin Factory. They took quite a drop in wages, but Indridi and Sigrid had no regrets. According to REGRET it was just as well they had got together, otherwise Indridi would have been killed outright in a car accident while Sigrid would have ended up an addict and drowned during a swimming-pool party.

While Indridi and Sigrid sailed through their days on a pink cloud, Sigrid's mother saw nothing but a black shadow looming over them.

"Sigrid dear, I've booked you an appointment with a specialist."

"Oh?"

"You're so young and innocent. It'll be such a shock for you when you break up."

"You needn't worry about me," said Sigrid archly. "We're never going to break up."

"Statistics, Sigrid dear," said her mother, shaking her head. "You can't beat statistics."

Indridi and Sigrid weren't about to let any statistics overshadow their love. Those who were interested could let their eyes wander and follow their lives in their cozy apartment at: Hraunbær90(3fm).is. A healthy and cordless modern person had nothing to hide (and nowhere to hide). If someone crushed or swore at the recording butterflies that flitted everywhere, people would ask: "What's he got to hide, anyway?" and rumors would begin to circulate.

Indridi and Sigrid lived in an endless apartment block, which wound around the old Coke factory that had been converted into the Puffin Factory. It not only bred puffins for the LoveStar theme park in Oxnadalur but also honey-scented roses. When Indridi opened the window in the morning the house was filled with the fragrance of roses and honey, and "Eat me! Eat me!" sounded from the Puffin Factory across the road and echoed all round the neighborhood.

The Puffin Factory was a gigantic space. The puffins not only had to be on show in the LoveStar theme park up in Oxnadalur, they also had to be conspicuous in the countryside on the way there. Trucks packed with puffins went out daily to distribute them on hillocks along Highway One. They could hardly be bothered to move and so were easy prey for predators, but that did not matter too much as the production cost of each puffin was small compared to the pleasure they afforded passersby.

The Puffin Factory was built following the unprecedented popularity of romantic movies based on Jonas Hallgrimsson's life, which LoveStar had produced at the opening of the Oxnadalur theme park. These were pretty powerful films. People who came to the country afterward had high expectations of being inspired or enthralled and often experienced severe disappointment. According to surveys there were two things that principally got on people's nerves. Firstly, LOVESTAR could not always be seen twinkling over the peaks of LavaRock and, secondly, the birds people saw from the bus window were nothing to write home about. When guides pointed to a puffin and said: "That's a puffin, the bird from the romantic poems, the bird from the romantic movies," some grumpy voice would always call out from the back of the bus: *"Das ist nicht der Vogel in dem Gedicht. Drichf thef of in fluc!* That ain't the bird I came to see!" And without fail the whole group would chorus the final verse uttered by the poet when his true love had been crushed by an avalanche, the love star had fallen, and the poet had thrown himself in despair from LavaRock:

O, black bird with the rainbow beak
Wings of love and feathers sleek,
So beautiful like babies' hands
Best of birds in all the lands
O, Puffin, sing your song to me
A dream of summer it may be
O, Puffin, will you fly with me?
Will you bring my love to me?

Even as the poet recited this verse, the puffin was flying to him through the snowstorm with a message from his true love in its beak: she had not died in the avalanche but lay trapped in a farmhouse. But just before the puffin reached him, the poet threw himself off LavaRock, and his lover starved to death in the snow.

In the movies about the poet, *Wings under the LoveStar* and *The Boy from Deep Dale*, CGI was used to recreate the puffin as it should have looked in the poet's time. The audience gasped with delight as the puffin hurtled through the storm and wept when it fluttered around the poet with the letter as he fell, and even the hardest-hearted were reduced to tears by its mournful song when the poet was crushed on the rocks.

The locals found it desperately humiliating when tourists asked repeatedly: "Oh, is that a guillemot?" Ornithologists (sponsored by a tourist authority interest group) opined that the puffin had repeatedly mated with guillemots or even razorbills or some other such lowly bird. There had been sightings, and photos were published in the papers. And of course there was no way of knowing what the puffins got up to in their overwintering grounds.

It was seen as a symbolic and patriotic act when LoveStar bought up the Coke factory and converted it into a puffin factory. The Puffin Factory scientists worked tirelessly for four years on improvements to the puffin until it would meet the approval of the most exacting tourists. The puffin was as big as a turkey (in fact it was 73 percent turkey, but that was confidential), a strutting and magnificent bird with a rainbow-colored beak. It was utterly delicious, laid brown-splotched eggs, and sang: "Eat me, eat me!"

Every day Indridi walked round the Puffin Factory grounds with a wheelbarrow and rake. He planted cinquefoil and forget-me-nots along the paths, combed out the heather, laid paving stones, and watered the cotton grass in the wetland. He pruned trees, pulled up chickweed, and cut the grass with a scythe. In late summer he picked crowberries and blueberries, took them home, and stirred them into Sigrid's skyr.

On sunny days the inhabitants of the neighborhood strolled through the factory grounds, lay down in the heather, looked up at the clouds, and listened to the song: "Eat me! Eat me!" It was all thanks to LoveStar's ideas and vision.

Indridi and Sigrid's lives had been a dance on honeyed roses for over five years. But suddenly everything had gone to the dogs, and Indridi didn't know whether Sigrid would be waiting for him when he got home. It was a long time since they had stroked their middle fingers together, and it was with heavy steps that he plodded up the stairs. His heart pounded in his chest as he opened the door and called:

"Sigrid? Are you home?"

LOVEDEATH

LOVEDEATH WAS INEXTRICABLY LINKED TO LOVE IN INDRIDI AND Sigrid's minds. On starlit winter evenings they often drove up to the Blafjoll ski resort just before closing time. When the floodlighting on the slopes was switched off, the most distant stars twinkled. They made themselves comfortable on a mountaintop not far from an iced-over hut half-buried in a snowdrift. On the roof was a billboard:

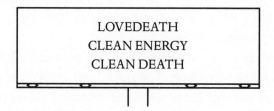

LOVEDEATH
CLEAN ENERGY
CLEAN DEATH

Indridi and Sigrid stared up into the darkness in silence or amid whispers, listening to their breathing and watching the steam rise from their lips as if from hot springs which sometimes gushed forth. Indridi and Sigrid gushed a lot about life and love as they lay on their backs up in the mountains, watching the twinkling stars and the yellow dome of light in the distance that eternally shielded the city dwellers from darkness and stars.

"There's Orion," said Indridi.

"There's Capricorn," said Sigrid.

"Where?" asked Indridi.

"Just below LoveStar," said Sigrid, pointing to the star that twinkled brightest of all in the sky.

At regular intervals they saw shooting stars. "Someone's just died," they whispered, watching the flash streak and burn up in the atmosphere, and they were quite right. If they looked it up in the morning paper, they would be able to see who had died and read the obituaries by their loved ones.

When the solar wind was favorable, the Northern Lights would appear, first as thin as an oily film, then dancing and fluttering as if someone had drawn a blue-green brain scan in the sky. The Northern Lights never lasted long. LoveDeath needed the energy. As soon as the lights appeared, there was a bumping and stirring in the hut, a light went on and an old man clambered out. He wore a fur coat and had a big mustache.

"Einar's awake," whispered Sigrid.

Einar said nothing as a rule. The snow crunched as he walked over to a mast, which stood on the mountaintop, and filled an orange balloon with helium. On it stood written in clear letters:

LOVEDEATH
CLEAN ENERGY
CLEAN DEATH

He tied the balloon to an endless roll of copper wire fastened to the mast, which was in turn connected to a power line that ran directly north to LoveDeath.

"Don't get in the way," grunted Einar, taking out a knife and cutting the cord that held the balloon.

The wire rattled off the drum at high speed and the balloon shot up into the black night. The Northern Lights had magnified in the meantime. They were like a greeny-white glacial torrent roaring over black sand, while the balloon resembled a float on a line. The old man was fishing, but before Indridi and Sigrid could wonder about the fish, the balloon had reached the right height, the wire grounded the Northern Lights, and a blazing electric river was sucked down the copper wire like a whirlpool down a drain. The mast stood blue as a welding torch in the darkness and the power lines hummed and crackled as the energy surged north along them to LoveDeath. Einar went back into the hut and turned out the light.

Indridi and Sigrid were left behind and watched the balloon glowing like a lightbulb or extra moon with a vortex spiralling around it. They listened to the hum as the energy streamed to earth and watched the odd flash of lightning dart around the wire. Indridi began to think about the float and river again. The old man had emptied the river like the bull in the folktale, while the stars lay like goldfish on the black riverbed. All around they saw balloons popping up from the mountaintops. LoveStar twinkled brighter than ever behind its cloud and a star fell.

"Someone just died," they both thought as one. Sigrid's eyes brimmed with tears, as it wasn't long since her great-grandmother, Kristoline, had gone the way of all flesh with LoveDeath.

When Kristoline died she was not simply lowered into a cold grave to rot away. Kristoline had been saving up for LoveDeath for a whole decade. Once all sign of life had vanished from the screen, they closed her eyes, and Indridi comforted Sigrid while the old woman was taken by lift down to a branch of LoveDeath in the hospital basement. A woman in a black flight-attendant uniform dressed Kristoline in a silver costume and put her in the black refrigeration unit outside.

The daily yield of the dead was collected from the city at 5:30 PM, and a transport truck thundered north with the bodies, turning left just before the theme park at a road sign that read:

Myrkarfjall.
LoveDeath launchpad no. 2
Rockets 18–54

← Loading   Viewing Platform →

The truck drove into a tunnel at the foot of the mountain and came to a stop in a white-scoured dome. In the middle stood an angled rocket with the words "LoveDeath" printed along its side. The rocket struck an odd note in the polished surroundings, looking fairly battered after countless launches and rough landings on land and sea. The doors of the craft stood open and Kristoline was rolled inside on a conveyor belt along with all the other individuals that the country had yielded that day, in addition to a large crop of Faroe Islanders, Danes, and Norwegians, who had already been loaded on board.

Indridi, Sigrid, and her family took their seats in a gallery on the fifty-seventh floor of the LoveDeath wing of the LoveStar theme park. There was a spectacular view through the glass wall over the glacier, the airships, and the launchpads lined up along the mountain peaks on the western side of the valley. Children ran and bounced cheerfully round the gallery after an exciting day in the company of Larry LoveDeath, a remorselessly cheery bunny in a space suit. A day spent with him helped them gloss over the shock of death. In fact it was so successful that there were few things children found more exciting than LoveDeath: "Great-grandma! When are you going to LoveDeath?" Sigrid's little cousin had asked Kristoline relentlessly in recent years. "My friend's lucky. She's met Larry LoveDeath four times."

Straggling from the shopping mall with their half-liter bottles of Coke, the teenagers slumped sulkily in the corner, played computer games on their lenses, or hung out on chat lines while their mothers scolded: "Your grandmother is making her grand exit, Magnus dear, will you please pay attention!"

The men got themselves beers at the bar before the big moment arrived and all eyes were fixed on the window. In the bowels of the mountain to the west of the valley the iron doors closed. The hydrogen rocket fuel ignited, and the earth shook as it lifted slowly off the peak before shooting up into the sky on a vast column of fire and smoke. Grieving yet captivated, the crowd watched the rocket swiftly disappearing through the stratosphere and ionosphere until nothing could be seen but a tiny bright light like a daystar. When the light vanished it was clear that old Kristoline had gone beyond the earth's atmosphere. There she and all the other bodies were released into the silent black void where they floated weightless for a single orbit of the earth, but that was not the main event. The magic lay in what came afterward.

The following evening all of Kristoline's descendants drove to the top of Mt. Esja, parked their cars, switched off their headlights, and gazed up into the clear September sky. Sigrid's father scraped frost off the circular view indicator, turned it to synchronize with the time, and peered at the constellation map with his flashlight. Then he looked up and pointed.

"She should appear high up in Ursa Major at eighteen minutes past eleven."

They all seated themselves on hillocks or rocks or lay on their backs in the soft carpet of moss. Sigrid blew her nose and Indridi put his arms round her. At 11:18 PM Sigrid's great-grandmother began her fall to earth. At that precise moment, at pre-booked coordinates in heaven, gravity exerted its pull and she fell according to Newton's law with accelerating speed, until a long, shining streak of white fire was etched in the silent darkness between the stars. "Shooting star!" whispered the children, and they made a wish. Everything was so poignantly lovely that their eyes filled with tears; death was so symbolic and beautiful. "Life is like a flash in the night," and the darkness that received death was not empty darkness. It was an infinite black space full of stars, and people were cheered because this was her last and greatest wish: to burn up under the heavenly plough, to fall like a blazing streak against the full moon, to shoot like an arrow from Sagittarius's bow.

As Sigrid's great-grandmother was 70 percent water, it wasn't really possible to say that she had burned to ash. She evaporated.

The star became a cloud, and Kristoline was reunited with her fallen husband who was also a cloud, and with all the other millions who had become clouds and rain, which waters the grass and flowers. Bone particles and cell debris fell as an excellent fertilizer for the earth's vegetation. Those who were not used to looking up at the night sky felt dizzy when they saw its unutterable depths and beauty. The mere fact that Kristoline's death united the family and gave them this time up on this mountain under this sky filled them with gratitude:

"Thanks for being born and dying before me and showing me how beautiful the world is and how fragile and short life is. I will never forget you, little great-grandma cloud. I'll take care of my little life and be diligent about saving so I can have myself launched to you when I die."

Parents pointed up at the sky for the children and said: "Now great-grandma has gone to heaven. She's in the clouds with great-grandpa. If you look at the clouds you might see grandpa's beard or false teeth. If you ask nicely perhaps grandma will make a whale-shape for you, unless they've flown to Africa to make a whale for the children there. You remember how keen they always were on Africa. Tomorrow you must lie on your back and see whether your great-grandma in heaven has made a shape out of the clouds for you."

It was LoveStar who got the idea for LoveDeath, or rather: the idea got him. The idea wouldn't leave him alone until he had fully realized it. The idea prevented him from sleeping, took away his appetite for food and sex, and pumped him up with chemicals that filled him with so much energy that it had to be born into the world. And although at first some people found the idea for LoveDeath far-fetched, it was actually very simple. The technology already existed: there were thousands of rockets lying around in the old superpower territories, just waiting to be put into service for LoveDeath. And it was no more difficult to launch a rocket in a gale-force blizzard up in Oxnadalur than it was to land a jumbo jet at Keflavik airport in the same conditions. It was all a question of money and marketing, possessing the energy to produce cheap hydrogen, and launching enough rich and famous people to attract the public's attention and create a mood. It was a question of the right man getting the idea. LoveStar did not actually need to know much himself. He had long given up working with his original field of study: the navigation skills and brain functioning of Arctic terns, butterflies, and bees. He didn't need to be an expert in hydrogen, launchpads, astronomy, solar winds, or cloud-drift. This knowledge could be bought. All he needed was the idea, a clear aim, funding, and the power of persuasion to drive a team of people to one goal. He didn't need advice or expensive opinion polls; he felt instinctively what would work and made it work.

The salesmen from LoveDeath's Mood Division sat oozing sympathy at the deathbeds of movie heroes and rock stars. They darkened the wards, turned on their laptops, and projected impressive interactive publicity films.

"LoveDeath will be a brilliant publicity coup for you; it's still so new that the launch will make international headlines. We'll make sure that a clip from your music video will be played during the evening news and, if you're lucky, a greatest hits CD will be released all over the world."

"It was only one song, I only had one hit," sighed the aged star on his deathbed.

"It'll be re-released. The record sales alone will pay for Love-Death in a week. You'll make a killing from this. Your name will be immortal. It'll live on among the stars."

At LoveDeath things were worded the right way and put in the right context. LoveDeath made death cleaner, grander, more glamorous, and simpler. It saved on land area. There was no grave to neglect, no guilt about weeds, no headstone to buy later. No stench, no horror or grinning skulls.

Creeping worms and grinning skulls became forever linked to the old method in people's minds after a successful advertising campaign in the early days of LoveDeath. The campaign's flagship was the award-winning advertisement *Rotting Mother*:

The first year beneath the soil is shown speeded up. A young mother is lowered in her coffin into a cold grave; her beautiful body blows up, turns blue, and rots, and in fast-forward her body seems to know no rest—it writhes and swells and her face is gnawed away by maggots until her corpse seems to scream. Then came the new method:

CLEAR SKY
SHOOTING STAR
LOVEDEATH

The clean method. Cleanness mattered. A simple, beautiful idea. LoveDeath was beautiful and the concept was easy to grasp even for children who couldn't understand why someone who was supposed to go to heaven should be buried in the ground.

> Child: Mommy! Where do the bad people go?
> Mother: They go to hell.
> Child: Where's hell?
> Mother: Hell's under the earth.
> Child: Is Granny going to hell, then?
> Mother: No, she's going to heaven.
> Child: Why was she put in the ground, then?
> Mother: Oh, you'll understand when you're older.
> Announcer: LoveDeath, now everyone can go to heaven for only thirty thousand points* (*per month for twelve years)
> LoveDeath: The high point of life!

— Dramatized radio advertisement —

The old method paled in comparison to LoveDeath. How can your granny, who's underground, buried in hell, be soaring in heaven like an angel? No, it didn't make sense. The old idea was not clean. The explanation was too far-fetched: the substance here, the spirit there. Was that an appropriate end to a beautiful life? To be lowered into a cold grave? To send your loved one to their final rest in a place where you would not feel easy for one moment on a dark night? To make your love rest in a place that was forever linked to darkness and horror? Who wanted to invest in decomposition? The matter was simple: the old idea was bad. The ceremony uncomfortable. The decomposition disgusting. It was hopeless from the start, a bad idea that was called tradition because no one had thought of anything better for sixty thousand years. No flowers or wreaths, please. Those who wished to remember the deceased were invited to donate their money to a more worthwhile cause. Death had potential that no one but LoveStar picked up on.

LoveDeath was initially the preserve of billionaires. In Hollywood LoveDeath was the next step when the plastic surgeon admitted defeat and said he couldn't correct the wrinkles, eyebags, varicose veins, cellulite, and droopy breasts; it was all downhill from now on and this was the right moment: to have yourself fired to the climax of life, submit to LoveDeath. The ultimate way to burn fat.

> Death is clean and LoveDeath is the purifying fire. Before becoming one with eternity you will burn up in the atmosphere. Then the spirit will be released from the bonds of the flesh.
>
> —Excerpt from LoveStar's farewell address
> on the launching of Pope Pius III

During the early years it made world headlines whenever anyone was fired with LoveDeath, and tourists and fans thronged to see the launch. But LoveDeath became so popular that the service improved, the cost came down, and the quality rose.

NEWSPAPER ADVERTISEMENT:
A man lies on his deathbed with a thought bubble over his head.
In it is nothing but black sky and the word
LoveDeath.
His relatives stand around, each with something different in
their bubbles:

LoveDeath	jeep	yacht	beach	summer house
o	o	o	o	o
o	o	o	o	o
o	o	o	o	o
man	son	sister	mother	uncle

CAPTION UNDER THE PICTURE:
Will they bother to send you when it comes time?

LoveDeath
The ultimate high.
— *Old slogan, LoveDeath spring campaign* —

The old method cost a million points or even two and hadn't changed for sixty thousand years. It wasn't long before LoveDeath became competitively priced; it was no longer one thousand times more expensive than the old method but only one hundred times more expensive, until eventually it was only ten times more expensive and that was when its operations really began to expand at a furious rate. In the end LoveDeath cost less than sending four hundred pounds of fresh fish to Japan by airfreight.

Of course, LoveDeath didn't appeal to all target groups at first, but by the time LoveDeath had become cheaper than the old method and Larry LoveDeath was introduced, it was no longer a question of appeal. LoveDeath was more economical, and more beautiful, and children wouldn't hear of anything else. Big stars elevated themselves above the masses by being fired in fantastically expensive costumes of precious materials that burnt at different temperatures:

ORDER

Magnesium outer layer to burn with a white flame, then a yellow layer of a sulfur compound to burn with a reddish-yellow blaze, then a pale-green layer of copper sulfate to burn like green glitter, then underclothes of a compound 60 percent polyester and 40 percent cotton to burn like a rainbow, and finally the body itself in its naturally sun-white blaze until two silicon pads explode like fireworks.

— Order for Pam An who fell so memorably over Hollywood after dying during plastic surgery at only fifty-three years old —

Colorful LoveDeaths were fantastically expensive exceptions and no one failed to notice them. Most people had to be satisfied with the natural blaze.

You could say that Sigrid owed her life to LoveDeath. Her mother was a fifty-five-year-old rocket engineer and had provided Sigrid and her sister with a stylish, well-designed home. When she told her daughters about the early years of LoveDeath, she closed her eyes and spoke about the glow and the mood and the novelty. LoveDeath was like the herring boom, and everyone in her generation was affected by LoveDeath nostalgia and pioneering arrogance.

"You might at least thank us. We were the ones who built all this up."

There was some truth to this. When the expansion was at its height and LoveStar was asked how many of his countrymen were on his payroll, he answered: "I guess about half."

Of course, the glow was greatest during the early years, while serious stars and millionaires were being fired with the appropriate media circus, retinue, and glamor. At that time most LoveDeath employees were young and up for fun and overtime. The best parties were held up north at LoveDeath, and it was at one of these very parties that Sigrid had been conceived. Her mother had sneaked out into a hollow with an electrician from Nordfjord while a wrinkled pop star with varicose veins sang an old hit in return for a trip with LoveDeath. Everyone drank to the star and thanked her for the swan song as leather-clad backup singers (from LoveDeath's female-voice choir) dressed her in a silver-leaf evening dress over an aluminium boiler suit. They led her out to the next rocket and, as Sigrid's parents rolled around in the heather, the flare lit up the summer night and the fine rain settled like dew on the flowers in the valley.

LoveDeath was ubiquitous. Every day LoveDeath transport trucks drove the day's harvest of the dead from the world's cities, and every minute a ship or plane set off with a full cargo, heading north for LoveDeath. Black freighters under Caribbean flags sailed to the country laden to the sinking point with corpses from every continent. The sky was striped white until late in the day after black jets had brought the European consignment. Russian airships hung over the country like black air-melons, carrying five thousand bodies with every trip. While the airships were being filled with helium their captains could never resist inhaling, ringing up a comedy radio show, and talking like Donald Duck in Russian.

LoveDeath was fabulous but could also be a bit eerie, especially in November and December when few living people made their way to the country, and some (for example people in the sensitive target group who cry over sad films) found it depressing seeing nothing but buses packed with Chinese or Swedish pensioners flocking in convoys north to LoveDeath, knowing for sure that none of them would return home alive.

Anyone worth their salt had been involved in LoveDeath or connected to it in some way. Fifteen thousand pilots flew LoveDeath aircrafts and eighteen thousand captains sailed people to the country and fished up the rockets that they came across out at sea. These were reused again and again. Two thousand bus and truck drivers drove customers north. Thousands worked in marketing, sales, packing, and distribution, even more in loading, calculation of firing coordinates, construction of new launchpads, and energy acquisition for increased hydrogen production. LoveDeath was insatiable as far as energy was concerned. All lines lead to LoveDeath, as the proverb said. Wind farms were erected out at sea, tides were harnessed, and geothermal heat fetched up from the magma chambers beneath volcanoes. All this was used to split water into hydrogen and oxygen and drive the simple chemical reaction: $2H_2O \rightarrow 2H_2 + O_2$.

During the early years growth was frighteningly rapid and there were often squabbles over the proceedings. Sometimes the freezer units on the container ships broke down and a ghastly stench was released when the holds were opened. Then everyone held their noses, but the people living in the ports were used to this and called it the smell of money. In the worst cases the cargo ended up as guano, but iSTAR made sure that the news didn't get out. Relatives never learned that what burnt so beautifully in the night sky was not their loved one but two hundred pounds of horsemeat.

The country may have been the center for death, but its image was as positive, profound, and clean as LoveDeath. In the world press the country was called the Ganges of the North and perhaps there was something in it. The country was Ganges, Bethlehem, Mecca, Graceland, or whatever they were called, rolled into one, all those holy places men had to visit before death. LoveStar could convert anyone to his cause. He managed to unite everyone under LoveDeath, whatever strange ideas people had about religion or death. When Indian gurus were launched, they were fired with electrolyzed water from the Ganges. When popes and bishops were launched, holy water was used, while Faroese oil barons were launched in monster spacecrafts driven by the crude oil that they had brought with them in tankers.

A large number of countries around the world wanted to offer LoveDeath and share in its operations, but the patent was held by the LoveStar corporation and no one could compete with the facilities at the LoveStar theme park in Oxnadalur. The deserts and reservoirs in the highlands and the immense heaving sea around the country made it unlikely that unsuccessful launches would land on towns or cities. The deciding factors were the inexhaustible reserves of clean, renewable energy and an endless supply of fresh water to split into hydrogen and oxygen, and then the rest was simple: Electrolysis! Load! Fire!

When the hydrogen burned there was no foul reek, only a clear water vapor that formed a mist on the northern moors. Although people were launched into the sky from the peaks around Oxnadalur, the stars could fall to earth anywhere on the planet. All around the globe convoys of vehicles wound up hills and mountains, and people sat silent and thoughtful around crackling campfires waiting for their loved ones to fall to earth in a blaze.

DON'T BREATHE

LOVESTAR SAT IN THE PLANE, TAKING CARE NOT TO CRUSH THE seed. He opened his hand and held it from him like dust that you mean to blow away, yet he hardly dared breathe in the direction of the seed.

He had become isolated from other people in the company lately. Almost the only people he had contact with were Ivanov, head of LoveDeath, and Yamaguchi, head of the Bird and Butterfly Division. Nowadays he saw little of the heads of other departments; they had made themselves comfortable on Pacific islands. He met them only at video conferences, but in recent weeks he had not bothered with most meetings. Now he was quite out of touch with the world. No film clip on the lens, no music in his ears. He looked at the seed with his naked eye.

He knew what ideas were making the rounds at the Mood Division and knew better than anyone that nothing can stop an idea. He was confident in his ability to stand up to them, but what would they do with the seed when he was dead? What should he do with the seed himself? He had been responsible for the search and expected to find a cave, ancient artifact, mountain, mound, pool. But a seed? What does one do with a seed? What would germinate from this seed?

> A seed becomes a tree?
> A seed becomes a flower?
> All as the one flower.

The search for what turned out to be a seed had taken seven years. Over the last few months LoveStar had spent most days at the office, waiting for the search party's reports. He did calculations to keep his brain working. He had to keep his mental pathways open. He drew patterns or a landscape. Always similar patterns and the same landscape. When he was in the grip of an idea he generally tried to preserve his mental health by doing calculations or drawing. Drawing was a form of meditation or overflow, an outlet for an unborn idea. He was also a collector: in his youth he had collected samples of handwriting from everyone that he could get hold of, even from abroad, as well as knucklebones from every kind of land animal, otoliths from every species of fish, and wings from every kind of bird, and the office was crammed with all these things. He had a yellow or fluorescent ring round his pupils, which shone in the dark like cat's eyes. He looked out over the unspoilt Oxnadalur valley. The office had a 360° view with windows on all sides, yet seen from the outside it was a black lava peak.

LoveStar's collecting mania had cranked up. He collected the world. He never acknowledged the fact himself, saying the world wanted to come to him. Above the valley hovered a red helicopter from a Norwegian oil rig marked Statoil. For a moment he mentally tried out his star on the helicopter with the legend below: LoveOil. He sent a short memo to the computer at iSTAR's asset management department: Statoil/LoveOil? Nothing more was needed. The computer would investigate the question, and if it proved profitable the computer would buy the company and simultaneously print out sticky labels marked LoveOil.

Below the helicopter hung a tarred stave church. A gift from the Norwegian state to LoveStar's Museum of the World. The gift was thanks to the Mood Division. They had managed to convince the world that anything not on show in the Museum of the World was worthless. Further down the valley the road had been closed and waymarkers and signposts had been removed while a giant Sphinx made slow progress up it on the back of a truck. All these things were on their way north to the vaults under LavaRock, and the magnetic pull of the LoveStar theme park seemed infinite. Infinity: ∞. He drew the symbol on the paper again and again. Infinity. He owned an infinite amount. He had waited an eternity, an infinite time, for the results of the search. An infinite sum of money had gone into financing it. If it all worked out, something infinitely great would be found. He turned the paper around and drew the infinity symbol over those already drawn on the page until the paper was covered with flowers.

LoveStar let his eyes wander over his realm. Polish welders snacked on Prince Polo crackers in one of LoveDeath's rocket hangars; a trawler hauled a rocket up from the heaving sea; a long-haired fly specialist from the Bird and Butterfly Division sat intently measuring the density of a mosquito brain while a colleague talked into thin air, apparently painting an invisible wall. In a concert hall on the outskirts of Bangkok, fifty thousand moodmen were disco-dancing at an international incentive conference held by iSTAR's press department. A crazy hubbub of rejoicing broke out and the moodmen flung their arms wide as if in a trance. LoveStar switched perspectives and saw what was happening. Ragnar Ö. Karlsson, former head of mood at iSTAR, was beaming at them from a giant screen and singing a duet with a stark-naked female pop singer in a live broadcast from the seventy-thousand-strong iSTAR music department conference in Moscow. LoveStar ground his teeth. There was no sign of Ragnar's standing within iSTAR diminishing, even though he had been demoted to head of the LoveDeath Mood Division.

LoveStar looked closer to home, watching a raven soaring on an updraft by the cliff, before passing inside the rock to where tourists were being shown to their rooms. In the inLOVE wings of the theme park, endless rows of lovers from all over the world could be seen cuddling up together inside the cold rock walls. Old people sat in rocking chairs, waiting for LoveDeath, resting their eyes on 3-D images of their childhood homes, or watching rocket after rocket shoot into space.

LoveStar roved around the world in this manner, changing perspective from Paris to Tierra del Fuego to Bologna, Tokyo, and Kiev. Everywhere towers rose like anthills from the suburbs and loomed over the old city centers. Although the towers were built variously from steel, stone, glass, or carbon fiber, the brand was instantly recognizable. They were imitations or stylizations of LavaRock, erected where there had once been cemeteries before LoveStar had taken it upon himself to "clean them up" and free the cities once and for all from *"los miserables restos de la época de descomposicion de los cadaveres de ceres humanos,"* as the Mayor of Buenos Aires put it: "The pathetic remains of mankind's age of decomposition."

LoveStar went nowhere near the daily running of LoveDeath. In a documentary about LoveDeath on CNN, LoveStar had said: "The satisfaction of seeing LoveDeath become a reality and watching Elizabeth II fired over Windsor Castle lasted for one day. It lasted from the first rocket being launched at six in the morning, until Elizabeth fell to earth at 3:00 AM the following morning. The moment the flash faded I became superfluous. Universities produce people in the tens of thousands who can, want, and know how to keep LoveDeath running and expanding. I had the sense to give them free rein."

That wasn't to imply that LoveStar didn't make demands on his people: "WHAT THE HELL DO YOU MEAN MICK JAGGER WAS BURIED?! HE HAS A SEAT RESERVED WITH LOVEDEATH AND IF HE DOESN'T GO UP ONE OF YOU WILL GO IN HIS PLACE!!!"

The cleanup job and tower buildings in the big cities were entirely the responsibility of Ragnar Ö. Karlsson and the Love-Death Mood Division. LoveStar roved from tower to tower and then rang Ivanov, head of LoveDeath.

"Have you found out what's supposed to go in those towers?" LoveStar asked.

"Don't worry, it's a safe project."

"But what are the towers supposed to house?"

"Hotels, offices, or shops, I expect."

"You expect?"

"This is the most valuable real estate in the cities and it's almost self-evident that the towers will house these kinds of businesses. Anyway, it's 100 percent Ragnar's baby."

"So you're not sure? I want to you keep a close eye on him."

"I can't stick my nose in everything. I had the sense to give Ragnar free rein. It's worked out well, as you can see."

"What about the cost?"

"The profit from the cleanup job covers the cost in full, and the bodies can go straight to the Million Star Festival."

"So you were paid for the bodies, got the land thrown in, and now you're supposed to sell the space in the towers?"

"I'm telling you, he's a brilliant moodman, Ragnar, unbelievably brilliant. The cities paid tenfold for the bodies, due to the decomposition, you see, and the Million Star Festival is a bonus. It's a mood boost, a pure image boost. It was a good idea of yours to transfer Ragnar over to us. I never dreamed that I'd live to see boomtime again at LoveDeath in my old age."

"So everything's going *well*?" asked LoveStar skeptically.

"The Million Star Belt is visible to the naked eye. Take a look."

"I'll look at it this evening."

"It's visible by daylight," said Ivanov.

LoveStar went over to the window and looked up at the sky where there was a gleam from something that lay like a broad arch over the vault of the heavens, like a stripe of glittering, powdered glass, like glitter or fool's gold on a riverbed. He picked up a telescope to see better. It was like a dense shoal of herring swimming far above the clouds. He switched perspective to the LoveStar satellite telescope. He shuddered at the sight that met his eyes: an endless shoal of LoveDeath orbiting the Earth, a hundred million gleaming silver bodies forming a Saturn-ring right around the globe!

"Isn't it fantastic?" said Ivanov. "It's equivalent to six years' worth of deaths."

LoveStar gulped, closed his eyes, and tried to breathe evenly. Ragnar had certainly not given up.

"Are you okay, by the way?"

"Yes," said LoveStar.

"You've been a bit preoccupied. You should talk to Ragnar more. I don't understand what you've got against him. Damn it, I reckon you've got an heir in that boy. It's time to let the youngsters have a go. It's not as if we're immortal."

LoveStar didn't answer.

"Hello? Are you there?"

LoveStar looked at the sun. It was sailing behind the Million Star Belt, its light reflecting from the shoal and forming a halo, a shining circular double halo with an additional sun to the east and another to the west. Two blazing red extra suns in the sky, like a burning sunset reflected in the western windows. "Three suns," thought LoveStar.

"Are you still there?" asked Ivanov.

"Three suns in the sky: a sign that evil is nigh," thought LoveStar.

IDEAS

NOT MANY PEOPLE FULLY UNDERSTOOD LOVESTAR, NOT EVEN HIS closest colleagues. Sometimes they couldn't tell whether he was joking or serious, but he got things done, whatever it took.

When asked about his ideas, he claimed he wasn't responsible for them. He did not get ideas; it was the other way around. The ideas got him. The ideas took over his body and used him as a host to launch themselves into the world, leaving him empty, worn, and tattered (and disturbingly rich and powerful, as those who had less sympathy with him pointed out). He said he had no control over the consequences when an idea took up residence in his head. "An idea is a dictator," he maintained in one of his best-selling books:

> An idea hijacks the brain, pushes away feelings and memo-
> ries, makes you neglect friends and relations, and drives
> you toward a single goal, that of launching the idea into
> the world. An idea takes over the speech centers, allow-

ing access only to itself, it steals your appetite, reduces your need for sleep, and induces the brain to produce a chemical that is stronger than amphetamines and can keep you going for months at a time. Once the idea is born, the person it possessed is left empty. Even if he tries to hang on to the idea, basking in its limelight and taking care to link his name to it, even naming it after himself, he will not enjoy the same sense of fulfillment. He who has felt an idea growing inside him, he who has been its slave for months and years, knows that there is no point in having once had an idea. To be content with having had an idea is like being content with having once had an orgasm, being content with having once eaten or drunk. Once someone has acquired the taste, he desires nothing more than to be enslaved by a new idea. Nothing is more pitiable than a man who has hit upon one tune, one story, one idea, and then no more. He will never be anything but a spent shell. It would have been better if he had never acquired the taste. Ideas are drugs. Someone with a predisposed weakness is doomed to put aside his nets or computer, throw away his wealth and belongings, and put everything at stake. When an idea says: "Follow me!" he follows it all the way.

He who is infected with an idea is not responsible for his actions. His only thought is to launch it. The idea permits no contradiction or doubt. The man is not responsible because he does not own the idea. The idea already existed. The atom bomb existed before it was worked out and built. It was imminent. It was biding its time. It had to be built. And it had to be detonated. Even though people calculated a 20 percent risk that the explosion would set off a chain reaction that would ignite all the oxygen in the atmosphere, they still had to try. It wasn't enough to calculate. They had to take it out into the desert, and, once they had seen its power, other people were seized with an uncontrollable urge to see it explode over a city. It was enough to do it once or twice. Someone who is possessed by an idea is beyond good and evil. His thinking is not on that scale. An idea is an uncontrollable hunger. An idea is a long suppressed lust. Those who get ideas are the most dangerous people in the world because they are ready to take the risk. They just want to see what happens; their thinking goes no further.

—*The Ideas* by LoveStar

LoveStar was not dangerous by nature. He sometimes said crazy things but that was only because they entered his head, not because he meant what he said. He just wanted to see what would happen.

LoveStar directed his binoculars away from the halo around the sun to watch the Statoil helicopter vanish over the mountains, minus the church. He turned to the glass table and drew a line on it. Above the line he began to sketch a bird but was interrupted mid-wing.

"The author's here," announced his secretary. "He wants to show you the first chapter of the biography."

The author from the Mood Division walked in. He was a rather foppish young man with round glasses and a frayed tweed jacket.

"Morning," said the author, looking at him oddly. LoveStar was appearing a bit rough; he hadn't slept for weeks and probably hadn't eaten either; his skin was a size too big for him. Realizing that he was staring, the author turned to the window that faced the Oxnadalur valley.

"Fantastic view," he said.

"Good," said LoveStar. "Look out the window. Not at me."

"I'll begin, then," the young man said and commenced reading.

"LoveStar was born the day that man first set foot on the moon. His birth lasted nine hours. As his mother, Margret Petursdottir, a thirty-year-old assistant nurse from Siglufjord, groaned from the first contractions, the world watched the astronauts bounding like overgrown children across the lifeless gray landscape. Five hours later his mother had dilated seven centimeters and begun to whimper from the pain, while the midwife watched in suspense as the astronauts fiddled silently with their machines, which for some unaccountable reason would not start up again. Four hours later the machines were still down and they were busy doing something around the lunar module, talking little and then only in technical jargon. But when there were only fifty minutes' worth of oxygen reserves left in the tanks, it became clear that they would not succeed in relaunching. The camera angle was adjusted and the astronauts cantered hand in hand toward the horizon. Their gait is unlikely to have illustrated their innermost feelings, but for some reason it was only possible to bound gaily on the moon. It took less than half an hour for them to disappear over the horizon. Their heads went down like three white suns. At precisely that moment, LoveStar's cranium appeared. After the astronauts had vanished from the screen, there was nothing to see but the naked landscape. They were still in radio contact but said nothing more; nothing but their breathing could be heard. Some would perhaps have taken the opportunity to convey an important message to the world, but they simply breathed slower and slower until they could breathe no more. At that moment LoveStar filled his lungs with air for the first time and screamed with all his life and soul.

"The image remained on the screen for the next hour. Gray sand, black space, and silence. During the following days TV stations and the president tried to convince the world that it had merely been a hoax, a modern televisual equivalent of Orson Welles's immortal *War of the Worlds*. Stanley Kubrick was persuaded to own up to the hoax. The film set was opened to the public. Here people could see tracks in the sand, the waxing earth painted on a black screen, and the rigid flag. 'This is the glue that was used to stiffen the flag,' said the female guides, allowing people a sniff.

"Since special effects this realistic had never before been seen on screen, few were willing to fall for this. So Kubrick received a ten-million-dollar grant to make a sci-fi feature film, proving not only that the hoax had been child's play, technically speaking, but that it could even be improved on. When the new movie premiered ten months later, people claimed they could see clear evidence of his signature style on the moon landing. Endless silence, heavy breathing, and a slow death.

"When people asked whether either of the superpowers were

aiming to win the real race to put a man on the moon, their spokesmen shrugged and asked why the human race should waste money landing on a barren gray rock when so much of life remained unexplored here on earth. It sounded like a reasonable question. Yet even today not everyone is reconciled to the events of that day and some cannot look at the moon without shuddering and thinking of the astronauts lying up there in a gray crater. It is less well-known that on that very day LoveStar was born. The man who has had a greater impact on the world than any moon landing could ever have had. The man who converted dead space into the climax of life with the magnificent LoveDeath program. The man who found love, not for himself, but for the whole world. The man who will always be linked to love and death in the memory of mankind.

"What do you think?" asked the author, looking over his shoulder but taking care not to meet LoveStar's eye.

LoveStar looked over the text and read a sentence aloud.

"'It is less well-known that on that very day LoveStar was born.' That's news. I myself didn't know I was born that day."

Blushing slightly, the author cleared his throat. "I felt we should link you in better with major events."

"Aren't there enough major events?"

"Not in your youth."

"Isn't it a cliché? To link someone's birth to a major event? You know I wasn't born that day; I was born the day the Reynimelur brothers died of exposure on Kjolur."

"The Reyni-what?"

"They ran out of petrol in a blizzard and froze to death because they were only wearing T-shirts."

"Never heard of them," said the author, scratching his head.

"Nothing was ever found but their bones and the skeletons of their jeeps. Someone had stripped the cars of anything valuable: engine, tires, winch, radio, all stripped. The remains can still be seen up above the Krakshraun lava field. The remains of the cars, I mean."

The author waited patiently but was plainly not listening. He put himself in persuasive gear. "As I said, I wanted to place you in a larger, more international context. The Reynimelur brothers are hardly headline material abroad."

"But it's not true; I wasn't born that day. It contradicts the documentaries, the homepages, and the other biographies."

The author shrugged. "Then we'll correct them; it won't take more than a couple of minutes to update your date of birth."

"But it's not right!"

"The year's right, which is more than can be said of most celebrities."

LoveStar stood up and regarded the author who was staring at the floor. "No! Not even the year is right! Must I change my date of birth just because you want to begin the story this way and not that? This chapter has nothing to do with me! It's bullshit! There was no television in the maternity ward when I was born."

"It's a question of mood. The guys at iSTAR said we needed to sharpen up the image."

"Wasn't my birth enough of a major event in itself?"

"Yes, of course, but . . ."

"It's so predictable! To draw breath just as they breathe their last. Why did you have to link my birth to such a depressing death?"

"That comes later, in the chapter called 'The Father of Death.'"

"'The Father of Death?' Is that supposed to be me?"

"LoveDeath was your idea . . ."

"Will you please leave me alone! Will you please get out!"

"Should I make changes?"

"You're not writing another word of this book!" announced LoveStar with finality. "The Mood Division should stay away from literature. It's supposed to sell books, pep them up, not write them."

"GOOD!" yelled the author, now looking LoveStar straight in the eye. "I'm not allowed to talk to friends from your childhood or schools, that's to say if you had any friends. I'm not allowed to use old photos or mention anything that could be classed as trade secrets. I'm not allowed to know why the Million Star Festival is being held. You forbid me to write about your parents, not a word about your sons or daughter, and nothing about Helga. I'm not even allowed to reveal your real name! WHAT THE HELL AM I SUPPOSED TO WRITE?"

LoveStar flushed crimson and trembled with fury. "GET OUT!"

LoveStar shook as the author stormed out. He strode back and forth across the room, then sat down at the glass table again but was too restless to draw.

"Goddam impudence," he muttered. "Damn fucking impudence."

He followed the author with his lens but retained his ears. Cursing, the author took the elevator down to the iSTAR headquarters. LoveStar hardly recognized the surroundings there; workmen had turned the whole place upside down. A few weeks ago the entire wing had been white; before that everything had been smothered in antique furniture and flowers. Mood people were restless by nature; they had shake-ups at regular intervals and chucked out all the furnishings. The author went into an office, threw up his hands, and tossed the manuscript on the floor. A moodman with a neat suit and dyed hair hushed the author and pointed out the recording butterfly in the corner. The author looked at the butterfly and, seizing a rolled-up poster, squashed it against the wall. Blinded, LoveStar rubbed his eyes, groped around in the darkness, and almost fell off his chair when normal eye-contact was re-established. He swore, grinding his teeth, and sent his secretary a message:

"Send the jerk a thousand Hail Maries and a Trap."

"A cry-trap, cramp-trap, heartburn, lumbago, pins and needles, erection, hiccups, or urination trap?" she asked instantly.

"Use your imagination!"

He activated a new butterfly and watched the author running bent double into the men's room, muttering ceaselessly: *Santa Maria madre di Dio prega per noi. Santa Maria madre di Dio prega per noi . . ."*

LoveStar's jet flew through the night. He had set in motion a chain of events with no end in sight and was feeling deeply concerned about the Mood Division. It was capable of anything. He had a lot to be grateful to the mood guys for; they had followed him through thick and thin. They looked up to him, flattered him, quoted him, and followed his ideas single-mindedly. They undertook the dirty work, dealing with any problems, whether they were accidents, ethical questions, politics, or religion. Moodmen managed to convert all ideas and discoveries into pure, clear Mood. Without ever specifying exactly what their goal was, they had gradually infiltrated the innermost core of the organization. LoveStar was confident he could control the moodmen during his lifetime, but what then?

The jet flew at three times the speed of sound at an altitude of forty thousand feet. Outside the sky was dark and a star fell. Someone's just died, he thought. In three hours' time more falling stars could be expected when the Million Star Festival began.

The instant LoveStar landed up north and the world was informed of the greatest discovery of all time, a hundred million stars would fall from the sky. A hundred million bodies would burn up in the atmosphere, illuminating the darkness like stardust in the spectacle of the century.

In LoveStar's hand was a seed and in the seed was a kernel and in the kernel was so much life that he was afraid that if the seed was damaged the world itself would crack like an eggshell.

INDRIDI AND SIGRID

INDRIDI AND SIGRID'S PERFECT WORLD CRACKED LIKE AN EGGSHELL several weeks before LoveStar found the seed. The cause was one little letter. It reached them one beautiful day, as all days appear to the eyes of those who believe they have found true love and happiness. When Sigrid came home at midday for a bit of word-synthesis, there was something strange in the air. When she opened the door, filling the apartment with the cries of puffins and the scent of honeyed roses, Indridi was not waiting in the hall to hug and kiss her as usual. Instead he was standing over by the window, his back to her.

"Hello?" called Sigrid.

Indridi stood still and didn't say a word. Poplars swayed green in the breeze outside in the yard and the swings swung to and fro. His eyes were red and he was plucking dry leaves from a dying yucca with trembling fingers.

"Is something wrong? Indridi, are you crying?"

"No," he said and carried on plucking.

"Indridi, don't be like that! Is something the matter?"

"There's a letter," said Indridi.

"A letter?"

"A letter came this morning from inLOVE."

Indridi picked up the letter and showed it to her. Sigrid beamed with joy.

"That's great, they've sent us a letter!" She ran to Indridi and made as if to jump into his arms but he recoiled.

"The letter's to you, Sigrid."

"To me?"

"Yes."

"Not to us?"

"No."

"What do they want with me?"

"They've calculated you."

"Me? What do you mean?"

"We don't match, Sigrid. I'm not your one and only."

Sigrid stood in the middle of the room, deathly pale. "You're joking!"

"No."

"There must be some misunderstanding," she said. "Your letter must be on the way."

"They say you can meet him up north at LoveStar next week."

"Who?"

"Your one and only. Your other half."

"You're kidding me, aren't you?"

"He's Danish."

"Danish?"

"Yes. His name's Per Møller."

Sigrid stared at Indridi in disbelief and felt a lump forming in her throat. "You're kidding me, Indridi. This can't be happening."

"It's true, Sigrid. It's quite true," he said in a low voice.

Sigrid went pale. Indridi stared silently out into the yard. It shouldn't have taken them by surprise. They knew, as all the world did, that it was pointless searching for love on your own. LoveStar took care of love and death. As no one had failed to notice, they should have followed the relationship counselor's advice and made a temporary contract: together until LoveStar calculates us apart. Together until LoveStar finds true love and happiness for us. They should have registered for a gym where uncalculated people could meet at midday and relieve their tension by doing it in the shower with a work colleague after an invigorating game of table tennis, instead of monopolizing one another day and night like fools.

It was a well-known fact that it didn't pay to entangle your life too much with someone else's before an official letter came from inLOVE. It was scientifically proven and no one argued with inLOVE any longer. inLOVE was the greatest discovery of all time. inLOVE was the essence of love and happiness.

"There are two phenomena in man that are halves," announced LoveStar at a press conference broadcast live around the world.

People were full of anticipation: news had been leaked, stories were circulating about volunteers who had taken part in scientific experiments up north and never been the same again.

"The sex cells are half cells," said LoveStar, "and need to meet another half in order for life to be created. Everyone knows that the urge to unite these cells is one of the strongest human drives. According to our research the same is true of the human soul. The soul is a half and needs to be united with another in order for life to be properly kindled. But the soul is infinitely more complex than the sex cell and what is more: every soul fits only ONE other in the world. Like a fragmented sign, like a key in a lock, like a split stone that fits exactly to its other half, there are two people in the world who fit together. We have found a way of calculating exactly which two people are suited to one another."

The reporters looked skeptical and were obviously about to give LoveStar a hard time. But then two journalists, a bitter double-divorcée from Norway's *Aftenposten* and a man from the Hungarian *Daily Socialist*, asked exactly the same question at the same moment. They broke off in mid-sentence.

"You first," they said in unison.

"But it was the same question," they said together and both fell silent at once as all eyes turned to them. Their eyes met across the room, their hearts sank like stones into their stomachs, they approached each other in total silence, and went away hand in hand.

The conference had been carefully planned. Every single journalist had their other half somewhere in the room and the meeting broke up in chaos and emotion, so LoveStar never had to give a scientific explanation. There was a short intermission in the broadcast while the conference guests recovered (they were never quite the same again). That evening LoveStar sat down in an old chair by a crackling open fire with beaming newspaper reporters all round him and talked serenely as an old grandfather:

"When we have calculated the world, love will flow like milk across borders. All wars and disputes will be a thing of the past, because a Swede who is united with a Chinaman is in reality half Chinese, and the Indian who is calculated with a German has become half German, and when every human child loves halfway across the world and has no need of anything else, there will no longer be any place for hatred or greed. No one will dare to drop bombs on strangers for fear of harming their one true love. Within two generations people will have ceased to define themselves by family, wealth, power, or nationality and will call themselves simply citizens of planet Earth."

LoveStar's experts had already begun to calculate the world. Of course, they couldn't calculate fast enough, the world was impatient. France first! Don't forget the smaller nations! It wasn't until an announcement came from LoveStar that the voices were silenced.

"THOSE WHO COMPLAIN WILL GO TO THE BACK OF THE LINE!"

LoveStar directed people north to Oxnadalur to be calculated and find their other half and happiness. Until then people were to live their lives as if nothing had happened. "Leave love and death to LoveStar," as the saying went, but apart from that people were free to do as they pleased.

inLOVE was built up with the same energy as LoveDeath. To attract enough attention and money to the game, stars and politicians were given precedence, along with critics, possible detractors, and satirists. For a long time calculation festivals at inLOVE were among the most popular TV shows in the world, broadcast live from the Oxnadalur theme park.

The inLOVE show featured no violence or sorrow, only perpetual love and happiness. The program producers captured the most unlikely people in their happynets and united them during live broadcasts. A malicious winner of the Nobel prize for physics, who deplored what he called LoveStar's voodoo science, and a religious leader who was insane with rage that people should be calculated regardless of gender, race, or religion, were persuaded to sit side by side in a Belgian TV studio on the understanding that they were to take part in a debate.

Viewers were able to watch as they melted like butter in each other's presence while struggling to maintain their composure. When they said good-bye at the end of the show they merged together, softened up, laughed and cried, and talked nonsense and hugged, and so they were carried together from the TV studio to the applause and cheering of the audience. Over the next few weeks the changes in their lives were followed via a recording butterfly. Together on a cycling trip, together on a beach, together on skis, or simply cuddled up in bed. That was the most popular. To lie and cuddle up together.

> It is simply impossible to describe the feeling. I have difficulty working out where I stop and she begins. We are one and there is no other way to express the feeling. People will just have to try lying and cuddling up themselves. I believe cuddling has been underrated in the past. Cuddling is a spiritual act. Two people lying

under a duvet or on a sofa and emptying their minds are
the closest you can come to Nirvana.

—Salman Rushdie's response to the question
"what is true love like?" after he was calculated with
the Norwegian skating champion Sonja Heine

It would be superfluous to quote all the articles and debates
that were generated in the first years after the LoveStar corporation found love. An uncalculated poet protested against this
cold scientific approach to the spiritual and irrational aspect of
man, but LoveStar was never lost for an answer:

There is nothing more physical than love. Nothing else has
such a decisive impact on the brain, heart, and lungs. Love
has a measurable effect on blood pressure, circulation, neural
impulses, corpuscles, and complexion. Love-deprivation is
more serious than vitamin deficiency and its consequences
for the body are more severe than scurvy. Love has an impact
on the immune system, metabolism, digestion, digestive
juices, appetite, mental health, zest for life, cell division,
enzymes, and hormone production. Love touches almost
every nerve and cell in the body and every single area of
medical science, but who was responsible for researching
love? Was it doctors? Nuclear physicists? Biochemists? No,
it was POETS and PHILOSOPHERS! They pondered it
for five thousand years without coming to a conclusion.
It's only to be expected that they should be feeling put out.

—"Of Love and Other Devils," excerpt
from an interview with LoveStar

The poets had never described true love because it was indescribable. They spent their time piling up inanities and were never really happy unless they were separated by a hopeless distance from their loved ones, who were preferably situated beyond mountains and seas or even beyond life itself. They described desire and sorrow and distance, but no one had ever succeeded in expressing true, living, mutual love. From the moment the poets made it into bed with the object of their love, not another word of love could be had from them. At best they would mutter grumpily: "Don't bug me. I'm writing."

Aristophanes' words about true love in Plato's *Symposium* came closest to the truth.

> When a lover stumbles upon his other half they both become strangely struck by the amazement of love and friendship and intimacy. They refuse to be separated for even a moment. They can spend their whole lives together but still words will not describe what they desire from one another. No one imagines the only reason is sex, that sex is what gives pleasure to their relationship. No it is an intense desire deeper in the soul, that words can not express.
>
> —Plato's *Symposium*, Greece, 380 BC

Indridi and Sigrid were enlightened, connected, and well educated. The concept and deeper impact of inLOVE should have been perfectly clear to them, but they were so naïve that they believed their relationship to be pure true love and confirmation by inLOVE a mere formality. While most uncalculated inhabitants of the planet looked on with envy as love gushed from the screen, and they saw the feelings, sincerity, and warmth that were lacking in their own failed relationships, the whole debate about true love had the opposite effect on Indridi and Sigrid. It strengthened them in their belief and they made no attempt to hide their love.

"What do you mean, 'have we legitimized our temporary contract of unscientific short-term relationship?'" asked Sigrid, deeply offended, when she went to open a joint account at the bank. "We've already found love."

"Do you have scientific confirmation from inLOVE?" asked the cashier.

"The confirmation's just a formality," said Sigrid in a gentle but firm tone. "We're quite sure."

The cashier shook her head. "You're taking a big risk."

Indridi and Sigrid avoided anything that could possibly cast a shadow on their relationship and drew a positive strength from anything that related to love.

"Huh," said Indridi, reading aloud an interview with a newly calculated couple. "Call that true love! It sounds like one of our bad days."

"Look!" cried Sigrid as they cuddled up under a blanket on the sofa, crunching popcorn and watching a young man calculated with a forty-year-old woman. "I felt just like that the first time we met. I felt like that then and I still do," she said, kissing Indridi.

"I think I know where happiness lies," said Indridi, indicating a point in the middle of his chest, just above his midriff. "It's here."

Sigrid felt his chest. "Where's happiness, Indridi? Show me where happiness lies. Is it here?" she asked, tickling him until he laughed. "Is love here?" she asked, tickling him with her gentle fingers.

Indridi suddenly turned serious and gazed into Sigrid's face. "Every time I draw breath I feel an ache and want to breathe in time with you forever."

"Your happiness is not there," whispered Sigrid. "That's my happiness. My happiness floats on your midriff like a sleeping eider duck, but your happiness is here." Taking his hand she laid it on her breast. "Your happiness is here," she said, and he touched her breasts, which were soft and warm and beautifully white below her sunburnt neck.

Some people found Indridi and Sigrid soppy, but they enjoyed being soppy. Being sincere, talking straight from the heart, and feeling the tickling above their midriffs.

The LoveStar theme park was not only the world center for death, it also became the center for love and scientifically proven happiness, and the origination point for well-calculated bliss after inLOVE was set up. Nowhere in the world was there so much contentment gathered in one spot.

After love had been proven, love letters were sent out all over the world and people flocked to and from the country in white cruise ships. These were a welcome change from the black LoveDeath vessels, and the smell of money they emitted was much fresher than the odor that clung to LoveDeath. The atmosphere of the town was transformed when hopeful individuals disembarked with a letter in their jacket pocket and a bouquet of roses in their hands, glancing around, quivering with anticipation, knowing that nothing but happiness awaited them. Scientifically proven love and happiness.

It was much more pleasant to see infatuated human sandwiches hauled on board the cruise liners under the Statue of Liberty than to see pensioners piled up in the LoveDeath buses. It could be awkward if someone forgot to put tranquillizers in their coffee and a whole herd of walking LoveDeath came to their senses, burst into tears, called home, and asked whether no one was going to come and give them a send-off or keep them company on the last lap. Even the LoveDeath method itself was undergoing a change. In the future, only twin stars would fall to earth.

Indridi and Sigrid sometimes lay cuddled up for whole days at a time, and for them the letter from inLOVE should only have been a formality. When the letter arrived they had intended to go and cuddle up for a few days in the vaults up north in a continuation of the love and happiness that would last until they fell to earth over the Blafjoll mountains in a blaze of love.

Sigrid's mother had warned her. "You can't beat statistics," she said, and the blow took no one but Indridi and Sigrid by surprise. It was only Sigrid who received the letter and she looked at Indridi as he stood, head bowed, with a handful of withered leaves.

"Are you going to go?" he asked.

"Of course not! How could you think such a thing?"

"I thought you didn't have any choice."

"Do you want me to go?"

At that point Indridi broke down into loud sobbing. "If you go I'm going to have myself sent straight to LoveDeath."

Sigrid went over to him and stroked his cheek. She gazed into his eyes, ran her fingers through his hair, and kissed his tears.

"My darling, we're one already. We're one and will be until the end of our days."

Sigrid took the letter from Indridi and tore it to shreds. They clung together as never before, unable to tear themselves apart until the sun covered them with honey the following morning and "eat me, eat me!" echoed around the neighborhood, and their love was stronger and more passionate than ever before. For the moment, at least.

VICTIMS OF FREEDOM

LOVESTAR WOULD HAVE SAID THAT INDRIDI AND SIGRID WERE among the last victims of freedom. They should have known better; they should have behaved rationally and waited their turn. Or as he put it himself:

> If any system was bound to fail it was the idea of a free choice of mate. The experiment lasted for around 150 years and ended in disaster. When civilization was established, mankind's first action was to abolish primitive man's so-called free choice of partner. Of course, there was nothing free about that choice. Primitive man had lived by the same system as the animal kingdom and the results were often laughable. He who had the gaudiest plumage, the reddest buttocks, the biggest horns, he who was strongest and most demanding got to mate with the females and reproduce himself.
>
> As mankind evolved, a better and more civilized sys-

tem was soon invented. A man let his parents decide; they made a cool, considered choice, independent of lust or strength differentials or ludicrous adolescent urges. To ensure the system and unconditional obedience, the parents said that he who divorced his mate or committed adultery would go straight to hell. This was a good idea and everything went smoothly for thousands of years. Those who were unhappy in marriages arranged by their parents could at least blame somebody else. If they fell in love with another they could meet that person in secret and run away together. Beautiful stories were written about adventures of this kind.

But these stories confused people and they began to believe that freedom of choice was always this exciting. To make your own choice was as exciting as making love in secret and eloping on a black horse. But in reality it was chance that ruled. People called this free will but that was far from the truth. People often seized the only thing on offer, or preferably as many as were on offer, because in reality people desired every other person they met in the street and were plagued with perpetual doubts about every choice. By sleeping with one person, people were denying themselves another thousand. Depressing stories were written about free will, about lonely middle-aged men, bitter unfulfilled women, self-accusation, and the children of divorce. It was a vicious circle that no one seemed able to break, and people became like animals once more with their ridiculous ape-buttocks. They competed for the favors of the opposite sex by enlarging their breasts and lips and wasting their energy on cultivating point-less stomach muscles. There was no returning to the old system of arranged marriages as there was nothing left any longer that could be called common parental desires, and no one believed in God or hell any longer. It was not until we at LoveStar discovered how to calculate people that all the problems were solved once and for all. Our system is better. We don't need any hell.

—"The Fetters of Freedom," interview
with LoveStar in *The Economist*

LoveStar and his experts were on a mission to free people from the oppression of freedom. If Indridi and Sigrid had been patient and waited for a scientific result and let themselves be calculated instead of deceiving themselves with their "freedom of choice," they would never have had to pay this emotional price. They should have known better.

REMINDER

INDRIDI AND SIGRID BELIEVED THAT THEY HAD HIT UPON THEIR one true love of their own accord and that if they didn't answer the letter, inLOVE would forget them and turn to more important matters. Ninety percent of the world was still uncalculated, and they assumed they would be happily forgotten and allowed to possess one another until the end of their days. But it wasn't that simple. Sigrid received reminders from inLOVE. They reiterated that her perfect match had been found and that Sigrid could meet him at the LoveStar theme park next week; enclosed was a booking number for Sigrid Møller, along with bus tickets and a color brochure about LoveStar. On the cover was a picture of LoveStar himself smiling broadly. The inLOVE timetable was listed along with interviews with recently calculated couples who had found a new life and true happiness. Indridi exclaimed:

"Sigrid Møller!!!"

"Calm down, Indridi!"

"Sigrid Møller! Have you ever heard such a thing? They've

booked you under the name Sigrid Møller! They're idiots! They're cretins! They're insane! Sigrid, we'll stand together. We won't give in!"

But of course they underestimated the corporate might of LoveStar. At LoveStar it was recognized that some people were quite simply afraid of happiness. When Sigrid failed to answer the reminders, the pressure on her was intensified. By a strange coincidence it didn't matter what Sigrid listened to or watched, the same problem was being discussed, whether on the news or a talk show:

Interviewer: But you thought you'd found the right person by yourself?

Interviewee: Yes, one can be so blind, but inLOVE had calculated that the situation could last a maximum of five years and seven months. *(Indridi and Sigrid had been together for five years, six months, and three weeks.)*

Interviewer: Where did you meet?

Interviewee: At a club.

Interviewer: That reminds me of what LoveStar said: believing you can find your perfect match at a club is equivalent to asking a bartender to perform heart surgery on you.

Interviewee: I never understood that quote. What has love got to do with heart surgery?

Interviewer: Of course, it could have been better phrased. But what he meant was that, when it comes to a phenomenon as important as love, people should act rationally and let the professionals take care of things, rather than dabble themselves; otherwise they're asking for trouble.

Interviewee: I was young and naïve and behaved like a dabbler, but then we came to our senses. We had ourselves calculated and we've never looked back. It's strange to think that only a few years ago there was no LoveStar or LoveDeath, let alone inLOVE. I mean, how did people cope?

Sigrid's evening shift was quiet once the old people had taken their sleeping pills, and she called her sister Hildigunn to ask for advice. Sigrid had never actually received any good advice from her, though Hildigunn was a year older. They had fought like cats and dogs ever since childhood, because they were as different as Coke and Pepsi. Sigrid listened to boy bands, Hildigunn to rap. Sigrid watched romantic comedies; Hildigunn stayed up late every night watching horror movies. Sigrid generally dressed in white or neutrals while Hildigunn was always in black or neon shades, and so on. The reason was not that they were different by nature. They could have been a perfect pair, but when data started to come in indicating that the older sister had become a rapper and a reliable consumer of everything pertaining to rap, an attempt was made to direct the younger sister down a different path. This was based on research that showed siblings of a similar age were, taken together, equivalent to no more than half a consumer. To prevent the sharing and recycling of toys, appliances, music, clothes, and cosmetics, every retailer worth their salt tried to point them in different directions.

"You're joking, right?" asked Hildigunn, when Sigrid asked for advice. She was still uncalculated and had failed to pick up a temporary boyfriend on the free market. "You've received a letter from inLOVE and you're not going to be calculated?"

"That's right."

"That's typical of you," said Hildigunn in disgust. "I'm going to be completely honest here. Indridi is so soft and nice that it makes me want to puke. I mean, planting cinquefoil and forget-me-nots around the Puffin Factory! What kind of man is that, anyway?"

"You've never given him a chance," said Sigrid.

"They've found your perfect match, girl! Doesn't it get your imagination going? Don't you lie awake at night? Doesn't your fantasy take flight? Haven't you imagined what he's like? What he thinks? What his touch is like? Are you totally dead?"

"I lay awake last night thinking about him," said Sigrid sulkily.

"What was he like?"

"He was almost exactly like Indridi except not as nice."

Hildigunn gasped. "Save yourself, Sigrid! Take Per! For God's sake behave scientifically! Do you really think Indridi will resist the temptation when he's finally calculated?"

Sigrid hung up on her and decided to watch a film to calm down. Specially recommended on the menu was "A hard-hitting documentary about inLOVE" and she began to watch it in the belief that it would be critical of the system.

The documentary followed a glamorous young French artist called Pierre. He was calculated with a woman called Sue from Arkansas. She was a down-to-earth, old-fashioned type who chose to remain faithful to her old husband, Bob. The viewers were left in no doubt that Bob was completely wrong for her. For example, he told his friends he didn't care if the old cow talked philosophy and art all day long, so long as he could come in her at night, which is exactly what he did. At night Bob lay on top of Sue and came inside her again and again, whether Sue was in the mood or not. Pierre, her perfect match, was a sensitive soul and had himself launched with LoveDeath when he heard that Sue didn't want to meet him, knowing that it was scientifically proven that in this case he would never again find true love and happiness. Several days after Pierre had burnt up in the atmosphere, Bob was calculated with a beauty queen from Texas while Sue looked on. The beauty queen told her friend she didn't care what kind of man he was, so long as he came inside her several times a night. It didn't take Bob long to give Sue the boot, and then she was alone because she had rejected happiness, missed her chance, and what was worse: she had behaved unscientifically. That was the movie's message.

Indridi moped around at home. As he listened to his favorite music station, a country song (released by LoveSong, a subsidiary of LoveStar) played over and over again about a man and woman who had gotten together the old way before they were calculated with their perfect partners. They were still good friends, nevertheless, laughing together at their foolish youthful infatuation, which, as it says in the refrain (loosely translated): never lasts longer than five years, seven months.

They sang a duet (again, loosely translated):

Man:	It's always hard when ways part. But the pain vanished as soon as we met . . .
Together:	Our perfect match.
Woman:	I met my perfect match and had to leave him for her. For a whole month he was . . .
Together:	Broken-hearted.
He:	It was a hard time but it deepened my feelings and I understood myself better.
Refrain together:	Puppy-love never lasts longer than five years, seven months.
He:	I'm glad she went, because right after, I met . . .
Together:	My perfect match . . .

It was quite clear to Indridi and Sigrid that they were under attack from all sides, that they would be continually deluged by propaganda until they gave in. Every single howler they met whispered or yelled at them: "Max five years, seven months!" "Set free the one you love, Indridi!" "Save yourself, Sigrid!" "Think of the world, Indridi!" They received the message subliminally wherever they went, but it only made them even more determined to stand together and resist being so easily calculated apart. Deep down they were sure they were made for one another, that their souls were already united. Of course, there were some odds against this happening: four billion to one.

Indridi was not the type who fell for images and film clips and he never jumped at special offers. It was a simple matter to compare advertising showing times on the one hand and dates on his Visa bills on the other to see how slowly he reacted to stimulation. iSTAR knew, for instance, that Indridi was a thoughtful man who regarded himself as intelligent enough to see through the hype. iSTAR knew too that his self-confidence grew every time he resisted being deceived. As a result he was sent a good helping of hype every day to increase the likelihood that he would swallow the reverse: hypeless ads that appealed directly to him as a man of intelligence and rationality. "You're enlightened and clever and you don't fall for gimmicks and special offers. We would never offend you by directing such ads at you, which is why we want to point out to you that as a thoughtful and responsible person you must see that now is the right moment to upgrade your car . . ."

Indridi and Sigrid did not give in, regardless of the methods that were used against them, but various aspects of their lives began to deteriorate. The media was filled with strange programming and all communication systems became slow and unwieldy. Then came the blow: Indridi was denied access to their joint bank account. It was in Sigrid's name, as she had originally opened it. But as things stood, LoveBank felt it imperative to separate their finances. At such a delicate time, Indridi could easily have emptied the account and made off with the money to prevent Sigrid from purchasing "an unforgettable calculation week of food, drink, massage, luxury, and endless cuddling." At the same instant as when Indridi's account was closed, he received a notification from the Student Loan Fund:

"According to our contract we are permitted to devolve responsibility for debt collection for your student loan to a third party if your loan creditworthiness is in doubt. As you apparently own no assets, we will have to resort to an organization that can collect payments in another form. iSTAR has taken over the contract and will be responsible for collecting the sum of 3,888,689 points."

Indridi reread the letter and choked on his morning coffee as he yelled out:

"HOORAY! I'M A HOWLER!"

He coughed and looked round. The noise had come from him. A text materialized in the air before him like a cloud. A cheerful voice sounded in his head.

"Hooray, you've joined iSTAR's payment service! Why struggle with payment installments when there's a much simpler way for you to clear your debt? Congratulations on becoming one of a team of millions of people around the world who let iSTAR see to their bills. We have paid the Student Loan Fund (*switch to a melodic female voice*): 3,888,689 points. (*Switch back to upbeat voice*) You needn't pay us a dime! We'll put a few words in your mouth and your debt will disappear. We'll exploit access to your speech centers and it may also prove necessary to activate your primitive biological reflexes. iSTAR is above all an easy and entertaining way to pay off your debts."

Indridi rang iSTAR immediately. He wasn't going to be any damned howler.

"iSTAR, good morning," answered a female voice.

"Good morning, there's been some mistake. I've become a howler."

"Welcome to doing business with us."

"No, you see there's been some mistake. My girlfriend was registered for our account . . ."

"Press one for orders, two for howlers."

Indridi pressed two. A man answered.

"iSTAR, Howler Department."

In the background there was a sound of waves and gulls mewing. A ship's whistle blew. The man who answered was sitting in his fisherman's jersey on the jetty in the village of Patreksfjord, smoking a pipe, fishing with hook and line, and talking into thin air. He was a cordless modern man.

"Good morning, I'm . . ."

"Indridi Haraldsson."

"Yes, exactly, I'm . . ."

"You're a howler."

"Yes. No. I'm not interested. I want to resign."

"Contracts can only be terminated with three months' notice."

"I never made any contract. I refuse to take part in this."

"According to the seventh clause of the eighth section . . ."

"Are you listening to me? Not a chance, I won't howl a single announcement!"

"One moment," said the man, "please hold a moment."

Indridi waited and heard nothing but gulls mewing and the sound of the sea and then the echo of a conversation: "Nothing but a worthless flatfish . . ."

"Excuse me," said the man, "there was someone else on the line. What were you saying?"

"I'm not going to say anything. I'm staying indoors. I'm locking myself in. Cutting out my tongue."

The man didn't answer. There was no sound but the slapping of waves and the chugging of a small boat.

"Are you still there?"

"I just wanted to give you a chance to calm down," said the man. "It's so soothing listening to the fulmars and the sea."

"I am calm," said Indridi.

"Good. I should inform you that more contracts have just come in. People obviously don't trust your ability to pay. We will also have to collect 50 percent of the rent for 90 Hraunbaer and 50 percent of your payments and insurance on a Subaru licence number R-72623, in addition to all your subscription fees, Visa bills, data transmissions, including optic nerve connections, and online-connection bills. You are in a state of total insolvency. Unfortunately you have also exceeded the howler limits: speech-center connections will not cover the payments. We will have to have a trap from you every week. You can choose the method."

"I'm not choosing anything!" shouted Indridi.

"Just calm down a minute. There's a brilliant campaign in progress. Xtremesport needs to expand the market for its autumn line. All traps laugh hysterically when they see anyone wearing a blue Millets anorak. If anyone asks the traps why they are laughing, they howl:

"I CAN'T BELIEVE THAT GUY'S STILL WEARING A BLUE MILLETS ANORAK!"

"NO! No way! It's all a misunderstanding!" yelled Indridi. "I'll sort it out at the bank later today. I'm not broke. I'll talk to my girlfriend and have money transferred to my account!"

"Be careful because the transfer will be registered as her gift to you. Gifts are liable to 30 percent tax."

The man let three waves crash and two black-backed gulls screech before continuing in a kind voice:

"There's a three-month notice period. You're legally bound to complete the period of contract. If you don't howl up your subscription fee we'll be forced to terminate your cordless connection and refer you to the old system."

This sounded like unfair terms but was actually a threat. It was possible to become a wire-slave and cease to be a cordless connected subscriber, but it was only a theoretical option as most home appliances were cordless, switchless, and remote controlled via lenses. Of course, one could pick up a phone and call 234.415.333.333 in order to turn on the tap in the bath (or was it 334?) and use the same number, but ending in 537, to flush the toilet, and it was possible to open the car door by calling 395.506.432.664 and tapping in a one-hundred-digit code for the car alarm.

"I have no choice," said Indridi.

"You're free," said the man. "Freedom is wonderful; you can do what you like." Eider ducks oohed in the background and a gull cackled.

"I have no choice," said Indridi.

"Good-bye," said the man.

Indridi wondered what to do but was only halfway through his thought when he suddenly shouted:

"DALLAS IS STARTING! DALLAS IS STARTING!"

"THANK YOU!" called the old man from next door.

Indridi flushed bloodred and paced the floor. The first notes of the theme song carried through the wall. Indridi listened to the tune, then put his hands over his ears and turned on his stereo full volume. The neighbor banged on the wall, but Indridi left the flat with everything on full blast. He tried to behave in such a way that no company would dream of having its name connected to him. Which is why he went up and down the escalator at the Kringlan shopping mall seven times naked. But the company observed the rule: "Bad publicity is better than no publicity," so that on his seventh trip up the escalator a woman noticed him. She was obviously in a target group that was interested in performance art because Indridi howled the moment he passed her:

"REMEMBER THE OPENING AT KJARVAL GALLERY! HAPPENINGS AND HAPPINESS!"

SECRET HOST

MOST PEOPLE WERE UNDER THE IMPRESSION THAT SIMON SMARI Magnusson was a cordless programmer with rather dubious taste in films; even his girlfriend Maria thought so after a three-year provisional relationship. No one knew that for over ten years Simon had been one of the most prolific spies and secret hosts of his generation.

When Simon was thirteen years old, it seemed clear that he would be one of the most sought-after and popular boys in the school. He was tall, handsome, tanned, amusing, and always looked as if he'd just emerged from the hairdresser's. He had a way with words, and it was obvious that he would lead the pack when it came to music and fashion. It was far more effective for shops to have him wear their clothes than to drape them over a dummy in the window. By the time he was sixteen, Simon had deals with a shopping center, two cinemas, and a telephone company, as he received far more phone calls than he made. It cost forty-six points a minute to call Simon, of which he himself received twenty-two points. It didn't matter which girl called him; he would let her stay on the line for as long as she wanted.

"Just hold a minute," he'd say, "I'm going to play an awesome track from the awesome new BOYZ CD while I slip into MY EVILS JEANS." Sometimes he'd talk to two girls at once without their knowing, letting them chatter on and listen to songs in turn.

He rarely invited girls with him to the movies, preferring to spread it around school that he was going to see a film with the boys. It was certain that ten to twenty adolescent girls from the lower grades would go to the same show in the faint hope of meeting him or his friends. The girls would then be followed by a bunch of nerdy boys from their own classes. When the groups met, Simon was always cheerful and self-confident, smiling his brightest smile and praising the girls for shopping at the right stores.

In the high season of spring, he would take a girl or two with him to the Kringlan shopping mall and help her spend her confirmation money. Nearly three-quarters of the markup went straight into his pocket, as it was only fair that the person who actually sold the goods should be rewarded for his pains.

"Buy both pairs of jeans if you can't make up your mind. You look just as cute in both," he said smiling, and the girl blushed and did as he suggested. "You could get a tattoo to match . . ."

Despite his success, Simon was rather isolated. He didn't know any other secret hosts and wasn't sure if he was the only one in his grade. However, he suspected certain people, sometimes everyone, and took care to smother all their attempts from the start. Ginger-haired Halldor had, for example, tried to get Simon to buy golf clubs and play on a course with him.

Simon took care after that to squash all Halldor's ideas or else turn them to his own advantage. If Halldor wanted to go to one film, Simon would fight for the gang to go to another. Sparks often flew between them.

Simon the secret host and spy couldn't share his success with anyone. All communications went through his home site at iSTAR and generally the offers came automatically via the computer system. He didn't know the people who ran the system, so Simon couldn't brag about how he made three thousand points by getting two girls to hold the line for fifty minutes while he took a bath and watched a thriller with one eye.

Simon drove around in smart cars and ate out most evenings, yet he had never bought a car, never paid for clothes or food in restaurants. He was registered everywhere as a marketing expense. He had never paid for a vacation abroad out of his own pocket. He always managed to infiltrate a group holiday, direct it to some other destination than originally intended, and get himself a free trip in the process. While the group was lying on the beach he would slip away and make a deal with a restaurant owner or shopping center, promising to bring along a group of ten if he got something in return.

Simon was popular but had few friends, meeting most of the people he associated with through Maria. They were in a couples' club that met up regularly, cooked, drank red wine, and had a cozy time, but he didn't regard anyone in the group as a real friend. Simon made an effort, nevertheless, to keep the couples' club going, as it was an important market. On couples' nights he collected valuable information for iSTAR; he planted information and recommended goods, but took care to be very delicate about the sale itself. He laid the bait but left it to others to reel in the fish.

You could say that everything had gone swimmingly for Simon until the day Maria came storming home. Simon lay on the sofa, leafing through a potential bestseller when Maria's shadow fell on him. She screeched:

"Simon! I got an offer from a plastic surgeon!"

Simon looked up from his book. "This is such a gripping read that I didn't hear what you said." He showed her the cover.

"I got an offer from a plastic surgeon today," Maria repeated.

"Really," murmured Simon innocently. "Are you going to accept it?"

"Do you know what he offered me?"

"I expect it was the thing you showed me."

"Exactly."

"Are you going to accept the offer?"

"How do they know, Simon?"

"Mm?"

"How do they know?"

"Are you sure they know?"

"They offered to help me get rid of exactly what I showed you."

"Did they make an offer on the area around the spot to the right of . . . ?"

"EXACTLY! How did they know?"

"I swear I didn't say anything to anyone."

"You're the only one who knew. You're the only person who's had their face down there. It was a secret!"

"Hey! Don't blame me! Are you sure you haven't told anyone else?"

"I'M SURE!"

"Well, then it's just a coincidence. Where are you going with the girls this evening? You should go to The Althing, the puffin sandwich there is quite . . ."

"Don't change the subject, Simon. Do you really believe anyone else has one of these? How can it be a coincidence?"

"Then you must have told someone, for goodness' sake . . ."

"I haven't told A SINGLE GODDAMN PERSON APART FROM YOU! I didn't even tell the girls about this! Did you tell on me?"

Simon looked down at his hands and said unconvincingly, "No."

"The offer came the day after you saw it!"

Simon flushed and said nothing.

"I trusted you! My God, you can be lousy! What deal did you make, you bastard? Thirty percent? Forty percent? The offer was for one hundred fifty thousand!"

Simon didn't know what to say. The iSTAR employee who was listening in to the conversation via Simon's invisible earpiece sent him a suggested response: "Hey! You should see a shrink!"

Simon didn't like it but muttered anyway, "Hey, you should see a shrink."

"CAN YOU RECOMMEND ANYONE? YOU SECRET HOST!"

Simon received a suggestion on his lens: [recommendation: therapist jonsson phone: 551 9550].

Simon was about to recommend the therapist when he realized what he was doing and blocked any further assistance.

"What's the matter with you?" he whined.

"Only yesterday you told the girls to go to a totally awesome film."

"Lots of people recommended it."

"They thought it was crap."

"That's their business."

"Have you no self-respect?"

He was silent.

"Answer me! Have you no self-respect?"

"People have different tastes. Why can't I?"

"But you haven't seen the film! They said you always recommended crappy films! You're a secret host, aren't you? Admit it! Are you a spy as well, maybe? Maybe you've got the line open at the moment? Is there someone listening to us?" Maria yelled in his ear: "HELLO! IS THERE ANYONE THERE? DOES ANYONE WANT TO KNOW WHAT I WANT? I NEVER WANT TO SEE SIMON AGAIN! DO YOU HEAR? I NEVER EVER WANT TO SEE HIM AGAIN!"

Simon went out. He wandered around town bowed and beaten, but he perked up a little when a teenager praised his new jacket.

"Wicked jacket!"

"Hey, thanks," said Simon. "I got it from Man of the World!"

Before the day was over several other people had slipped him compliments. The team at iSTAR, who had overheard everything, arranged for nine compliments to be howled at him in order to calm his feelings.

"You're a world beater. Don't give up, Simon!" said an old graybeard.

"You're so cool, Simon!" shouted a woman with a baby carriage.

"Thimon!" came from the carriage (it was considered cute if

children said something too, especially if they were babies and hadn't yet learned to talk).

Several weeks later Maria had received so many offers from plastic surgeons, information, advice, and so on that she decided to go for it and let them sort out the thing that no one knew about except that damn spy and secret host Simon. He received his percentage in the end (30 percent), in addition to a fifty-thousand-point deposit for a final report on the details of Maria's life.

Part 12B: She doesn't know where Africa is. She can't stand Swedish thrillers. More sympathetic to sick dogs than sick babies. Pizza sauce always goes bad in the fridge (N.B. smaller containers). She likes it best doggy-style (film clip attached, N.B.! Don't sell it within her target group). She knows nothing about science but believes anything that sounds scientific (market hair products with chemical formulas).

Simon worked out that the emotional cost had been reasonable relative to the profit. Maria couldn't be his one and only anyway. It was scientifically proven. A month later he was still emotionally battered so he called REGRET and had it calculate what would have happened if he hadn't blown his cover, if he had carried on servicing Maria and her friends. He asked for a brief answer:

"You'd have died."

"How?"

"You'd have been run over by a tram on the 18th of February." He closed his eyes and tried to concentrate. "It was a good thing I blew my cover, otherwise I'd have been run over by a tram on the 18th of February. It was a good thing I blew my cover, otherwise I'd have been run over by a tram on the 18th of February." But it didn't matter how hard he concentrated, he couldn't fill the void that Maria had left behind in his heart, not even when his jacket was praised for the fourth time (belated praise led people to believe that the relevant garment was a classic of its kind and a good investment).

Maria had left and with her went many of his best customates. Now he would have to move, find a new group, build up trust, and get better established. Chain-friendship was the fate of secret hosts. He made a friend, concentrated on him for a while, then turned to his friend's friend, and *his* friend the following year, and so on. The current chain-friend enjoyed his undivided attention for a time but then his attention was gradually directed elsewhere. Simon had put himself through five groups of friends in seven years and so had a wide but rather loose-knit net of acquaintances. After he lost his customates through Maria, his turnover tumbled and his personal rating at iSTAR took a dive. He was forced to concentrate on his family for a while.

"Dad, you should try a Saab. Mom, who on earth cut your hair? Grandma, I'm not going to give you a lift to Bonus. You should go to 10-11; it's quicker and cheaper."

His dream was to scale the heights at iSTAR, quit the mean streets, get into the creative side of advertising, become part of the ideas team, draw up campaigns, even get a job as a service rep or follow a target group from youth to adulthood, instruct, remote control, categorize, and record them. But all his applications were turned down and all the ideas he sent to iSTAR were bounced straight back. Nevertheless, he lived with the hope and got butterflies in his stomach every time there was a message from iSTAR. One day he received the following special assignment:

[Problem category: Victim of freedom.
Individual: Sigrid Gudmundsdottir, calculated with Per Møller.
Problem: SG refuses to be calculated because of Indridi H.
Goal: Essential to bring SG north to meet her one and only.
Budget for information, announcements, AdHosts, traps, stuntmen, etc.: one hundred sixty-seven thousand points.
Budget subtracted from sales commission.
If a satisfactory result is not achieved, the cost will be subtracted from your balance at iSTAR.]

Simon got straight back to iSTAR.

"Yes, hi there!" he said breezily. "It's about the assignment. Don't you have anything else for me? You see, Indridi and Sigrid are friends of Maria's and mine, and I would hate to . . ."

"No problem," answered a man's voice brusquely. "We'll get someone else for the job."

"That would be great, thank you. I just need to lay off my immediate vicinity . . ."

"Your refusal will be recorded in your application for the position of secret-host marketing advisor at iSTAR. Do you want an explanatory note attached? Are there any other limits to your capability?"

Simon was speechless. "No, no. I just wanted to see whether there was anything better on offer . . ."

"Refusal is accompanied by a mandatory week's leave."

"Since when?"

"It's new policy. It's difficult to get good people for the tough cases. The system won't work if people only opt for the fun assignments."

"I'm sorry," said Simon. "All I said was that they were friends of Maria's and mine."

"It's been two months and three days since you last met your friends and according to my information you're no longer with Maria."

"We're having temporary problems . . ."

"That doesn't fit with my information. Are you shirking responsibility? Can I put that on your application?"

Simon crumpled. This was an unusually grumpy moodman. Why did he have to bring up the application and Maria?

"I'll think about it," said Simon, preparing to hang up.

"I'll hold," said the moodman.

"What?"

"Your week's leave begins in two minutes."

A clock appeared in front of Simon and started to count down the two minutes.

"Two minutes?"

Flustered, Simon hurriedly looked over the special assignment and weighed up the choices. "If I don't do it someone else will," he thought to himself. "That someone else could be a brute of a debt collector who uses extreme methods."

"I'll take it on," said Simon dully, with only fifteen seconds remaining.

He received instant total access to Indridi's and Sigrid's personal media. At first it seemed a bit of a dirty job to Simon, but he convinced himself that he was mainly doing Sigrid a favor that she would appreciate later. Then his guilt gave way to a pure spirit of competitiveness. He went energetically to work, directing appropriate documentaries, propaganda films, and ads their way. He adjusted song lyrics and talk shows before forwarding them: "True love never lasts beyond five years and seven months." He pulled a few strings to make their life a bit harder by influencing the banking system and timetable of shifts at the geriatric unit.

But Indridi and Sigrid were stubborn, unbelievably stubborn, and his budget was running low. If things went on the way they were going he would get nothing in return and his personal rating would drop even further. He'd soon be reduced to being a trap or howler. Simon decided to invite Indridi to lunch and assess his will to fight, see whether his defences hadn't lowered enough for an ordinary lecture to do the trick.

"RAVEN LIQUORICE," answered Indridi wearily when Simon called. (It was Thursday, when iSTAR would hire out part of the howlers' daily vocabulary. A company could have its name substituted for hello, bye, really, yes, no, black, or white. This turned conversations toward the brand.)

"I was wondering whether we could meet up at lunchtime?" said Simon.

"SINALCO, I'm afraid not," said Indridi. "I'm meeting Sigrid for lunch."

"I sent Sigrid an e-mail," said Simon. "She said it was okay by her."

"MANGO ZEST, she said that?"

"Let's say twelve, at The Althing, the new place in the old parliament house. Bye."

"COUNTRY COOKIES."

Simon briefed himself well in order to exploit the lunch to the fullest. He went carefully through all the reports about Indridi. He was recorded as a down-to-earth, honest, and loyal individual. According to the service rep who managed Indridi, he was borderline autistic from a marketing point of view. No doubt that explained why he clung so tightly to Sigrid. Indridi could be relied on to buy blueberry yogurt, Bounty bars, Adidas shoes, Grandma's Pancakes, Blizzard skis, liver paté, and Co-op bread. If he went out at lunchtime he generally bought soda and olive bread at the Norwegian place in the old City Jail downtown, or chicken at the Indian place in the old Ministry Offices. He read the *Morgunbladid* newspaper and ate ham and pineapple pizzas. He was filled with insecurity if the packaging of his favorite brands was changed or production stopped due to technological advances or low sales. It generally didn't pay to pester Indridi, but when a new invention or product line came on the market there was everything to lose. Indridi had a strong sense of sympathy and generally sided with the underdog or those who were badly treated in some way. The reports said: "Never buys mega-bestsellers, tries to even out the share of those which are good but sell less."

Indridi looked rough: unkempt and unshaven with shadows under his eyes. The waiter brought a complimentary beer for Simon while Indridi devoured a puffin sandwich. Simon had recommended it wholeheartedly.

Simon put a book on the table. It was a bestseller that had sold millions of copies within certain target groups. Indridi picked up the book and examined it.

"Great book," said Simon. "Shame it's been overshadowed by

other titles, just because they're better marketed. It's sad when sales hype matters more than quality."

"I've heard of it," said Indridi. "Wanted to read it."

Simon employed his closing tactic. "I'm in a book club. I could have it sent to you at club price."

"FRESH HADDOCK, thanks," said Indridi, which Simon took as acquiescence and closed the sale on the spot.

They were sitting by the window in The Althing chamber. Above them was a screen with a direct link to the Democracy machine. It was connected to the pulse of the nation at iSTAR and provided such a complete picture of the people's wishes that it had replaced both parliament and government. The nation's views on motions, which the government firms (mostly owned by iSTAR) placed before it, were updated hourly. There weren't actually that many motions and some were only there to amuse the restaurant customers. Indridi watched the letters moving across the screen: Do you want to add the LoveStar symbol to the national flag? Yes: 69%. No: 11%. Motion carried. . . . Do you want an oil war with the Faroe Islands? Yes: 49%. No: 51%. Motion rejected by a narrow margin. . . . Do you want rebirths and spare copies to be legalized again? Yes: 81%. No: 10%. Motion carried. . . . Do you want to cut your standard of living and provide better services for the disabled? Yes: 15%. No: 69%. Motion rejected. . . .

Simon cleared his throat and turned to the issue at stake. The book sale was only a warm-up, his way of getting in the mood. While they were sitting there the topic of conversation edged ever closer to the center, like a needle on a record, closer to the goal where it would all end.

"How are things going with you and Sigrid?" asked Simon, sipping his beer.

"Sigrid and I didn't calculate together," said Indridi sadly.

"Shame," said Simon, "but, look on the bright side, you have to be glad for her. It's impossible to feel sad about other people's happiness."

"PRINCE POLO, perhaps not," said Indridi.

"Your time will come, Indridi. Be sure to remember LoveStar's philosophy: Free the one you love. To me these words contain an important truth. Maria and I decided to see whether we could free each other. It was hard at first, but now we're fine. I've never had so many compliments from complete strangers." (He got a lump in his throat merely from thinking about Maria.)

"But our case is really special," said Indridi. "You don't understand how it is between Sigrid and me. Our relationship is unique."

"Unique? What do you two talk about?"

"Talk about?" Indridi thought. "Just, lots of things. Sometimes we lie around all evening talking."

"But what do you talk about?"

Indridi thought but couldn't remember any particular topic of conversation. "I don't know exactly," he said.

"But what do you do?"

Indridi thought and shrugged. "What anyone does," he said. "Live, and cuddle when possible."

Simon had difficulty hiding the fact that he had always found Indridi and Sigrid rather nauseating. Nauseating was perhaps putting it too strongly. Indridi and Sigrid were incredibly sweet together and okay in most ways, even fun, but they were somehow so steamy. Always had their hands down each other's backs, grabbing each other's asses. There was something in their eyes and the way they kissed for no reason. Even when they weren't French-kissing, their kisses were lewd with wet, pouting lips and half-closed eyes that looked creepy with only the whites visible. If they behaved like that in public you could bet they went a lot further in private. Simon felt uneasy shaking their hands, as if he had touched a soiled doorknob in a public restroom—there was no telling where their hands had been.

Simon looked at Indridi, who was raising his index finger to his nose. Simon grimaced. He suspected them of wiping each other's scent on their fingers or the backs of their hands before they went to work. They both had a strange nasal twitch that reinforced his suspicion. He was sure they sent each other regular messages saying when they should both sniff: "Sniff me." He suspected them of being in constant audio contact, even when they weren't always talking to one another, just to be sure that the other was alive and breathing. If Simon bumped into Sigrid at a store she often referred word for word to the conversation Indridi had had with him earlier that morning. Simon tried not to let them get on his nerves, they were all right and he had nothing against them really, but it didn't alter the fact that Indridi and Sigrid were steamy and he always sensed something desperate and doomed in their behavior.

"I would do what's scientifically right," said Simon. "According to the statistics, love like yours lasts a maximum of five years and seven months. You can't beat statistics. After inLOVE is completed and the world has merged, love will flow like milk across borders and all wars and conflicts will end. We all have to do our bit."

"I'm never going to let her go," said Indridi. "I wouldn't survive an hour without her."

"There goes the global argument," thought Simon. He watched Indridi raise his finger to his nose, sniff it, and slide it into his mouth. Simon felt sick. No doubt he was now getting the message: "Sniff and taste me." Simon took a sip of beer before carrying on.

"I'm your friend and I would never tell you to part unless I knew that it would be best for you both. The introductory offer only lasts until the new year, then the price goes up and what'll you do if your love fades and you want to meet your perfect match? You'll lose hundreds of thousands of points."

"Sigrid is priceless to me," said Indridi, shaking his head. "Love can't be measured with money."

Simon clenched his toes. The financial argument didn't work. Nor did the global argument. He sighed and grasped at his final straw: Indridi's sympathy for the underdog.

"I just hope he survives this," said Simon.

"Who?"

"I hope the man who was calculated with Sigrid has a strong character. You never know . . ."

"Never know what?"

"Some people won't want to live," said Simon carefully. "You must understand . . . suicide."

Indridi stared down at the remains of his puffin. Simon looked at him gravely:

"I wouldn't say this unless I knew it was for your own good. If Sigrid's other half dies and you're calculated shortly afterward, a disastrous chain reaction will have been set in motion.

Think carefully, Indridi. This is no game. You must see the bigger picture."

Indridi sat silent and pensive until he howled: "DON'T FORGET YOUR MEETING, SIMON!"

Simon looked at the clock. "Thank you," he said. "I almost forgot. Better get going. See you!" Simon hurried down the corridor.

"Could you possibly lend me some money?" Indridi called after Simon.

"Haven't a dime, sorry," he said, vanishing from the room.

Indridi considered his situation. "Disastrous chain reaction."

He remained sitting at the table, not knowing what to do with himself. He wanted to take a peep at REGRET and get confirmation that everything was how it should be, but gave up the idea when he saw the people sitting on the benches in Austurvollur square. There were always some victims of REGRET, people who became seriously ill from the bleak answers it gave them. Those who sank deepest into REGRET spent all their money on it and became hyperaware of what would have happened and therefore what might happen. They hugged the walls so as to have as little impact on the world as possible, always weighed things up carefully in advance, and had anxiety attacks when it came to making a decision or a change of policy because the end of the world lay literally at every step. When they subsequently examined their life on REGRET, it always transpired that every single decision they had made (generally after two hours of thought) was the right one. It was a good thing I put on the red trousers, otherwise I'd have been killed. It was good to be careful, it was good to talk quietly, it was good to not disturb the world, and it was a good thing I checked with REGRET.

Although those who were dependent on REGRET tried to have as little impact on the world as possible, it was these people who were most noticeable: the woman who sat in Laekjartorg square, waiting for a bus, but refused to board when the bus came because she hesitated and thought: "Its route could lead to certain death." So she decided to wait for the next bus, and so on, until she sat down on a bench, accepted a drink from the down-and-outs, checked REGRET, and received the instant answer: Every single bus would have led to certain death.

A tightrope walker must never look down or he'll lose his balance. These people always looked down. Stared down into the abyss and lost their balance.

Indridi was on the point of losing his balance and took care not to look down. The waiter came to the table. He was wearing a black cloak and a wig. Indridi sat looking in embarrassment at the waiter who loomed over him like a British judge.

"Can't pay; can I wash up?" asked Indridi.

"I'm afraid there's no washing up on offer," said the waiter sternly. "You can pay by howling. Ten howls for a puffin sandwich."

"Bloody hell, what a rip-off," thought Indridi, and bargained: "A single trap?"

"Epilepsy trap with a text, during Friday's rush hour," the waiter said shortly.

"Epilepsy trap with a text?" asked Indridi.

"A rare and effective trap. Really makes the text stick in the recipient's memory."

Indridi agreed to the conditions with half his mind. Sometime on Friday he would have an epileptic fit in a busy place and the announcement would be engraved on the recipient's memory: "YOU'LL HAVE A FIT IF YOU MISS OUT ON THE ALTH-ING'S PUFFIN SANDWICH OFFER!"

Sigrid was in a bad mood when Indridi came home. Her lunch break had been spent arguing with the furious neighbor about the noise from their apartment.

"You left the music system on full blast! I thought you'd died or something! What were you thinking of?"

"I met Simon at lunchtime."

"Why didn't you tell me?"

"Simon said he let you know."

"I didn't know anything. I'd have eaten at work."

Indridi was going to tell her about the howler business. That he had become a howler and might start talking complete gibberish, but before he could say a word he began to sing "Yesterday" again.

"YESTERDAY, ALL MY TROUBLES SEEMED SO FAR AWAY!!!"

Indridi bit back the song, fled into the bathroom, and locked the door, but the song persisted. Sigrid stared after him.

"ARE YOU DRUNK?"

Indridi turned on the shower but could still be heard from the corridor: "NOW IT LOOKS AS THOUGH THEY'RE HERE TO STAY!"

Sigrid banged on the door. "WHAT'S GOING ON?"

"International song week next week, sing and be happy!" he burped through clenched teeth.

Indridi and Sigrid faced blows and pressure from all sides. Indridi was sent home from work for singing. Sigrid had to take ten night shifts due to staff "illness," so they no longer had any time for word-synthesis. Sigrid came home tired in the morning and went to sleep just as Indridi woke up, foul-breathed and musty.

When Sigrid had been humming along to some unusually good tune on the night shift it was more often than not announced as "a request by Per Møller." When she admired her favorite actor, a text bubble appeared saying: Per Møller's favorite actor. According to the information, Per had seen every single one of his films at least twice, and so had Sigrid.

Of course, Indridi saw nothing of this—the program was only visible to the eyes watching it. Sigrid had stopped mentioning the Møller ads aloud, as Indridi went berserk every time he heard Per Møller mentioned and she hardly recognized him in this mood. She spent quite some time checking out Per's information page at inLOVE because it had links to almost everything she was interested in. She didn't know that each time she visited his page, Indridi received a notification:

[sigrid is checking out information about per møller. heard it from a friend who's a systems manager. thought I should let you know. regards simon.]

Indridi felt as if he'd received a kick in the stomach, a dagger in his back, a needle under his fingernails. He writhed and suffered.

[she's still on the page. regards simon.]

To Sigrid it all seemed perfectly innocent, as she wasn't reading up about Per himself, nor could they get in touch with one another except through the mediation of inLOVE.

Indridi was on tenterhooks. Every time he opened his mouth, some nonsense might fly out. Every time he came home he was terrified that Sigrid would have gone north to have herself calculated.

"Sigrid, are you home?" he called.

"I'm here, Indridi."

Indridi entered the flat to a wholesome smell of baking. Sigrid was in the kitchen and his heart leapt with relief. She was sitting there with her hair in a bun, newly bathed, and wearing an ugly old dress. She was braless and her hands were covered in flour. Indridi touched her hand gently and kissed her softly on the neck. She smiled, darted him a look, and had just puckered up her lips when he barked:

"PRETTY DRESS! YOU WERE SMART TO BUY SUCH A PRETTY DRESS!"

Sigrid looked at him strangely. "Are you making fun of me? You've seen it before. I wear it for baking and crafts."

"Yes, now I remember," said Indridi, smiling awkwardly.

The dress contained a chip the size of a butterfly brain with five howler compliments attached. They were all unused because Sigrid had never worn the dress in public. An hour later Indridi walked past the kitchen and called:

"PRETTY DRESS! YOU WERE SMART TO BUY SUCH A PRETTY DRESS!"

Sigrid jumped and gave him a dirty look but two hours later all was forgotten. They cooked supper and laughed at something ridiculous and the meal ended with a deep kiss. Indridi removed her dress and it fell to the floor. While she was pulling down his fly, Indridi accidentally trod on the dress and crushed the butterfly brain. He felt the announcement arrive with full weight. He locked his jaw, grew red in the face, and tears sprang to his eyes with the pressure. The announcement thrust upon his speech centers, harder and harder until his head was bursting and he yelled: "PRETTY! DRESS! YOU! WERE! SMART! TO! BUY! SUCH! A! PRETTY! DRESS!!!!"

The phone rang and Sigrid was called out on an extra shift. She left without saying good-bye. There were cracks in the defensive barriers that Indridi and Sigrid had raised around themselves and, though neither let on that they had noticed, they had been together for exactly five years and seven months.

I WOULD WITHER AWAY

"THE SEED IS WITHERING," THOUGHT LOVESTAR. HE LOOKED around. His heart pounded in his chest. "The seed mustn't wither," he thought but didn't dare move. He didn't dare breathe on the seed. He didn't dare stand up to fetch a drop of water. He looked at his hands, which were closed around the seed. They were old hands. The sky was bright with stars, but he covered the window so he didn't have to watch any more LoveDeath.

His body had rejected LoveDeath. So it was with most of his brainchildren; he wanted little to do with them once they had been born. As chairman he was the most senior official at LoveDeath, but in reality he hated it every time he was forced to give LoveDeath an additional moment. LoveDeath's gestation had taken five long years and during that period death had expanded inside his head until nothing else could get in. He roved around the world searching for experts and cheap, secondhand rockets. It was difficult to find governments willing or able to give away the technology. In underground vaults in the bowels of the Urals there were thousands of unused launchpads and long-range missiles left over from the Cold War. The nuclear cores were believed to have been destroyed, and many of them were in danger of dilapidation. They were fairly small rockets that could easily be converted to shoot up a deceased rock star.

In the Florida swamps rockets lay scattered like flotsam after a series of hurricanes, most of them overgrown with vegetation and probably inoperative, but they might provide spare parts for LoveDeath. Then there were rockets in storage that hadn't been used for decades, not since birdwaves did away with the satellite industry. This was one of the factors that made things difficult for LoveStar. He was hated by rocket engineers and space scientists. The LOVESTAR satellite constellation that twinkled behind LavaRock was the final humiliation in their eyes.

Of course, LoveStar attended to other business and the administration of the company as needed, followed up on the birdwaves and mankind's liberation from cords, gave speeches at conferences, promoted new technology and the company's future vision, but the same thing applied to these activities as to LoveDeath later on: his passion and greatest talent was for new ideas and that's where he wanted to stay, instead of wearing himself out on the daily grind of business. Every free moment was spent on LoveDeath, and sometimes he was abroad for months without coming home.

On the final day of the gestation, LoveStar had been on his way from Vladivostok to Los Angeles where he had a meeting booked with a plastic surgeon who wanted to run the first Love-Death branch on the west coast of America. He had an hour to visit home, see the family, and fetch some data. The taxi stopped outside his villa. The boys were obviously home because their Mercedeses were in the drive—one of them badly bashed up in front and scratched all along the driver's side. The garden was a mass of weeds. The front door opened automatically.

"Helga?" he called as he went inside. "Boys! Helga? Is anyone home?" LoveStar had a look around. The house had changed. The sitting room had been painted in darker shades. The boys were nowhere to be seen. He went upstairs.

"Helga?"

Helga appeared on the bedroom landing. LoveStar hardly recognized her. She had grown so thin . . .

"Were you asleep?"

"No, I was dyeing my hair black," she said.

"Where are the boys?"

"They're still in Croatia."

"Still?"

"They sailed up the Adriatic, north of Greece, and past Albania to Croatia."

"You mean they're not back from their world tour yet? Hasn't school started?"

"Don't you read the tabloids?" asked Helga.

LoveStar looked round as if he was still expecting to see the boys somewhere in the house. A sentence darted across his lens and disturbed him:

< . . . RESULTS OF APPLICATION FOR LOVEDEATH
PATENT DUE WITHIN 5 MIN . . . >

His thoughts returned to LoveDeath. His heart pounded. He was making a mental review of the business plan that he intended to present to the plastic surgeon when Helga repeated the sentence:

"Don't you read the tabloids?"

"What?"

"Don't you read the papers?"

"Sorry, I've lost the thread. What papers?"

"The Ukrainian rocket engineers have destroyed our apartment in Copenhagen."

"What are you talking about?"

"A woman who was with them has accused them of rape."

"THE BOYS?" asked LoveStar.

"No. The engineers."

"I wasn't asking about them."

"The television was found out in the garden," said Helga.

"For God's sake, we were talking about the boys, not the company. They're all right, aren't they?"

"The boys have created havoc on the island of Murter. They beat up a bouncer. No one would accuse them of rape in Croatia. They're rich and the police are corrupt . . ."

LoveStar took a better look at the woman facing him and felt as if he had never seen her before. He couldn't grasp what was going on and was thrown completely off balance when a ribbon of text appeared on his lens:

< . . . LOVEDEATH PATENT AGREED WITH REFERENCE TO APPLICATION 12B. OPERATING LICENSE GRANTED ON FOUR CONDITIONS . . .

MINIMUM DISTANCE FROM BUILDUP AREA . . .
NOISE REDUCTION . . . >

"THE PATENT!" he shouted. "Helga! THE PATENT! Love-Death is home free! Ivanov will . . ."

"You're leaving in half an hour," she said dully.

"Didn't you hear? We've just got the patent."

Helga smiled but the smile didn't reach her eyes. "Congratulations. Then perhaps you could look in on your daughter."

"My daughter?"

"She's asleep in her crib."

"Yes, right away. I just need to let Ivanov know."

LoveStar prepared to call, but Helga grabbed both his hands. "You think about nothing but death," she said, looking him straight in the eye.

"What?"

"You think of nothing but death," she repeated.

"No . . . well . . . I mean, sure. I think about lots of things."

"You spend your life on death."

"Don't be like that."

"I mean it; you're surrounded by death."

"Hey! You know what I'm like, it's just an idea. I won't be a free man until I get rid of it."

"Yes, I read the book. 'An idea is a dictator. When an idea calls, you put aside your horse and hound, neglect friends and family . . .'"

LoveStar lost the thread. The letters "IVANOV" flashed on his lens. Ivanov was clearly waiting for the news. He made to answer the phone, but Helga wouldn't let him past.

"Your father was asking after you."

"What did he say?" asked LoveStar.

"He can't be reached any longer . . ."

"I'll try and visit him later this week."

"Orvar, look at me!"

LoveStar looked at her. There weren't many people who called him Orvar. She was one of the very few who did so without hesitation. Old friends always stumbled over the name "LoveStar."

"You've missed him. You could have reached him last week. The doctor doesn't think he'll wake up again."

LoveStar stared at the floor.

"Do you understand what I mean now? You postpone life and devote yourself to death. Death can wait. Life can't."

LoveStar was silent for a moment, then he looked at the clock.

"I must see him before I go to Los Angeles."

"I was the last person to make contact. He asked after you. You've missed him, Orvar."

LoveStar looked at her angrily. "They gave him several months! There was no need to fling this in my face! Do you think I have no feelings? Why didn't you let me know?"

"I tried," whispered Helga, "but I couldn't get through. You would only talk about death. Sorry, I didn't mean to be cruel. Sorry."

Her eyes filled with tears. She had become so sensitive. Too soft, his grandmother would have said. LoveStar tried to rearrange his view of the world. The house, Helga, his father, the boys, his daughter, but all the time "IVANOV" was flashing on his lens. He meant to ask more about his father, but his eyes were continually drawn to the flashing letters and LoveStar had major news for Ivanov. The LoveDeath license was home free. Construction could begin. He who is infected with an idea can't think normally. A strong idea attacks anything that threatens its existence; it has its own immune system. At this moment the idea was at the height of its power. LoveDeath was a hairbreadth from entering the world, the contractions were at their height, and LoveStar's head was ready to burst.

"Sorry, Orvar," said Helga. "I didn't mean to be cruel." She put her arms around him but LoveStar didn't feel her. His skin received the touch but his brain couldn't process the stimulus. LoveDeath closed down all transmission of neural messages from skin cells to brain and directed attention to "IVANOV," which was still flashing on the lens.

Immediately after the phone call, LoveDeath could abandon its host and live an independent life out in the world where anyone could buy or sell it. Anyone could build up LoveDeath and make it grow and thrive while the host, who had been vital for the idea, would become like any other shareholder. LoveStar could be at most a temporary director, sadly superfluous in all likelihood. In the worst case, his offspring would cast him off. As soon as he had answered the telephone call and had completed his trip to LA, LoveDeath would be officially born. Ivanov would take over the baton; after a five-year gestation, LoveStar would be a free man. For half a second a battle was fought in his mind in which the idea wiped out all the worries that the man Orvar Arnason—original user of the brain in his body, original inhabitant of his body—felt about his dying father, his sleeping daughter, and his withering wife. Slowly but surely his mind became as clear and cold as a starlit November sky, which was only waiting for a blazing body to shoot through the darkness. LoveStar answered the phone call from Ivanov with LoveDeath on his brain.

"Great news, Ivanov! The patent's been approved. No one can take LoveDeath away from us!"

Helga let him go. For a moment she had believed that she had managed to retrieve her husband. He noticed neither the embrace nor when it ended. He carried on regardless.

"There's more! Elizabeth II is going to fall over Windsor Castle. And the Jaggers are going to fall over New York! It'll be sensational!"

Helga had stopped traveling with him. Formerly they had traveled around the world together, but then he began to add strange detours to their route. Not fun surprise detours for the boys or secret detours for her—instead he accepted invitations, coffee, or dinner with aged billionaires. Sooner or later, without fail, the conversation would turn to death. Again and again she sat in a grand room while Orvar listened patiently to some old man whining and complaining until the right opportunity came and the lure was cast: but death? What about death? Then she shuddered and wanted the earth to swallow her up, tried to withdraw herself, pretended to be excused. If the boys were there she would sneak outside with them, show them the ornamental gardens, swimming pools, statues, and sports cars. Sometimes the visits ended with a butler escorting LoveStar to the door and angrily ejecting them. But LoveStar didn't give up. He sought out all the more zealously those who stood closest to death, not in order to learn from their lives but to obtain a share in their deaths.

Finally his work and thoughts had borne fruit. The patent was home free and Ivanov was on the line.

". . . The death rate in the West is almost ten in every thousand inhabitants. That's about twenty million people a year, nearly two million tons of bodies. That's like four times the national cod quota," he said, inspired, to Ivanov. "Imagine the revenue. If people pay half a million for each body we're talking about an industry with a $10,000 billion annual revenue and even then I'm only talking about the West, and I have an idea for an advertisement! We'll film a beautiful young woman rotting underground. The world will turn against the old method. LoveDeath will be the only alternative."

Helga felt sick.

"Which woman are you planning to use?" she asked.

"Sorry, Ivanov," said LoveStar, turning to Helga.

She looked at him with eyes full of disgust and sorrow. "Who is going to donate her body for the advertisements? Who's going to rot for us?"

"It's the way everyone ends up anyway; there's no point hiding the fact! Can I finish my conversation with Ivanov?"

"You think about nothing but death."

"Ivanov, I'll talk to you later . . ."

"You don't talk about terns and butterflies anymore. It's all worms and maggots now. You used to be interested in everything that lived; you were a specialist in life. You watched the boys and were amazed by how they played without words. You taught them to know their birds. You told them what the moors were like before the terns disappeared. You were preoccupied but you had a head full of butterflies."

"I haven't changed. We're sorting out LoveDeath, then I'll have time."

This was not true. It was not Orvar who spoke. LoveDeath was trying to kill the conversation. Orvar was seldom allowed to reach the surface. Orvar had been ill when they met. She fell in love with a man who had bird and butterfly waves on the brain. Now the vessel was the same but the content was LoveDeath. The birdwave invalid had been preoccupied and forgetful, creative, funny, and amusing. The LoveDeath invalid was hard and cynical, a pure businessman. The bird-waves and LoveDeath used the same body and same head, so perhaps it was only to be expected that Helga muddled them up.

"The boys call you LoveStar. What kind of name is that, anyway? They just say LoveStar, like the people who read about you in the papers, the man who freed mankind from cords . . ."

LoveStar went into the kitchen. He closed his eyes and pleaded. "Let me finish LoveDeath! I'll have time as soon as LoveDeath is completed."

"Leave death to the dead. Go back to the birds. LoveDeath's not science. LoveDeath's engineering, business, marketing. LoveDeath's technically possible but has no magic. Rockets are just buses. Anyone can shoot dead bodies into the air."

He didn't answer. He was writing a letter to Ivanov. He hid his fingers so she couldn't see what he was up to.

"The birds were science but LoveDeath is greed."

LoveStar looked at her angrily. "You'll never understand. Was Beethoven greedy when he composed the Ninth Symphony? Weren't eight enough? Was it greed that drove Shakespeare to write more plays after *Hamlet*? Hadn't Einstein had enough ideas by the time he was thirty?"

Helga didn't answer.

"You should have got yourself an ordinary husband. You'd have been happy with a man who came home from work, mowed the lawn, and barbecued with the kids. I'm not like that and I can't do anything about it."

Helga shook her head. "Do you remember when we stayed in the old deserted farm on Melrakkasletta?"

He remembered. They had been testing new equipment for measuring birdwaves. The equipment enabled people to identify individual birds in a flock without needing to tag them. Every bird gave off a unique wave or aura like a fingerprint.

"Do you remember when you measured the pair of great northern divers?" said Helga. "You couldn't distinguish their waves. Every bird was supposed to give off its own identifying wave, but they gave off the same wave and measured as one and the same diver. Do you remember what I said then?"

"Yes."

"Perhaps it's love, I said. Perhaps that's why they only mate once, only love once, why if one dies, the other withers away, because no one can live as only half."

"I remember," said LoveStar.

"Do you remember what you said to me then?" asked Helga. "Do you remember what you said?"

"Yes."

"I would wither away if you died, you said."

"I remember."

"I've been thinking about death so much recently. Even when

I have our baby, our little life in my arms, I think about death. I've sometimes wondered whether you would wither at all. Would you wither at all if I died?"

GREAT OFFER ON MELONS

INDRIDI HAD ONLY HAD ONE GIRLFRIEND BEFORE SIGRID AND THE relationship had been a miserable failure. He'd met her when he was seventeen and his father had got him a summer job producing electricity at the aluminium plant (LoveAl), which sprawled over the southern lowlands. He was fired in a matter of weeks for refusing to slaughter chickens and sprinkle their blood over the electrodes, although it had been scientifically proven that this would improve conductivity by around 3 percent.

Indridi worked on the treadmill in the mornings. He soon became super fit, as he ran thirty miles a day, producing close to 100 kW an hour. On Wednesdays he wrestled with employees from the souvenir factory on the sands between the aluminium plant and the national highway for the benefit of passing bus passengers. On Mondays he put on a Viking helmet and had sword fights (staged, obviously) with employees from the windmill factory for the entertainment of Japanese and German pensioners. The windmills, which were cast from the aluminium that

Indridi smelted, had been raised all along the coast and extended beyond the horizon to east and west. They turned with the wind in their thousands like giant daisies.

Sometimes Indridi's job involved walking along the shoreline, gathering up the birds that had collided with the sails. He collected the birds, categorized, counted, and skinned them. The skins went to the taxidermist at the souvenir factory. He sent the breasts to the kitchen, while the entrails and bones were minced and boiled down for fox feed. Then he told the girl at the hatchery how many birds he had found. The hatchery was by the southern wall of the plant. It was cheaper and more humane to rear and release birds to be stunned by the blades than it was to raise chickens in cages. The staff had game for lunch four days a week. The game improved energy production by around 0.5 percent (although excessive game consumption increased the employees' sex drive by 5 percent, which in turn reduced their productivity by 1.3 percent). The chickens were eaten on Fridays after the sacrifice. Fridays could be quite lively, and there was a general scramble to take part as feathers, heads, and blood went flying, while the director yelled over the loudspeaker:

"SACRIFICE!! The metal craves sacrifices!"

Indridi stumbled into a relationship with the girl from the hatchery. She had raven-black hair and an owlish stare. Birds sat screeching on the dropping-splashed ledges that lined the wall and a strong fish-oil stench of fulmar vomit filled the air. Indridi visited regularly to read out his list. It was important to release the same number of birds as those that were stunned, so as not to upset the balance of nature.

"Forty puffins, a black-backed gull, fourteen kittywakes, eight fulmars," he shouted, handing her the list.

"There's no *y* in kittiwakes. Why did you put a *y* in kittiwakes?" the girl yelled back.

"I thought it was funny."

"WHAT?" she shouted, "WHAT DID YOU SAY?"

"I THOUGHT IT WAS FUNNY! I THOUGHT IT WOULD MAKE YOU LAUGH!"

Chances to be funny were few and far between, and the girl seldom smiled at him.

Now the gannets were making a ruckus, each trying to out-squawk the other as a greater black-backed gull landed among them. They were forced to raise their voices still further:

"KEEP COUNTING!"

"Seven eider ducks, two drakes, a skua, an Arctic skua, an oyster catcher, three great northern divers, a swan, and a heron."

"A HERON?" she yelled.

"Yes, a heron. You can see it at the taxidermist's."

"Are you sure it was a heron?"

"Unless it was an overgrown whimbrel."

"An overgrown whimbrel?"

"One of the whimbrels that fly to Ireland in the winter and eat the worms around the nuclear plant."

"You know we don't release herons. Herons don't belong here. No one comes here to gawp at herons."

"I just thought you'd be interested . . ."

Not listening, the girl flounced down the corridor and returned with a cage. Judging from the smell, there was a fulmar inside. Indridi took it and put it on the back of the truck while she went and fetched more birds. When the truck was fully loaded they drove out to the beach together to set the birds free. Indridi took a black-backed gull in a firm grasp, carefully avoiding its beak, released the wing-bands, and threw it into the air. They watched it soar in the direction of the windmills.

"Can I tell you something?" asked Indridi.

No answer.

"Did you know that the windmills are driven by us runners? Everyone thinks the wind produces the energy and that we runners are producing electricity, but in fact the waterfalls, hot springs, and Northern Lights take care of all the electricity."

The girl released a diver and pretended not to hear anything over its hooing.

"The diver's making a terrible racket today," she said. "I can't hear anything over its hooing."

Indridi raised his voice. "Seriously! The outside world is impressed that the factory is man-powered, otherwise all these people wouldn't come to see us, which is why we're made to run. But those aren't real windmills; they're fans!"

The girl looked at him without interest and said nothing.

"Yes! We're producing wind for the old people on the buses who have paid for gales. They expect wind, so they get wind."

"Does it matter whether you smelt aluminium or produce wind?" she asked grumpily. "It's all the same in the end."

"Probably not."

"All the people on the buses are on their way north to LoveDeath anyway. They're just killing time until then; some are sent around and around the country until they die of boredom."

By rights this should have been quite a romantic time, but Indridi was as far from being her perfect match as one could imagine.

"Just because I play squash with you doesn't mean you own me," she sometimes snapped at Indridi, as she chopped up a raven's egg for a sandwich.

They generally sat together at lunchtime and played Yahtzee; sometimes they had sex, at other times they played squash. They went to the cinema together on weekends but never had anything to talk about, either on the way to the cinema or on the way home. They made out to pass the time; then at least they didn't have to talk, but after the making out there was always a long silence because every sentence that Indridi struggled to produce ended up somehow dead, forgettable, and meaningless.

Indridi had often told Sigrid how oppressive and awkward his relationship had been with this girl. It proved to him just how special his relationship was with Sigrid. Yet this girl touched some nerve with Sigrid. Indridi said he'd hardly recognize her if he met her on the street, but then one day they bumped into her at the shops. Indridi would have preferred not to greet her; he meant merely to nod at her but instead he yelled out:

"GREAT TITS! WHERE DID YOU GET SUCH A GREAT BOOB JOB?"

The praise did not go unnoticed. The whole shop turned round and looked at her bosom. The girl smiled sweetly; the compliments that came with her boob job were intended to have exactly this effect: to make a whole shop turn around and stare. Her breasts were a classy pair in the latest fashion: full-bodied but nipple-free. Nipples were regarded as unsightly, like underarm hair and droopy labia.

"Hi, Indridi," she said smiling. "Long time no see."

Indridi tried to extricate himself but even from inside the milk cooler Sigrid could hear the girl inviting him for a game of squash.

"We should play a game of squash for old times' sake," she screeched chirpily. She spoke unnaturally loudly, as if her hearing had been impaired at the hatchery. "EH? PICK UP THE OLD BALLS AGAIN!"

It was Thursday and Indridi could use neither yes nor no. Instead of no, he used the only word he could think of:

"Maybe."

He grew flustered when he saw Sigrid's expression as she stood frozen by the freezer, hurried to say NO loud and clear, but instead howled:

"GREAT OFFER ON MELONS!"

Sigrid knew only too well what squash meant, and although Indridi had repeatedly told her how boring this girlfriend was and how unexciting their sex life had been, she was unconvinced. Sigrid had begun to suspect that Indridi might just be thinking of himself in making her wait. That he would make a beeline north the moment he himself was matched. Of course, Sigrid didn't know that Simon had asked the girl to be in the right place at the right time and paid her with ten additional compliments.

Indridi and Sigrid undressed in silence that evening and went to sleep without kissing each other good night. The neighbor had it in for them after missing a repeat of Dallas. He had declared war and spent his pension on ordering howlers, compelling Indridi to shout out in his sleep at hourly intervals: "IT'S ONE O'CLOCK! GOT TO WAKE UP IN SEVEN HOURS' TIME! IT'S TWO O'CLOCK! GOT TO WAKE UP IN SIX HOURS! IT'S THREE O'CLOCK! GOT TO WAKE UP IN FIVE HOURS!"

Finally Sigrid rammed her elbow in his chest.

"What's the matter with you? Do you think this is funny? You're unbearable! You can sleep outside if you're going to be such a pain!"

WAVE ON A SCREEN

"WOULD YOU WITHER AWAY IF I DIED?" ASKED HELGA, AFTER they'd measured the pair of divers that time on Melrakkasletta. Their boys, then ten years old, were paddling in the bay a short way off. Orvar was too scientifically minded to leave it at that. In the evening he went out to the patrol jeep and aimed the monitor at Helga who was sitting outside the tent reading a book in the light summer dusk. He climbed out of the car and sat down beside her so the machine could measure their waves.

He had a knot in his stomach when he opened the jeep door to see the results. She had soft, rounded waves. He had sharp, peaked waves, like the jaws of a savage wolf, he thought. No. Like the peaks of Hraundrangi. Exactly like Hraundrangi. They each had their own individual wave, their own individual land-scape. He went to bed without turning off the monitor. Helga came across the screen the following morning.

"Orvar!" she called. "Orvar!"

"What?"

"Look at the screen! Did you hear anything last night?" She gazed at the screen, entranced. "It's as if a falcon and a ptarmigan had flown through the sensor!" She glanced around. "What a shame to miss a falcon."

"Would you wither away if I died?" Helga asked, seven years later, but before he could answer a black BMW honked outside.

Their daughter woke up crying in her room. Helga hurried to her. When she came back, LoveStar had left for Los Angeles. LoveDeath was nearly home free. All that remained was the technical side, which others would sort out. Trial launches, earthmoving and the excavation of tunnels, the installation of launchpads on the mountaintops around the property in Oxnadalur. Then there were the power plants. Endless power plants, hydrogen production, packing, body transportation, and the battle against reactionary forces. Last but not least there was the mood. The Mood Division would smooth image over everything and distract attention from potential problems.

LoveDeath was breaking out of its shell and from now on the idea would live an independent life. LoveDeath would take up residence in Ivanov's head. He would be managing director of LoveDeath. For the next weeks and months LoveDeath would compel him to employ thousands of men and women, and all these people would get the same symptoms. Technicians' heads would be filled with technical solutions, transporters' with logistical ideas, businessmen's with business plans, and every branch manager in the world would do their utmost to ensure that every single millionaire in their market area would be launched with LoveDeath. They would all work as one toward expanding the empire, cutting costs, and improving service.

LoveStar himself needn't worry about a thing. All he had to do was sit back and watch the outcome.

All over the world people received phone calls from Ivanov and became infected with LoveDeath, but LoveStar was cured that night as he lay alone in his Los Angeles hotel room. As if a fog had cleared in his head. It was late at night when he came home and got into bed beside his sleeping wife and baby. At that very moment their sons were dancing the night away at a disco on the Croatian island of Murter in the Adriatic, before going on to screw cheap whores and suck cubes of golden Chicago honey.

For one moment LoveStar's mind was pure and clear as the sky, but in the sky there was a bird.

"Apply your mind to the birds," Helga had told him.

Their own chick was asleep. He stroked her head before going down to the basement. The monitor that he had used to measure the divers lay among a jumble of wings, otoliths, and old computers. He drew a line in the dust with his forefinger. His nerves were going, his home was breaking up, Helga was wasting away, and the boys were on the fast track to ruin. He needed to get his bearings, rest his mind, take a holiday, and recover from LoveDeath. But there was something that drew him to this monitor: the monitor harbored an idea. It hadn't been designed to measure human waves, yet it seemed to do so anyway. He put the monitor under his arm and took a taxi to see Yamaguchi, head of the Bird and Butterfly Division. Yamaguchi came to the door. She was stunning, with a smooth cap of silky-black hair, white skin, slanting eyes, and fiery red lips. They had met in Paris, in mutual pursuit of Arctic terns. She had spent long periods at the terns' overwintering grounds in southern Africa. She was tern-like herself: petite, delicate, yet more determined than anyone else he knew.

"Is everything okay?" asked Yamaguchi. She was standing in the doorway in her dressing gown.

LoveStar stood hunched over, the monitor in his arms.

"I think I've found love," he said with tears in his eyes.

Helga never knew that Orvar had love on the brain while Love-Death was coming into being and everyone was wondering at the developments in the Oxnadalur theme park: the extravagance, glamor, madness, lunacy. While the media spotlight was directed at the liberation of mankind's hands, the inexorable technological advances, the Statue of Liberty, the Puffin Factory, the films, and cordless Russian rocket engineers who trashed apartments wherever they were lodged, the Bird and Butterfly Division had something extraordinary up its sleeve. Its emissaries set up sensors on the busiest streets of big cities. They recorded major events, protests, and mass meetings all over the world, measured the waves emitted by as many people as they could; they collected the results and processed them in the research wings in the bowels of Oxnadalur. Gradually patterns began to emerge, real results. They invited people north and witnessed incredible scenes.

"How do you feel? Is it love?" Yamaguchi asked the first people to be brought together after being measured with the same wave signal.

"It's love," they replied. "I've found my other half."

"Could you describe the feeling?" she asked after they'd been together a week.

"It's more than sex. Words can't describe the feeling."

"How do you feel?" LoveStar asked people after they'd lived in a derelict farmhouse for a whole year.

"Better. We get on better and better together."

By then everything had long ago broken down in the control group. The control couples had been made to live together under the understanding that they had been measured with the same wave—but in fact they were opposites. Healthy, beautiful, lively people began to bite, beat, and hit one another after only half a day in isolation.

"How do you feel?" a psychologist asked a woman from the control group.

"I feel sick just thinking about him. I sweat and shake, I get headaches, stomachaches . . ."

"Would you like to meet him again?"

The woman grabbed the psychologist and stared crazily into his eyes.

"SAVE ME! DON'T SEND ME BACK TO HIM! THIS CAN'T BE LOVE!"

Doctors came and measured the woman in every conceivable way. "Physical rejection," they noted.

Those couples who genuinely had the same wave almost merged into one being.

"Well, now she's gone and you'll never see her again. How do you feel?" Yamaguchi asked a man who'd spent a year in a derelict farmhouse with his perfect match.

He didn't answer. He lay in a daze like a heroin addict. "Véronique!" he moaned, "Véronique!"

"There's hardly any pulse," said the assistant doctor. "I'm

concerned about him. He's got a serious physical dependence on her. You must reunite them."

Everything is material. Everything is physical. Somewhere in the body was a primitive sense that could pick up birdwaves as the eye senses light, the ear senses sound, and the tongue senses taste. A sense that processed the waves and auras emitted by other people. The brain had no words for the feeling.

LoveStar never got to tell Helga about the inLOVE plan, which was not made public until seventeen years after LoveDeath. She was dead by the time the LoveDeath division of the LoveStar theme park was opened, two years after that telephone conversation with Ivanov. Queen Elizabeth II and the Jaggers were not the first people to fall to earth with LoveDeath. That honor went to Helga Thorlaksdottir, a thirty-seven-year-old mother of three and wife of Orvar Arnason of LoveStar for sixteen years. No one knew this except two Russian engineers and LoveStar himself, who sat in his Hummer on a black sand dune in the middle of the Odadahraun desert, watching her burn up in the atmosphere. No one noticed that the coffin that was laid in the earth in the old graveyard in Reykjavik was full of sand. The boys were too brain-fried to carry it.

It was twenty-nine years since Helga had died, and LoveStar's hands had begun to wither away. In the cold darkness outside the gleaming body of the plane, the Million Star Belt could be seen like a glittering nebula. Around the moon a silver halo formed as its rays were reflected by the costumes, which flashed in turn as they rolled and revolved in the vacuum. LoveStar held a seed in his withering hand. He had only one hour and fifteen minutes left to live.

RANCID COD-LIVER OIL

FOR SOME REASON THE HONEY THAT THE MORNING SUN POURED
over Indridi and Sigrid had begun to resemble syrup—not maple
syrup, golden as amber, but cheap corn syrup: cloudy, cloying,
and sticky. But that was better than what followed over the next
few days. The syrup grew sour and the mornings, far from being
sweet, resembled rancid cod-liver oil. Waking to the sound of
bluebottles buzzing around them with their metallic sheen,
blue-green and gross, and with a foul taste in their mouths,
neither felt like kissing. They turned away from each other's
sweaty body odor mingled with the dried-fish genital stink of
days-old sexual juices that they had not yet washed off. Their
conversations became perfunctory and their silences were no
longer harmonious, intimate and mutual but separate, so that
when one of them broke the silence, the other was generally
pensive and preoccupied and said:

"What?"

"Doesn't matter," came the refrain, although it often mattered a great deal, more than anything else in the world, a question of life and death, love and happiness.

"What?"

"Doesn't matter."

Even the "eat me, eat me" sounds from the Puffin Factory were accompanied by a strangely deep, harsh undertone, a "Grrryap! Grrryap!" that intensified every day until nothing but "Grrryap!" could be heard, filling the streets with fear and trembling.

At eight o'clock one morning there was a knock on Indridi and Sigrid's door. Indridi went to open it. Or rather, he was over by the front door because Sigrid was taking a shit with the bathroom door open and he wanted to air out the apartment. Outside stood a smiling woman dressed in a red flight attendant uniform with the inLOVE logo on her breast. Indridi showed her into the sitting room. Sigrid slammed the bathroom door. When she came out she shot Indridi a poisonous look.

"Have I come at a bad moment?" asked the woman, trying to hide her disgust as the foul smell reached her. She looked about for a chair that wasn't covered with piles of dirty laundry.

Sigrid didn't answer but Indridi replied dully: "No, not at all."

"I understand you've got a problem with being calculated," said the woman, sitting on some crumpled shirts. "I may work at inLOVE but I'm human too, which makes me an impartial advisor. I thought perhaps you'd like to talk to someone you could trust."

"It's only me who's been calculated," said Sigrid. "Indridi hasn't."

"She's not going," said Indridi, looking determinedly at the woman. "We don't need your help. She's not going north."

"Can I speak for myself, please?" asked Sigrid, looking at the woman and trying to smile. "I'm not going north."

"Are you unhappy with the inLOVE service?"

"We've found each other," said Indridi.

"But why were you on the list if you didn't want to be calculated?" (Few people could face the bureaucracy involved in removing themselves from the inLOVE list, as de-registration resulted in all sorts of inconveniences and loss of privileges.)

The woman's speech was a bit stilted. She was probably reading a text or parroting something that was being whispered in her ear. Valuable negotiators did not waste their time paying house calls. They eavesdropped from a distance and fed stooges like her with well-chosen phrases.

"Naturally we wanted scientific confirmation; we never dreamt we wouldn't match up," said Sigrid.

"You don't have any children, do you?" asked the woman glancing around.

"We wanted to wait until we were calculated," said Indridi.

The woman's next line emerged rather stiffly: "You do realize what you're doing?"

"Yes," said Indridi.

"There are two people out there who will miss out on happiness because you didn't want to be united with them."

Silence.

"Do you want to miss out on happiness?"

"We *are* happy," said Indridi.

"You mustn't be selfish. You might think you're happy but you're only thinking of yourselves as halves, not as a whole."

"A whole?"

"The whole is you and your scientifically selected other half. You must think of mankind as a whole. You know the inLOVE plan: when the whole world has been calculated and love flows across borders, races, and genders, then all wars and disputes will be history. Don't you want a better world? Do you want to break the chain?"

"Of course not but . . ."

"It really ought to be illegal not to participate in inLOVE. Otherwise the world will continue to burn with misunderstanding, racial hatred, war, and selfishness. It only takes one unhappy man to send the whole thing up in flames."

"But Sigrid is my other half; I've known that since the first time we set eyes on one another."

"If she's your other half, she won't have eyes for anyone else, will she?"

"N . . . no," said Indridi.

"So what are you afraid of? If she goes north she can talk to Møller, break it to him gently that he's not her one and only, and come home again! Then you'll have been proved right and that'll be great!"

"Great, eh?" said Indridi. "Unbelievably great, yes. I don't know of anyone who has gone north without getting hitched."

"Indridi, dear, if they get hitched, then she'll have found her perfect match! Or do you want to deprive Sigrid of happiness? Perhaps that's it? Are you holding on to Sigrid because you yourself are still uncalculated?"

Indridi looked at Sigrid but she looked away.

"Of course it's understandable if you don't trust her," said the woman.

"Don't trust Sigrid?" said Indridi.

"Yes. Don't you trust her?"

"Don't you trust me?" asked Sigrid.

Indridi nodded. "Of course I do."

"She wouldn't be your perfect match if you didn't. Would she?" asked the woman triumphantly.

"No."

Indridi and Sigrid sat silent and thoughtful on the sofa. Sigrid looked at the clock and left for work without saying good-bye. She walked down the street without looking over her shoulder. She took an extra double shift. They didn't meet until near midnight. They lay in the same bed without touching. Sigrid tossed and turned. Indridi stared at the ceiling and felt every fraction of a second pass like an hour. He lay awake for three thousand years and the moment he fell asleep, Sigrid silently dressed and crept out into the dawn. Half an hour later she boarded a bus headed direct for the deep valley where LOVESTAR twinkles behind a cloud.

GRRRYAP!

INDRIDI WOKE TO FIND HIMSELF ALONE IN BED. SIGRID'S CLOSET was open and bare. Indridi lay rigid, a bad taste in his mouth. A thick glaze of fat clung to his palette as if he'd been chewing leather or a fatty sausage. A storm lashed the window. There was no scent of honey roses filling his senses, and instead of "eat me, eat me" echoing round the neighborhood, there was only the intolerable "Grrryap!"

It was sinister and menacing, and a disgusting stench like dog shit seeped through every keyhole and crack in the apartment. Indridi lay alone in bed, trying to think clearly. He flinched at every "Grrryap!" Tried to concentrate but the noise kept breaking into his thoughts: "Grrryap!" He looked out of the window and saw that the sound was coming from the Puffin Factory. All the doors stood ajar and workmen were piling plump, well-fed puffins on to transport trucks, while on the other side of the road the glass was being torn off the honey-rose greenhouses. Thick steel grilles were being welded on to the structures.

Indridi ran outside, trying to shelter himself from the rain. He tapped the shoulder of a workman with a yellow helmet and red stubble.

"Are you taking the flowers?" he asked in a choked voice.

"They've given up on the flowers; it's foxes now. Zoos have started replacing lions and polar bears with our VikingCenturyFoxes."

"The honey roses were my favorite flowers," said Indridi sadly.

"That's just the way it is."

"But what about the puffins?"

"The puffins are going north. They're not happy near the foxes. They get stressed out. Stop laying."

"The puffins are going north?"

"Yes, are you deaf?"

"Why don't the foxes go north? They're used up north as well, aren't they?"

The man with the red stubble thought: "Simbi! Why aren't the foxes going north?"

"They're bred out east and west, they're bred here, but it's banned to breed them up north."

"Why?" asked Indridi.

"Why's it banned, Simbi?"

"Because of LoveDeath. They go crazy over the smell of 'money.'"

"Where's Grim?"

"He was here a minute ago. I don't see him now."

A yellow bulldozer came roaring around the corner like an old rhinoceros. It sank its teeth into the lawn and Indridi watched it gnaw and chomp the flowers he had planted earlier that summer. The bulldozer trampled the heather and moss and chewed up the mountain avens, yarrow, and spotted orchids. Indridi wanted to stop the digging, but the the machine was remote-controlled from Korea by a cordless excavation engineer. Close to tears, Indridi ran into the factory.

"Grim! Where's Grim?"

Grim was the factory manager. He would often come out into the grounds, chat with Indridi, and ask him about his gardening duties. Sometimes Grim would give him honey roses or puffin eggs to take home to Sigrid, but now Grim was nowhere to be seen. Indridi went into the hall that used to be the friendly Puffin Factory. It no longer bustled with life and spring. Minus song and feathers, it was a cold steel hangar; iron doors slammed, sending echoes around the hall, and welders were erecting vast cages for the foxes. Two men stood using a high-pressure hose to sluice feathers, droppings, and fishbones from the floor.

"There are ten puffins left! What's to be done with them?" shouted a man from inside the hall.

"Destroy them!" called another. "The truck's full. Throw them to the foxes!"

The man busied himself with wringing the puffins' necks and chucking them onto a heap behind him. Then a bell rang. "COFFEE BREAK!" called the overseer. The hall emptied into the cafeteria and the man threw a puffin at Indridi. It was soft and warm.

"Don't just stand there like an idiot! Throw that to the foxes!"

"What foxes? I don't see any foxes."

Indridi was left standing in the middle of the hall. Then he heard the terrible noise behind him.

"Grrryap!!!!"

He looked around and saw an open door. The bloodcurdling sound came from next door, where the storeroom had been emptied of puffin feed. Under a slender steel bridge there was a deep pit like an old-style swimming pool. It was divided up with steel panels and each compartment contained the most terrifying beasts he had ever seen. Foxes the size of polar bears yammered and circled, slavering and growling.

Indridi had little interest in foxes, and for some reason no one had seen fit to tell him what was going on: that the foxes would take over the factory, that the honey-rose greenhouses would be pulled down, that the garden would be laid to waste. Perhaps no one had known how to tell him, how to "find his angle" in this matter. Now every imaginable fact about foxes appeared automatically before his eyes with explanatory diagrams:

> When the Vikings (*check out Viking gear?*) discovered the country (*buy woolen sweater?*), it was full of giant foxes the size of polar bears. The Vikings invariably killed off the larger beasts and so the fox diminished in size with every generation because the smallest animals were more likely to survive and reproduce (*see theories?*). In the end only foxes the size of cats remained (*read about cats?*) because they could hide in clefts. In the countryside (*see countryside?*) the memory of the ferocious Viking-CenturyFox lived on, which is why farmers got their picture in the papers whenever they brought down a fox.

[PICTURE OF A FARMER AND HIS SON WITH A FOX IN ONE HAND]

PICTURE CAPTION: *Before the VikingCenturyFox declined it was one of the most dangerous predators on earth.*

The VikingCenturyFox was first bred for the LoveSaga (*see ad?*) Theme Park in Fljotshlid (*buy Njal's Saga?*). Thanks to a careful breeding program, by which the trend was reversed and the largest animals allowed to live, the VikingCenturyFox has recovered its former dimensions. It is sure to prove a powerful draw for the National Museum (*virtual tour?*) on its reopening in the LoveStar theme park. The VikingCenturyFox weighs some 1,500 pounds, can bite a crocodile in half with its jaws, and pierce a two-inch-thick aluminium sheet (*watch video?*). It can outrun a horse (*buy a horse?*). The VikingCenturyFox was one of the most dangerous predators on earth.

Listening to the soothing recorded tones of the voice reading the text, Indridi stared at the ferocious gray beasts that growled, grrryapped, and snuffed the air as he approached with his human scent. Bloody carcasses hung on chains from the ceiling and were lowered at regular intervals; the foxes attacked the carcasses, tearing off thighs or sections of spine, then lay down with their booty and gnawed at it. The floor around them was littered with bones and blood, mixed with straw, puffin feathers, and shit. The stench was almost unbearable.

"GRRRYAP!" said the foxes in the pit. Poor Indridi stumbled backward, tightening his grip on the puffin. Then he inched his way warily along to the middle of the bridge. There were gaps in the floor and he could see the foxes directly below him. They snapped at the struts until they clanged, trying to shake him off. The foxes had jaws that could have bitten off a man's head in one go, short sturdy legs, and pelts as soft as fur coats.

Soft as fur coats. Indridi hadn't slept for three hundred years. His soul had been splintered in two, his heart was shattered, his diaphragm was like concrete, and his eyes were drowning. He was tired and wretched; every fraction of a second felt like an hour. He was so tired he no longer saw the foxes' teeth, he saw only soft fur coats all around him, furs that lay on the floor like rugs, cushions, or sofas, growling, purring soft furs where one could snuggle up and go to sleep. Indridi put down the puffin, climbed on to the handrail, aimed for a fur, closed his eyes, and let himself fall into the pit. He never reached the bottom. A fur coat lunged toward him and Indridi looked into a vast, moist, red cavern before the jaws closed with a snap.

"GRRRYAP!!!"

SIGRID

AT THE VERY MOMENT INDRIDI WAS DISAPPEARING INSIDE A FIERCE fur coat, Sigrid was sitting on a bus hurtling north over the highlands, where geysers spouted, volcanoes erupted, gales blew, sands stretched out, and waterfalls skipped before LoveDeath sucked all the power to itself. Long before Oxnadalur appeared in all its glory she saw the LoveDeath rockets shooting into the sky. She watched a rocket vanish in a white glow in the blue sky, shooting like a nail through a hand-shaped cloud.

Sigrid knew she should be excited about meeting Per Møller at last, but she was listless, tense, and empty inside, her mind dwelling on everything that she and Indridi had done together. She remembered their eye-meets and how they used to rub their middle fingers together and their trips up to Blafjoll. She thought about the laughter and tickling and silence, which was not hollow but deep as a bass note. Sigrid called Indridi but got only the message: "This number is no longer connected."

She tried to imagine how he felt and what he could be doing.

Of course she hadn't a clue that at that precise second he had vanished into the maw of a famished savage beast twice the size of a polar bear.

A feeble old man sat behind her coughing. He was talking on the phone.

"You'll get there on Thursday, then? Didn't little Gusti want to come? (Cough.) Yes, I understand, of course he's outgrown Larry LoveDeath . . . The keys to the jeep? Oh dear, I seem to have brought them with me . . . Yes, I'll make sure they're not fired up with me . . ."

Sigrid strained her eyes as yet another rocket shot up from LoveDeath. The driver said over the loudspeaker that there were an unusual number of launchings at the moment due to the Million Star Festival. Soon the heavens would be ablaze, a million stars would shoot from the sky simultaneously, and the most momentous discovery in history would be announced to coincide with the opening of a new division of LoveStar. It would be bigger than inLOVE and LoveDeath combined.

Sigrid was happiest in a restful, cozy environment, and so one might have thought the LoveStar vaults would be too intimidatingly vast for her. But this was not the case. LoveStar was designed to suit everyone. Sigrid was registered as someone who avoided bustle, large airports, and city centers, but was in her element in safe suburbs and small towns. So she was given a room in a small grouping excavated in the mountainside on the edge of Oxnadalur.

She was let out on the main road and from there she followed the orientation marker that appeared on her lens. She jumped a ditch, climbed over a rusty fence, and walked up a grassy slope until she reached a rock face. There she stood at a loss for a few seconds until a door opened and a long tunnel appeared before her. It was cold and damp and smelled of water, moss, and stone, but soon she reached a warm room clad with wood paneling and plush velvet. A fire crackled comfortingly in the hearth. A man sat by the fire reading a book. He looked up and smiled.

"Sigrid?"

"Yes."

"You're in room twenty-seven."

Through a glass wall she could see a newly calculated couple sitting in a jacuzzi, while behind them another couple sat at a heavy wooden table playing Ludo when they weren't gazing into one another's eyes. A dark-haired man was restlessly pacing the floor in a freshly ironed suit. Sigrid got butterflies in her stomach when she came face to face with him. She looked into his dark-blue eyes. (Looking into the eyes of your other half is like looking in a mirror reflected in a mirror reflected in a mirror reflected in a mirror, some said.) There was no connection. Breathing easier, she walked down another passage until she reached room twenty-seven. The door opened automatically to reveal her dream room (information obtained from a report by Sigrid's childhood friend Dora). The room faced a gully overgrown with woolly willows and blueberries; a stream babbled in a narrow bed, disappearing here and there under the grassy bank. Seen from the outside, the window of the room probably appeared as a boulder or rock; it was a bay window so she could sit in it and watch the horses or lambs grazing outside. The animals did not react even when she tapped the glass. "It's like an aquarium," she thought to herself. Light streamed in through glazed cracks in the ceiling. Sigrid tried out the cozily made bed, then took a shower and stood under the stream of water for half an hour while remote-controlled swans flew in V-formation up and down Oxnadalur. On the radio someone was reading a traditional love poem: "Oh bright maid, deep under the blue mountain, prepare to meet thy lover . . ."

WOLF! WOLF!

GRRRYAP!!!

As Indridi had never been anywhere near a live fox in his life, let alone a VikingCenturyFox, he could hardly be expected to know that it was to no VikingCenturyFox that he had thrown himself. To the right of the steel bridge lay a fully grown vixen with a cub that would have made short work of Indridi, but Indridi had thrown himself to the left of the steel bridge. There awaited him the Big Bad Wolf, which was being developed by the Puffin Factory for a subsidiary company and theme park in Bavaria: GrimmsLove. The Big Bad Wolf had been specially designed to wolf people down in one mouthful, which was exactly what this wolf did. It wolfed Indridi down in one mouthful.

The Big Bad Wolf had not yet been publicly unveiled. It had been specially bred and genetically engineered to play the leading role in a magnificent staging of the Red Riding Hood story at GrimmsLove. The Big Bad Wolf must on no account digest the actors it swallowed because it was wasteful to have to train new people for the roles evening after evening. Naturally Indridi knew nothing of this. He was held in the dark, moist warmth of the wolf's stomach and believed that this was how the Vikings had felt when they were devoured, skin and bone, by the VikingCenturyFox. Time moved slowly as he awaited his fate, and his life passed many times before his eyes without the wolf's digestive system ever seeming to get going.

It was actually most uncharacteristic of Indridi to throw himself to the Big Bad Wolf. He had always been a happy, optimistic soul, but the last few days had sapped all his strength. Indridi could hear the beast's rapid heartbeat just above his left shoulder while its guts rumbled beneath him. He waited for the gastric juices to gush over him and burn through his skin like battery acid. He was suffocating from lack of air.

"This is like being sewn up in a haggis," Indridi thought, as he fumbled at the stomach lining. Suddenly he felt the beast's heartbeat slowing and heard a tremendous snoring. By a specially programmed instinct, the wolf flopped on its back and went to sleep as soon as it had swallowed a human. As it snored its jaws opened and shut, and rays of light filtered between its fangs, blinding Indridi, while its teeth stood out against the green-painted roof like snow-white mountain peaks. Fresh air rushed in like a southerly breeze, but the sunbeams did nothing to improve Indridi's mood. He imagined the morning sun dribbling over Per and Sigrid Møller like golden Tuborg beer. He pictured them together, crawling out of bed like an eight-footed spider, trying to tear themselves apart in order to go to work, and talking and talking and talking, and finally making love on the bathroom floor. He pictured Per laughing affectionately when Sigrid told him about the old folks at work and her summer in Sicily as an exchange student when she was seventeen, and his eyes would brim with tears because her stories would be like the most cherished nourishment for him. Her stories would slip down his throat like Gammeldansk aquavit, he would chew them and lick them like pork crackling. Later they would have a little boy and a little girl and Sigrid would comb the girl's golden locks while Per built a Lego digger with the boy (or vice versa, to be politically correct).

Rage boiled up inside Indridi. He felt as savage as a wolf and regretted having let the fox eat him. He was filled with regret. He should have killed Per, blown up the inLOVE experts who calculated him and Sigrid apart, shot LoveStar himself, or caused a riot at the theme park. He should have abducted Sigrid, but now he was trapped in a fox's belly and even if he managed to get out and run away with Sigrid, there was no escape. The world was so exhaustively recorded that there wasn't a turd in the sea that couldn't be traced back to its owner.

Indridi was losing control over his feelings; he had given way to regret. It was illogical to feel regret and be unreconciled to the past. He checked REGRET: What would have happened if he hadn't shown Sigrid the letter from LoveStar? He requested a quick answer, which appeared instantaneously on his left lens:

"It was a good thing she saw the letter, otherwise I and S would have died in a plane crash a week ago."

He checked REGRET again. What would have happened if she hadn't gone north at all but stayed at home with him and slept in:

"S would have crept out and thrown herself to the Viking-CenturyFox at 8:17 am."

Indridi was still alive half an hour later, but there was no point ringing the police or even a woodcutter. No doubt this was fate. Indridi wept, the wolf snored, and his only love had left him.

The phone rang. His Mom was on the lens:

"Hello, Mom," said Indridi dolefully.

"Is everything all right, Indridi dear?"

"Sigrid's left me, Mom." Indridi fought back tears. "She left me."

"Are you taking it very hard?" his Mom asked sympathetically.

"I'm dying, Mom."

"My darling boy," sighed his mother. "Your father and I probably overprotected you. Perhaps we shouldn't have sheltered you from all the bad news."

"What bad news?"

"We had you blocked against plague, flies, endangered animals, diseases, nuclear power, the environment, and Rwanda."

"What happened in Rwanda?"

"You don't want to know, Indridi dear. Where are you, anyway? Shall I come around and give you a hug?"

"There's only room for one in here."

"It's no good being alone, Indridi dear. You must take part in inLOVE. It's best for everyone; you know that when inLOVE has been completed and the world unites . . ."

"I know all that, Mom . . ."

"Come by our house this evening. Your father and Xing are coming over." Inevitably, every fourth person was matched with someone from China. "You should talk to them. Your father's a whole new man since he was calculated; he's not even grumpy in the mornings. Carlos wants me to stop dieting. He likes me plump and he saw a picture of my old nose and . . ."

"I can't make it, Mom," said Indridi.

"Where are you, anyway?"

"I'm in a fox."

"Where's that?"

"In the old Coke factory."

"Never been there. What's the food like?" She was obviously keen to divert the conversation to more cheerful topics.

"You know the sort of thing, Mom. The food's good," he said, thinking of himself lying in the fox's stomach. If anyone could save him it was Sigrid. He closed his eyes and called her. The only answer was:

"This number is no longer connected."

Indridi logged off and tried to empty his mind. He was assailed by a fit of silent weeping. The heat made him sweat, his hands were sticky, his hair was wet and slimy, and a sour fluid ran down his face. "Now the digestion is starting up," he thought. Something hard and sharp poked him in the back, and he assumed the stomach must be like some kind of mill that would grind him up from below and press the mush through the guts like a mincer, yet it didn't seem to hurt. He groped behind him and felt a piece of metal. It was a zipper. It was the zipper in the Big Bad Wolf's stomach! Indridi unzipped it carefully and stuck his head out through the gap, squinting up into the glare, before crawling slimy and weeping from the belly of the wolf, which woke up and licked his face from a genuine instinct.

The Big Bad Wolf was actually a she-wolf: the male prototype's penis had shocked preview audiences in Bavaria. Like most female mammals, the Big Bad Wolf would lick clean anything that emerged from her body alive, as if it were her offspring. She didn't connect this offspring with the man she had devoured earlier, and this was one of the main reasons why the Big Bad Wolf had not yet been sold abroad. People found it crude when she licked Little Red Riding Hood and her Grandmother with her long tongue. It was thought crude because the rough tongue tickled and the old Bavarian actress squealed with pleasure, slipping out of character, when the wolf pawed her like a cub and licked her under her skirt. Indridi had not been licked on the face since he was twelve, the day before his dog Snotra was put down. "Don't cry, Indridi," his mother had said. "We're not putting her down, we're postponing her. We can have her again when we have time."

Despite his sobbing, the wolf's tongue tickled so much that Indridi chuckled inside. Her whiskers were soft, her eyes were large and dark and deep, her ears were big like her mouth, her teeth were sharp, her pelt tickled, and Indridi wept. The Big Bad Wolf curled around Indridi, who buried his sobbing face in the dark-gray fur and thought about Snotra and Sigrid while the wolf licked away his tears with motherly tenderness. Indridi was lying sound asleep, enfolded by the she-wolf when Grim found him half an hour later.

GRIM

GRIM HAD ALWAYS SUSPECTED THAT INDRIDI'S RELATIONSHIP WITH Sigrid would end in disaster, but he never imagined the consequences would be this dire. Indridi was a hardworking employee but rather too preoccupied with Sigrid. When he was engaged in simple tasks, such as mowing the lawn or weeding, he could be directly linked to her for hours on end, and if he wasn't talking to Sigrid he was talking about her. When a monologue of this kind seemed imminent, Grim would light his pipe, lay his spectacles on the table, and listen patiently while Indridi prattled on and on about Sigrid this and Sigrid that and about their shared obsession with having found one another and true love and happiness.

Grim called the Puffin Factory's head of security, who came running up with a ladder. Trembling at the knees he put on a pair of chainmail overalls, a red crash helmet, and iron gauntlets, before climbing warily into the pit. He stepped cautiously to the ground and gave the wolf a gentle pat. He didn't even flinch when the wolf growled and showed her teeth. He unwrapped two bundles of fodder (secretly packed meal from the LoveDeath guano-processing plant), poked some sleeping pills into them, and eased them in through the stomach opening with a long pole before zipping it up. The wolf growled fiercely when Grim tried to rouse Indridi. A genuine instinct prompted her to protect her offspring. But now the mill in the wolf's stomach started up, audibly crunching and grinding the bundles, and soon her eyes grew bleary and she fell sound asleep.

The security guard helped a slime-covered Indridi up the ladder. Grim met him at the top and took him back into the main hall, neither speaking a word. They closed the door on the VikingCenturyFox and were halfway across the old puffin hall when Indridi fell to the floor. He rolled his eyes up until only the whites were visible. His throat rattled and he jerked around like a trout on a riverbank, bit his tongue until the blood trickled out of the corners of his mouth, moaned and lost control of his bladder, releasing a yellow stream.

Grim knelt beside him. "Help!" he shouted. "Somebody help us!"

Workers rushed over and crowded around Indridi, but before anyone could react, the fit ceased and Indridi howled:

"YOU'LL HAVE A FIT IF YOU MISS THE PUFFIN SANDWICH WEEKEND OFFER AT THE ALTHING!"

He turned blue in the face when he pronounced "puffinsandwichweekendoffer," as the word had begun before he could draw breath. "Shit," somebody exclaimed. "Damn," said another. "That was quite something," muttered a man from the Puffin Factory Mood Department. He clearly appreciated the aesthetics and science behind such an inspired trap. People returned to their jobs. Indridi lay like a wrung-out dishcloth in a yellow puddle.

He turned his face to the floor, closed his eyes, and was carried into the cafeteria. Grim brought him a set of orange overalls and sneaked a pink pill into his coffee cup.

When Indridi woke up an hour later, Grim was sitting beside him, filling his pipe.

"So it's over between you two," he said sympathetically. Indridi didn't speak, just brushed the hair from his eyes and burst into tears again. Grim put a fatherly arm around his shoulders.

"Indridi, son . . ." Indridi didn't answer. "Is there someone we can call?"

 "Sigrid was my best friend."

This was true. Sigrid was his only confidante. He and Sigrid had mutual friends, but as an individual he didn't really have any. He and Sigrid had only met up with their friends when numbers were even; he would never call one of the guys from the group. He didn't know them as single entities.

"There must be someone."

Indridi shook his head.

"I'm going straight to LoveDeath," said Indridi, and he called them at once. "Hello, is that LoveDeath?"

Grim interrupted and broke off the conversation.

"Just hang on a minute, Indridi," he said. "You'll get over it. Rest assured, LoveStar will find your other half."

He dialed inLOVE.

"Hello, is that inLOVE? I'm calling to check whether Indridi Haraldsson is due to be calculated with someone soon."

"Indridi Haraldsson?" answered a voice. "iSTAR has him down as a bad example. His girlfriend was taken from him and speed-calculated to Denmark."

"But what about him? How long will it be before he's calculated?"

There was a long silence before the answer came.

"Four percent chance of being calculated within a year. We believe his other half is in Laos. We haven't got an agreement with Laos yet. It probably won't happen until the king dies. He's a tough nut to crack, the King of Laos."

"Yes, he's a tough nut, the King of Laos," mumbled Grim. According to inLOVE's data, his own other half was also in Laos, too.

Indridi shook his head and stared gloomily out of the window. The bulldozer had ploughed away all the greenery from the factory grounds. Dumper trucks arrived and dumped piles of rubble over the mud.

"They have to expand the factory because of the foxes," said Grim apologetically. "Perhaps we should have let you know, but you weren't here last week."

"Don't you need a gardener anymore, then?"

"Indridi, son, you're a trained web designer."

Indridi shrugged. "I'm going straight to LoveDeath. I'll apply for a mercy trip."

Grim hurriedly tried to think of something to cheer Indridi up and distract him.

"Indridi, I've got something amazing to show you before you go."

"What's that?"

"I'm going to show you an absolute secret, much more amazing than the puffins or honey roses. I'll show it to you if you stop crying."

Indridi dried his eyes and blew his nose on a facecloth.

Grim stressed: "This is a top secret project and you must promise not to tell a soul. We're working with mice. Sigrun! Would you come here a minute?"

Sigrun, overseer of the Mouse Research Department, was pale and highstrung with faded gray eyes. They took an elevator down to the basement. The building didn't look particularly large from outside, but it seemed the lift would never stop. Sigrun opened the security door with a sure hand, unlocked another, drew back a bolt, and opened yet more doors until she came to a sliding door that opened automatically. She showed Indridi into a room full of skeletons, skulls, and body parts in jars. At the back of the room Indridi was greeted by a familiar face in hundreds of cages. He had never seen anything like it. This was unlike anything else; this was like a fairy tale.

"It! It's . . ."

"Exactly . . ."

Indridi threw up his hands. "It's Mickey Mouse! It's Mickey Mice! You've created a real live Mickey Mouse!"

The Mickeys sat there waving, each a foot and a half tall with big eyes and black button noses. Indridi wanted to take them all in his arms and cuddle them. But he didn't.

"Why are they white with red eyes?" asked Indridi, approaching one of the cages. The Mickey waved and smiled and Indridi was drawn nearer.

"I'm a scientist. These are laboratory mice. What do you expect?" asked Sigrun dryly.

"Do you find the Mickeys more appealing than cats?" asked Grim, regarding the cages with something approaching a shudder.

Indridi admitted he did.

"The Mickeys are the Mood Department's pet project. They're supposed to take over the market for cats and dogs," said Grim, rather gloomily.

"And the foxes are supposed to take over the fur market," said Sigrun. The VikingCenturyFox and the collaboration with the National Museum were merely intended to generate good publicity and secure the approval of the Democracy Machine. They've created a new image: humane furs. One animal. One fur."

"They want the next generation to be shaped like a woman," sighed Grim, "it'll save on tailoring."

Indridi noticed posters on the wall:

> Mickey! Better than man's best friend!
> Mickey food for your Mickey!
> Mickeys! More fun than cats and dogs!
> Mickeys! Their urine doubles as cleaning fluid!

"That's how they work," said Grim, knocking out his pipe. "First they make the ad, then they tell the scientists: this is what we want."

Indridi was about to open a cage and pat one of the Mickeys. Grim grabbed his hand in a hard grip.

"Careful, mate. The mice aren't finished. They've got to breed up a better temperament."

"Really?"

"They're savage. They eat children."

"Yes, of course," said Indridi. "My hamster Fluffy was forever eating its babies."

"No, I don't mean it like that," said Grim. "They eat children."

power of his cousin Svenni. Insurance—lots of insurance. A turkey of a film needed a good word on the street. Discounts, announcements, but then the following text popped up:

> [Cool competition for secret hosts!
> Assignment: Indridi Haraldsson. Mercy trip with Love-Death. 75% commission.
> Million Star Festival, special offer: 190,000.
> Regular launch: 250,000.
> Night launch: 300,000.
> Additional frills: Magnesium: 25,000. Aluminium: 34,000.
> Nitrate: 12,000.
> First come, first served!]

Simon called iSTAR at once.

"What's this about Indridi Haraldsson and LoveDeath?"

"One moment," answered a man with a German accent, humming cheerfully. Cowbells clinked nearby (the man was lying in a grassy meadow in the Austrian Alps). "Here it comes, dum de dum," he hummed, and read out: "Indridi H. called LoveDeath this morning. His girlfriend has been matched with someone else; he was just inquiring about a mercy trip when the connection was lost. It's a simple assignment. The fish has nibbled the worm, as we say here in the Alps."

"But Indridi's not ill. I know him," said Simon.

"Autistic from a marketing point of view, it says here. . ."

"That's a character flaw, not an illness! It's not sufficient grounds for a mercy trip. I'm not going to send my friend on a mercy trip, damn it!"

"We can't ban a man in full possession of his wits from going up with LoveDeath. We don't think for people. We just do what they want."

"What'll happen if I take up the challenge?"

"You'll persuade him to go with LoveDeath."

"What'll happen if I refuse the offer?"

"Someone else will take up the challenge. It's an open hunting license!"

"Open hunting license? I've never known LoveDeath issue an open hunting license before."

"Progress," said the man.

Simon examined the page more closely. According to this, ten hosts had already registered for the competition to persuade Indridi to go with LoveDeath. "What nonsense is this?" wondered Simon. LoveDeath didn't need to chase after customers. LoveDeath was above all reliable, secure, effective, and unavoidable, but now there seemed to be a change of tune: somewhere out there ten hosts meant to compete to see who could get Indridi to LoveDeath.

"Where's Indridi now?" asked Simon.

"The coordinates will follow if you take up the challenge."

Simon registered himself and a yellow smiley face flashed on a map of the city. Indridi was at the Puffin Factory. Simon ran out to the car and roared off. On the way he received a belated text message from Binni.

> [sorry, no go, maria's coming out to squash with me and sjonni what a girl!
> p.s. easy to get the hang of her, got good info from iSTAR (and a nice video!) ;-)]

Simon deleted the message and did an intensive search for
Maria. She wasn't at work, nor at her mother's. He roved into
the gym and saw her sitting in a Jacuzzi with Sjonni and Binni,
laughing at something, then she stepped out of the water, stark
naked, bent over, turned her ass to the Jacuzzi, and shot a tan-
talizing look at Sjonni, who rose up and went over to her. The
counter shot up to twenty thousand viewers and rising as Sjonni
rammed away at Maria until Simon yelled "FUCKING HELL!"
and switched off. He couldn't take any more, and now for the
first time something really began to crack inside him. The car
radio blared. *Last chance to take part in the Million Star Festival!*
His application for iSTAR had been turned down . . . *A hundred
million stars will shoot from the skies!* His network of customates
had collapsed . . . *Be prepared, don't miss the spectacle of the century!*
He was almost in a mood to book a mercy trip for himself.

Meanwhile, back at the Puffin Factory, Grim reckoned it was
safe to let Indridi go home. He put an arm round his shoulders
and escorted him to the front door. "You'll get over this, son.
Everyone has to go through their first heartbreak."

Indridi had no sooner left the puffin hall than a cheery fellow
popped up and took his arm.

"Hi, Indridi!"

"Do we know each other?"

"Come with me," the man said, taking his arm. "I can get
you quickly and safely north to LoveDeath. The connection
was lost before you booked, so I thought it would be better to
discuss this man to man . . ."

A neatly dressed woman in her thirties stormed in through the door, seized Indridi's wrist, and tried to drag him in the opposite direction.

"Don't listen to him," the woman said. "I've got a car. I'll give you a ride north." She stood on tiptoe and whispered in his ear. "We could stop on the way and satisfy your last wishes . . ."

A rumpled old woman with a headscarf came in and tugged at Indridi's sweater. She had long gray fingers.

"Don't listen to them, my boy. They don't wish you well. Trust me. Come home with me and I'll tell your fortune and then we'll see what's in store for you." The woman stroked his back. "I see a bright, shining future! Come with me . . ."

Indridi looked in bewilderment at these people who were having a tug of war with him. From inside the factory came a pitiful, long-drawn-out howl. The wolf had woken up. Hands fumbled at Indridi and voices promised him mercy and a fiery exit. More people came in. Indridi tried to back into the puffin hall again but the secret hosts gripped him tighter so he couldn't break their hold. The wolf howled louder and Indridi was spun around four times before he managed to tear himself free with a sharp jerk and flee back to the Big Bad Wolf, back to the safety, softness, and warmth. Grim ran after him along with the head of security, who called out:

"STOP! HEY, STOP! DON'T GO BACK!"

When they arrived Indridi was lying in the wolf pit again, patting the wolf affectionately while it licked his face with its huge tongue and growled at anyone who approached.

"Don't growl, dear wolf, they're not wicked people," said Indridi sadly, scratching it behind the ears.

The security representative didn't dare to go down. He stood on the bridge, scarlet in the face.

"If you keep patting the wolf like that it'll stop being fierce!" Indridi pretended not to hear him.

"Get out of there, boy! If it stops eating people and starts fawning on them like Lassie we stand to lose 500 million and five years' work and we'll have to begin all over again."

"We should have left out the dog's heart," thought Grim with a sigh. "A wolf with the heart of a dog . . ."

The secret hosts were still standing in the entrance lobby, banging loudly on the door to the puffin hall.

"Open the door! I'm his friend," echoed around the hall.

"Indridi, dear! Could I have a quick word?" Indridi recognized the voice. It was a friend of his grandmother's.

"Are these his friends?" asked the security representative.

"Indridi hasn't got any friends," said Grim. "He only mixed with other couples and his girlfriend has been matched elsewhere."

Simon parked his car outside the Puffin Factory. More and more hosts kept joining the group to take up the LoveDeath challenge. A pale man stood to one side, puffing on a cigar. A woman waited in a car with smoked glass windows. Two teenagers loitered outside the fence.

"There's something wrong with the Mood Division," thought Simon. He had never seen so many secret hosts exposing themselves in one place. He called Indridi but got no reply. In the entrance lobby of the Puffin Factory, he was met by a crowd of people.

"Indridi, it's all right! It's your cousin Anna here! I haven't seen you since you were small."

Simon managed to force his way through the throng to the glass door and caught sight of Indridi as he was escorted into the puffin hall between two men, one of them wearing a white coat, the other clearly a guard. Simon made eye-contact with Indridi and called:

"Indridi! I'll get you out of here, Indridi!"

Indridi smiled dully at him. Simon was shocked at how drawn he looked.

"Do you know that guy?" asked Grim, pointing at Simon.

"He and his girlfriend were friends of mine and Sigrid's," said Indridi.

"Is he one of them?" asked Grim.

"I think he's a programmer," said Indridi.

"People claim to be all sorts of things," said Grim. "Is he to be trusted?"

"Who can be trusted when it comes down to it?" asked Indridi.

The security guard drove the secret hosts back and let Simon in.

"We were here first!" a woman hissed at the security guard.

"Bribed you, did he, the bastard?" a man shouted. "I'll offer more!"

"Are you okay?" Simon asked Indridi. "Has Sigrid left?"

Indridi didn't answer.

"Indridi had a little accident," said Grim.

"What happened?"

"It doesn't matter," said Grim. "I just want you to keep him away from LoveDeath."

"Of course," said Simon.

Grim drew him aside and glared at him. "I'm serious! I'm

the manager of this company. I see things that you stooges on the street don't know! Can I trust you to keep him away from LoveDeath?"

"What do you think I am?"

"You're a secret host and a spy."

"I'm a friend, his man!"

Simon barged through the throng of hosts pulling Indridi behind him, out into the rain, and into his car. The security guard had his hands full shooing frantic hosts away.

"Don't take him!" called the rumpled old woman. "I've got a bad feeling about this boy!"

Indridi sat in the front seat and a plastic bag containing his wet clothes was chucked in the back.

"Watch out! He means to take you to LoveDeath! Come with us!" shouted the teenagers.

Simon slammed the door. "There's something wrong with the Mood Division," he thought.

"It sounds as if the wolf's howling," whispered Indridi dejectedly, straining his ears. The Big Bad Wolf howled desolately somewhere in the bowels of the factory.

Simon drove into town. There wasn't much that could be done. He was driving a nine-year-old Toyota. It was the best he had been able to wangle out of the agency.

"You'll have to sell it within a week," the agent had said. "If not you'll have to pay rent for the use."

"Don't you understand?" said Simon. "This is ME driving a Toyota. It's good for Toyota."

The agent looked at him pityingly and shook his head.

"You're not at high school any more, young feller. It's not as if you've got celebrity ratings."

Indridi sat in silence in the front. Simon drove down the high street and then back and forth around the harbor area. From the right foot of the Statue of Liberty to its left foot. Rolling down the window, he called out to a man in a woolly sweater.

"Great choice. No outgoings. No payments to speak of."

They were hit by a cloudburst. Indridi stared dully out to sea until he came to his senses and looked at his watch. It was nearly five. A green helicopter the size of a bus hovered over the town. Two immense rotors held it in the air while below it hung the replica Viking Age Farm that used to stand in front of the National Museum. The helicopter flew over the town and vanished into a black cloudbank that was forming over Mt. Esja.

"Everything's going north," said Simon.

"Everything except me," sighed Indridi.

"Your time will come," he said.

"Sigrid's meeting Per Møller at eight." Indridi closed his eyes. If his soul was a ship, it was drifting rudderless toward this rock. He hid his face in his hands. "All hope is gone."

Simon looked at the road ahead and a number of thoughts passed through his mind while the offers piled up on his lens. More dirty offers than he had ever seen before. Somewhere Maria was feeling rejuvenated after a refreshing game of squash with Sjonni and Binni. He received a message on his lens:

[congratulations! indridi h. is within reach. confirm trip with LoveDeath? seventy-five percent commission on offer. nb! eighty percent for additional magnesium and aluminium nitrate! last chance!]

[CONFIRM NOW!] flashed before his eyes. Simon looked at the clock and muttered. "Damn it, if I don't do it nobody will."

He made a U-turn at the next junction and veered a sharp right at a crossroads onto the highlands freeway. Indridi sat in front, frail as a bird's wing, and asked: "Where are we going?"

Simon looked at the road ahead. "You know I've never really liked you much."

Indridi didn't answer, only drooped his head.

"You know I've never called except to make money out of you."

Sigrid had sometimes claimed to see through Simon, but Indridi had always tried to look on the bright side. He believed in the good in people.

"I can't stand the music I've inflicted on you. I've suffered on those trips to the movies. I hate the books I've recommended. I'm allergic to puffin sandwiches and I love Maria!"

"I understand," said Indridi, sighing hopelessly. "So you're going to take me to LoveDeath, too."

"No," said Simon. "We're going north, to the rescue of love."

Indridi looked at Simon and from what he could see he seemed perfectly sincere, so he nodded.

"I believe you. Thank you very much," he said.

Simon felt as if a great stone had lifted from his chest and he experienced a frisson and lightness when he breathed. And so they raced along in a nine-year-old Toyota over the mountains, along the broad, straight road to Oxnadalur, where love is proven, death is light, and LoveStar twinkles behind a cloud.

"TO THE RESCUE OF LOVE!"

Unscientific, foolish love was at stake, and the Big Bad Wolf's maternal love was so strong that she sensed Indridi moving further away. She felt as if a rubber band was stretching from her heart and if the band broke, it would snap back with an indescribable pang. She writhed and panted as the band stretched until, unable to bear it any longer, she howled, raged, clawed, and snapped at the wall, while the foxes went crazy and grrryapped and the Mickeys went mad and mickeyed as if their lives were at stake. "Mickeymick! Mickeymick!" The head of security crept trembling along the steel bridge and shot a tranquilizer dart into the wolf. Peace was restored, a Swedish bioengineer showed up, and together they began to tie the wolf down, unaware that the shot had gone wide. The wolf lay on her back with her tongue hanging out, but when the right opportunity arose she bit the arm off the screaming security guard, then bounded onto the steel bridge, through the old puffin hall, and out on to the street. Led by her maternal instinct, she took the shortest route north.

Grim stood on the steel bridge between the main office and the Puffin Factory, following the wolf with his eyes.

"There goes the wolf," he muttered and lit his pipe. "Who would have thought it: the Mickeys turned out bad and the wolf good." He laid his brow against the windowpane. "All on their way north to that black hole," he sighed sadly.

The sky over Mt. Esja was unusually dark.

PLUMBING SACRED DEPTHS

WHILE LOVESTAR FLITTED FROM ONE IDEA TO ANOTHER AND WAS caught up in the mood and glamor around iSTAR, the Bird and Butterfly Division stubbornly plowed its own furrow. While iSTAR created a new image for itself at three-monthly intervals, the Bird and Butterfly Division never got around to inventing a snappy name or striking brand for itself. Every week the bird specialists made amazing discoveries, and iSTAR took the results and marketed faster, smaller, and more sensitive gadgets for the cordless human race. The Bird and Butterfly Division avoided packaging and design and anything that did not serve a purely scientific purpose. Meanwhile at iSTAR packaging was the be-all and end-all. The two departments were irreconcilably opposed, but neither could survive without the other. iSTAR thrived on bathing itself in the limelight of the newest discoveries by the Bird and Butterfly Division, while the latter's research was founded not least on the profit made for the company by the moodmen's powers of persuasion.

The bird specialists discovered that the waves were not merely waves but were themselves composed of smaller waves, and if these were examined more closely it could be observed that their innermost units were substances, colors, and forms. In this way the bird specialists plumbed the depths of love to explore its smallest constituents, from there delving even deeper until they plumbed its sacred depths, with the result that LoveStar was now sitting on a plane like a withered plant with a seed in his hand.

It was midnight in midwinter and Arctic winds were blowing around the cold rock walls of the theme park when Yamaguchi summoned LoveStar to the research wings. He took the elevator down. The research wings were an extensive labyrinth where the preference was for everything to be visible and transparent. Cables were on show, pipework was external, research appliances tended to be black or see-through boxes, if people could be bothered to cover their inner mechanisms.

LoveStar walked past research cubicles, tanks of liquid, birdcages, greenhouses, and cafeterias full of old, unmatched furniture and staff members who lived in their own world and seemed not to know whether it was day or night outside. Few had the presence of mind to worry about their appearances. Body hair was either shaved off or allowed to grow unmolested, and most were pale from their indoor existence, though among them could be seen the weather-beaten faces of Arctic biologists and sundried crocodile experts. LoveStar walked past a vast tank, an old basking shark following him much of the way. A blue radiance emanating from the tank fell in rays across a spacious hall, and in the center of the hall was a tiny computer, which was busy calculating the world. iSTAR promoted its calculations under the brand name inLOVE.

There were two men watching over the computer: one had long gray hair, the other was bald. They didn't look up when LoveStar walked past. They sat lost in thought, each at his own chessboard, engaged in remote combat with distant opponents.

Yamaguchi greeted LoveStar and showed him into a sound-proofed room. A young man was sitting on a chair with some-thing resembling a woolly hat on his head. The material of the hat was spun from fibrous wires. Behind him was a wall on which was projected a white line on a blue background; not a still of a straight line but a moving image of a living line, like the surface of a calm sea. Perfectly horizontal.

"What were you thinking now?" asked Yamaguchi, looking at the wall.

"I was just wishing that the experiment was over," said the man wearily.

"It's almost done," said Yamaguchi gently and pulled his hat down over his eyebrows. "Think one more time. Just an ordi-nary thought." The man closed his eyes and thought, without the surface of the sea behind him showing a ripple.

"Try wishing for what you did just now."

The man made a wish, but nothing happened. LoveStar watched attentively.

"Look," said Yamaguchi, pointing at the wall. "He's wishing, but it's having no effect on the line."

"How interesting," said LoveStar sarcastically.

"Just wait," said Yamaguchi, giving him a light nudge with her elbow, "It's not finished."

"Wish again."

The man wished again and still nothing happened.

Yamaguchi had various results projected on the wall. Nothing happened when the man felt hungry and wanted food, nothing happened when he was horny and wanted sex, nothing happened in the silence when he longed for music, nothing happened when he was afraid, when he got angry or was disgusted. LoveStar looked over the list and the effect that the stimuli had on the line, or rather the effect they did not have on the line.

"This is interesting," said LoveStar again.

Yamaguchi looked at him. "No, that's not interesting," she said. "The interesting bit comes now."

She went over to the man.

"Can I ask you one more thing?" she asked. "Try doing as your grandmother taught you. Try praying."

"For what?"

"Anything. Pray for us. Pray for your grandmother."

The man closed his eyes and prayed.

LoveStar watched the line on the wall and saw it ripple in waves. He went over to the blue wall and moved his finger carefully along the upper margin of the wave.

"Does the wave only appear when he prays?"

"Yes," said Yamaguchi.

"So?"

"We thought perhaps it was the remains of some brain center that people needed billions of years ago. When man was a fish or an amoeba, remains of something that was lost with evolution."

"That sounds plausible, doesn't it?"

"No," said Yamaguchi.

"Really?"

"Animals can't pray."

"What?"

"At first we assumed it was a primitive system, but then we did more research into prayer. *Animals can't pray.* Only man can send forth prayers."

"I see," said LoveStar.

"And part of mankind still uses these waves. All over the world old women are teaching their grandchildren to send out waves like these. Surely there must be some reason for this?"

"What do you think it could be?" asked LoveStar, watching the prayer ripple on the wall.

"I've got a theory, but it's a bit crazy," said Yamaguchi, "so I want to hear what you come up with first."

LoveStar looked at the wave and memorized it before returning to his office. He stayed awake all night and all the next day, drawing. He drew a mountain like Keilir in the distance and birds and spiders hanging from the sun and clouds. He walked around the room, lay down on the floor, looked out over the cold, windswept valley, and thought. His thoughts wandered to and fro until they began to form rings around one focal point and he was filled with a pleasant sensation, like intoxication, like half a teaspoon of golden honey passing through his body. An idea was grabbing hold of LoveStar and suddenly he leapt to his feet and sent Yamaguchi a message.

"Come here at once!"

Yamaguchi came without delay.

"Where does the prayer go?" asked LoveStar, stumbling over his words. "Where does the prayer go when a man prays? Does it go in any particular direction? Is there any recipient?"

"Go on," said Yamaguchi. She was clearly pleased by his words.

"If we could trace people's prayers to their destination," said LoveStar. "Like a phone call."

"Like a phone call," repeated Yamaguchi.

"Then we ought to find . . . GOD?"

LoveStar shivered. He walked over to the window. Hail lashed the rocks; a huge LoveDeath airship floated past his eyes. Three rockets thundered into the air in a bright blaze and vanished into the blizzard.

"Have I gone crazy?"

"It's all part of the same thing," said Yamaguchi. "It's all the same field, the same branch of science, the same bird science."

"The birds led us to love and from there it had to be a short step to God. Love, God, flowers, birds, butterflies, and bees. Everything has substance. The supernatural does not exist. We have always found everything we went looking for. In every corner of the world people have for some reason sent forth prayers. The prayers must have a destination. This is no crazier than love, is it?"

"It's just as crazy as love," said Yamaguchi.

"What now? Should we trace the prayers? Should we look for the place?" LoveStar got gooseflesh at the thought.

Their eyes met. He didn't really need to ask. Nothing stops an idea.

"If we don't do it, someone else will," said LoveStar.

LOVEGOD

OVER THE NEXT MONTHS YAMAGUCHI AND LOVESTAR DREW UP the guidelines for the newest and most hush-hush department of the LoveStar empire: LoveGod. They avoided saying the name of the department aloud and never committed it to paper. The only ones who knew about LoveGod were a handful of the most brilliant scientists at the Bird and Butterfly Division, their director Yamaguchi, and LoveStar himself.

Thousands of searchers were sent out equipped with highly sensitive monitors, but none of them knew exactly what they were looking for. So as not to awaken suspicion, their orders were not only to walk around churches, chapels, monasteries, and mosques, but also motorways, shopping malls, schools, factories, and playgrounds. The monitoring team had no screens: all they had to do was flick a switch and the results were sent to databases for processing. The Indonesian mathematicians who processed the data did not know how their calculations related to reality. The Indian computer operators who collated the mathematicians' results had no idea what data they were collating or what company they were working for. There was no need for Ivanov at LoveDeath to know anything, and Yamaguchi insisted that Ragnar, head of iSTAR, should be kept as far away from LoveGod as possible.

Ragnar Ö. Karlsson had taken up the gauntlet when it came to the rift between iSTAR and the bird specialists. The latest gambit by the iSTAR fashion department had infuriated Yamaguchi. It was the marketing of the "Bird and Butterfly Look," which was really nothing more than an in-joke on the part of the iSTAR management. It was a "style-free line" of clothing and interiors, inspired by the "style-free and liberal" spirit of the Bird and Butterfly Division. A new "philosophy" of design and architecture was promoted around the style-free look. The "style-free" line was an immediate hit and was sold in a thousand carefully style-free stores around the world.

Ragnar had been director of iSTAR for four years. LoveStar had always worked closely with the heads of iSTAR and got to know them well, but most of them burned out in five to seven years. Lately he'd found it hardly worth getting to know the iSTAR management and so had little personal acquaintance with Ragnar or his predecessor. This did not affect their ambition and, if anything, distance only served to increase their respect for LoveStar. Ragnar had succeeded in thoroughly surpassing all his predecessors; no moodman before or since had shown such vigor in expanding the LoveStar empire.

Ragnar held quarterly meetings at which he went over the state of affairs with Yamaguchi and LoveStar. On this occasion he was grave. The meeting was about the company's growth potential, or rather diminishing growth potential. LoveStar and Yamaguchi entered the meeting room. Yamaguchi, who was wearing a lab coat and old tracksuit pants, growled when Ragnar grinned and praised her for her style-free look. Ragnar then became deadly serious and showed them projections of graphs, bar charts, and slides: "There's good news regarding hosts, traps, and spies. The systems are working well. They've returned substantial results, and should continue to do so for the near future. The media branch is flourishing, thanks to improved access to our production materials, and LoveDeath has reached full capacity, as you know. We take what death provides and there's not much for a moodman to do, particularly since the EU and AU (African Union) health committees banned the old method. However, I have to report very worrying results from iSTAR's latest research into calculees. inLOVE has more far-reaching side effects than we realized. Unfortunately, calculated couples have proved intractable subjects for iSTAR. There's almost nothing you can sell a calculated couple because they already have everything they need. They score lower than twin brothers with identical interests, lower than hippy or monastic target groups. Calculated couples gaze into one another's eyes, pick blueberries, and stroll on beaches. Calculees can hardly be bothered to put in their lenses. It's enough for them to see each other. Retail and service industries have collapsed in densely calculated areas, and, as if that wasn't enough, calculated retailers have thrown in the towel. The howler and trap markets have taken a dive in these areas, and information about calculated people has proved worthless. We researched the response to sexy car ads among newly calculated couples. There was no response. We researched the reaction to "Are you unhappy with your appearance?" stimuli, aimed at forty-year-old calculated women in the 200- to 250-pound weight category. There was no response. We researched their interests: their partner. We researched how they wanted their partner: as he is. If you could change anything about him, what would it be? Nothing! answered 97.9 percent. The world economy will collapse if things continue this way. Although a percentage of mankind remains uncalculated due to premature death and famine in parts of the world, inLOVE is nothing but opium! I have to ask: should we raise the calculation age? Is it justifiable to match people so exactly? Are we on the right track? You must see how the order of priority has been muddled! Could it be that happiness is in fact the road to ruin? What do you want to do about this?"

LoveStar was silent for a while before saying clearly and decisively:

"Nothing."

"Nothing?" repeated Ragnar.

"That's right."

"What do you mean? We must do something!"

"No. We're going to wait."

"Wait for what?"

"We're going to wait for the results of the search."

"What search?" Ragnar pricked up his ears.

"Don't tell him!" cried Yamaguchi, shooting LoveStar a forceful look. "Don't tell him why!"

Ragnar gave LoveStar a sharp glance, and the latter thought for a moment before saying:

"LoveGod."

"LoveGod?"

Yamaguchi clenched her fists under the table and LoveStar turned to her.

"Yamaguchi, fill Ragnar in about LoveGod. He'll have to deal with it anyway, sooner or later."

"I don't understand what you mean," said Ragnar, looking bewildered.

"We're on the brink of something magnificent; we don't know what it is, but until it happens we're not going to make any radical decisions."

LoveStar left the meeting room and, against her will, Yamaguchi explained the LoveGod project to Ragnar.

LoveGod assailed Ragnar's waking and sleeping life. He could no longer keep up with the daily mood, fashion trends, design, branding, slogans, and catchphrases because everything paled in comparison to the possibilities inherent in LoveGod.

There came a point when Ragnar could take no more. He pepped himself up. Had himself praised to the skies, polished his shoes, brushed his teeth, and dressed according to the latest fashion: style-free shoes, style-free jeans, style-free matching T-shirt from the same manufacturer. His hair was carefully casual. He booked an appointment with LoveStar and walked into the office looking like self-confidence personified.

"I've got certain ideas in relation to LoveGod," he began.

"It's too early to draw up mood strategies, Ragnar. I thought I'd made that clear," said LoveStar firmly. "We'll let you know when it's ready . . ."

"I've been thinking about this business of the prayers. The way they all go to the same place. What are you going to do with the place, if it's found?"

"We haven't discussed it," said LoveStar. "We can't decide anything until we know where the place is and what it's like."

LoveStar had done little else recently than picture for himself where the prayers of the world might end up. He had imagined a being, a pyramid, a tower, rock, shrine, mountain, palace, forest, spring, pool . . . He had imagined all these things and the place assailed his dreaming and waking life. In all his dreams he was standing in a desert where he cast no shadow.

"But you are assuming that they all go to one place?" said Ragnar.

"Everything points that way."

"So the prayers must be stored there, mustn't they?"

"Presumably."

"And if we can find the place, we'll be able to read the prayers?"

"It's not improbable but I must ask you . . ."

Ragnar interrupted him:

"Imagine what a goldmine that would be for iSTAR. We could get right to the heart of every human being. We could get direct access to their longings, wishes, and innermost desires!"

"We'll have to proceed very cautiously, to say the least," said LoveStar firmly.

". . . and if we can send prayers to such a place, then we've found a natural inbuilt communications system? Haven't we?"

It was obvious LoveStar was becoming impatient.

Ragnar spoke faster. LoveStar had never seen him like this.

"Can you imagine what an invaluable system we would have

our hands on? Cordless, gadgetless, inbuilt direct access. Imagine you were hungry. You close your eyes and pray: Dear God, I want a pizza with ham and pineapple. We receive the message and have an exclusive contract with Dominoes, for example, and if you say Amen, it means the order's confirmed. The pizza will be sent out instantaneously! It couldn't be simpler! Technologically speaking, iSTAR can only harness primitive biological reflexes. We can make people howl and writhe and cry, but they're just reflexes, unconnected to the soul. When traps cry they're not really crying. If we unlock the technology perhaps we can send the advertisements deeper. Have you thought of that? Imagine if we could send a message back the same way, if we could send people some kind of revelation, inspiration, or sensation! If we could speak to the heart like a thunderous voice from heaven! If we could speak directly to the conscience. Imagine what a company would pay for guilt! If you felt guilty for walking past some product!"

Horrified, LoveStar stared at Ragnar and saw that he was on fire. LoveStar had lain awake for a whole week, trying to ward off similar ideas. He had suppressed them in the hope that they would suffocate and vanish to the four winds, but ideas do not die. He of all people should have known that. They had all popped up in Ragnar's head and he was beside himself. It was as if he was drunk. As a rule he was lively and cheerful; now he was something else. He was speeding on ideas.

"Are you listening to me?" babbled Ragnar. "Is everything all right?"

"Yes," said LoveStar, looking at him, frozen.

"You see," said Ragnar. "Of course, it won't just be business.

We'll help people, too. Let's say you come face to face with some thugs who are going to attack you. You send up a prayer." Ragnar became involved in his story, mimed being threatened, fell to his knees, and pretended to pray: "DEAR LOVEGOD, HELP! THERE ARE FOUR BIG UGLY BRUTES ABOUT TO BEAT ME UP!!!"

"Dear LoveGod?"

"Yes, it doesn't matter who it's addressed to. The prayers all go to the same place, don't they? Whether you say dear God or Buddha or dear Bob! We could just as well say: Dear LoveGod. Save me! And what happens? The message goes directly to the Angels! THE ANGELS COME TO THE RESCUE!!!"

"The Angels?"

"Yes, we'll set up special squads called the Angels. Subscribers to the LoveGod service can call on the Angels. The rest will have to call the police or pray to God to help them."

"Shouldn't we help them?"

"Those who are not subscribers will have to trust that God will help them or the police, if they manage to dial 999. Otherwise we couldn't finance the Angels."

"Subscribers?"

"Those who get to pray, they're subscribers."

"But everyone can pray."

"Nothing's free. Who do you think paid for those medieval churches? St. Peter's is still standing, raised on the profits of absolutions! God could have destroyed it but he didn't. A giant colossus raised in times of poverty and famine. We'd be doing what the Church did. We'd be creating mood around him and encouraging people to pray."

LoveStar regarded Ragnar with horror. It was hard to take in everything he said. He had never seen a moodman sink so low. Ragnar was seriously ill. Everything he mentioned was a direct consequence of LoveGod. But it was inevitable that this would happen when they found the prayers' destination. Nothing can stop an idea; nothing can prevent a possibility from being exploited to the full.

"But . . . God," whispered LoveStar. "What about him?"

"He'll benefit most. We can pep him up. He'll get a crazy surge through his system. We're talking about a billion hits a day. It'll be like in the old days when the Church took him under their wing. It worked for him for two thousand years. But then science came and took charge and the Church couldn't make him popular any more. But LoveGod will combine science with God. Except that rather than only appealing to a small target group that believes in things—whether it's God, Elvis, ghosts, or aliens—we'll also reach all the rest whom science drove out of the Church. We'll find the place, bring him here, and make him famous. We can do it! And everyone'll benefit! He'll benefit and we'll benefit and the subscribers will benefit and everyone'll be happy!"

LoveStar had foreseen this. It was clear that the moment the prayers' destination was found, it would be possible to find a way of moving it here. Then everything would be in one place: LoveDeath, the center of death; inLOVE, the center of love; and LoveGod, the center of everything.

Ragnar counted on his fingers.

"Then we'll have Love, Death, and God in one place! Have you ever heard of anything like it? We'll have a billion visitors a year. Mankind united on earth, calculated through inLOVE, fired up with LoveDeath, and finally all with a direct line to LoveGod. We're talking LoveWorld. The world. The earth. LoveWorld. It'll be awesome. WON'T IT?"

Ragnar waited for a reaction, but LoveStar was speechless. As a rule it was LoveStar's role to talk like this. As a rule he was the one enslaved to the idea, but now LoveStar just looked at Ragnar and thanked him politely.

"Thank you," he said as formally as he could. "I'll let you know when we have a use for your energies."

"Isn't it awesome?" asked Ragnar. "Isn't it fantastic?"

LoveStar knew that Ragnar was in a dangerous state. If he received Ragnar's ideas too enthusiastically, it would be like pouring oil on fire. If he received them too coolly, it would be the same. Ragnar could explode either way. It couldn't be helped. Even if he picked up a gun and put a bullet between Ragnar's eyes, the idea would evaporate through the hole. It would find itself another host, make him come crawling and saying: "Excuse me, LoveStar, I've got some ideas about LoveGod . . ."

"I'll be in touch, Ragnar," said LoveStar. "You've got some interesting ideas."

Ragnar walked out slowly, his expression unreadable; apparently he'd expected a stronger response. His eyes were glowing, the pupils filling his irises. LoveStar knew the symptoms. He had to ask him one final question.

"Excuse me, Ragnar. Can I ask you one final question?"
"Yes."
"Why?" asked LoveStar.
"Why?"

"Yes, why should we do this? What for?" asked LoveStar. "What's the point?"

Ragnar looked at him baffled. The answer couldn't be clearer. "JUST BECAUSE!"

"But what do you think he's like? Who receives all this? What does he do with the prayers?"

"You pray for something: a harvest, long life, love, happiness, luck, success, good fortune. There's a demand for what money can't buy. If he listens to the prayers he can improve what's on offer: more sunshine, rain, better harvests, or fertility, making the customer happier and reaping more believers and more prayers."

"Then why are there famines and failed harvests?"

"The prayers end up in one place. So God is probably only one entity. There's clearly a need for more gods. If there were two of them they would compete for prayers. If people could send them somewhere else, then the original would have to improve his service, enhance the quality of life on offer. Wouldn't he? He must have some goal, mustn't he?"

"I see," said LoveStar, staring rigidly out of the window. Ragnar was much sicker than he had realized.

"So another God is needed?" asked LoveStar.

Ragnar the moodman gazed at him with glowing eyes.

"I believe YOU ARE God."

FIREFLY

"I BELIEVE YOU ARE GOD," RAGNAR HAD SAID, AND THAT WAS when LoveStar stopped sleeping. He sat in his office, waiting. There was nothing he could do but wait. He lay on his couch, staring up at the ceiling. He sat at his desk, drawing. He sat in a chair, doing mental arithmetic. It was too late to stop the search, and somewhere out there in the night an idea had gotten a man. He kept Ragnar under surveillance, trying to follow all his movements, all his texts and messages.

At times LoveStar was overtaken by such a fit of trembling that his legs refused to carry him and his hand wouldn't write. At those times he sat down on a comfy sofa and rested his eyes on a pool in the Indian jungle. Ferns covered the floor of the forest. White lilies bloomed in the water. A frog floated with its eyes above the surface. The canopy of leaves filtered the sunlight; it was ideal lighting for the eyes—he need neither squint nor peer into the shadows. He breathed, listened to the buzzing of the flies, and cooled his sight in the clear water.

"Where are you?" asked a distant female voice. It was Yamaguchi.

He sent her the coordinates.

"Beautiful," she said.

"Where are you?" asked LoveStar.

"I'm the firefly."

A firefly darted across the water.

"Where are you?" he asked again.

"I'm with you," she said. He felt a body sit down beside him and a hand crept into his. It was a delicate hand that he knew well.

"I think we're losing control of the Mood Division," said LoveStar. He watched a drop fall from a leaf and form rings on the surface of the water.

"I warned you about iSTAR," said Yamaguchi.

"We wouldn't be as big without them," said LoveStar. "Mood converts everything to gold."

"They want to build a gadget out of every single thought we have in the Butterfly Department. They can see no beauty in the thought itself."

The firefly settled on a lily.

"Why are they like that?" asked LoveStar. "Ragnar was a philosophy student. How could he change in such a short time?"

"There's a biological explanation," said Yamaguchi.

"You explain everything by biology."

"They live in a dead cycle. You drive their brains to produce surface and packaging, and if they don't take care their internal world ends up becoming the same as their external one. The surface becomes the depths. Do you understand what I mean? The packaging becomes the content. The emptiness becomes the filling. The brain lacks something but doesn't know what, so it begins to function like that of a starving man; the thoughts desire the same as the body and as a result the brain starts to burn up."

A gray tortoise crawled onto a rotting tree stump. LoveStar was silent for a while and they continued to hold hands.

"You're shrewd," said LoveStar. "You've never been able to stand iSTAR."

There was a parrot perched in a tree. A noisy beetle buzzed in the treetops.

"Can we abandon LoveGod?" asked LoveStar. "Can we behave as if it had never occurred to us?"

"What do you think?" asked Yamaguchi.

"If we stop, someone else will continue the search."

The frog dove. They heard a distant rumbling.

"We'd better get going," said Yamaguchi. "The bulldozers are here."

"What bulldozers?"

"Bauxite. Under the jungle and pool there's a sixty-five-foot layer of bauxite."

"Can't we stop them?"

"LoveDeath's renewing the fleet. For that they need bauxite."

LoveStar looked over the pool where he had so often rested his eyes.

"I'll cancel the bauxite order," he said.

"There's no point," said Yamaguchi. "Someone else will buy it. iSTAR had the area photographed; it'll be saved in the mother computer. The surface, at least."

They transferred their vision back to the office. Yamaguchi

was still holding his hand. LoveStar rested his head on her shoulder.

"What are you going to do about Ragnar?" asked Yamaguchi. "What ideas did he have?"

"It doesn't matter," said LoveStar. "I'm going to try to explode him. I'm going to transfer him to LoveDeath."

"He won't explode," said Yamaguchi. "He'll quit."

"He won't quit. I'll have to explode him."

EXPLODING A MOODMAN

"ARE YOU SENDING ME TO LOVEDEATH, MY LORD?" ASKED RAGNAR
when LoveStar gave him the news. He kept his face perfectly
still, though his voice broke a little.

"I'm putting you temporarily in charge of mood at LoveDeath,
and don't call me lord."

"I'm grateful for the faith you're showing in me, but wouldn't
my energies serve LoveStar better in overall mood at iSTAR or
. . . LoveGod?"

"You'll take over mood at LoveDeath and carry on doing
what you do best."

"I'm sorry, Lord LoveStar, but I hope you appreciate that
LoveDeath doesn't need a moodman like me. As head of iSTAR
I've had an overview of mood at the corporation, and I promise
you that at LoveDeath there's nothing for a serious moodman to
do. The image is ingrained. There are no real challenges. Trust
me, it wouldn't be worth the expense of trying to reach the tiny
minority who for some reason don't choose LoveDeath."

"You'll find something to keep you busy. Not a word more on the subject."

Ivanov appeared behind Ragnar and escorted him down to LoveDeath, where he was shown into a dusty office. There he sat, trying to buck up. He was surrounded by furnishings that were so hopelessly out of fashion that he felt his self-image being eroded every minute he remained among such horrors. He was far from all the glitz surrounding inLOVE, far from cordless innovations; he'd lost sight of the beautiful people, sharp suits and sex, chicks and convertibles. The LoveDeath Mood Division was largely automatic and computer-driven; the few people who worked there were so completely burnt out that they held ideas meetings about the wording of regular death notices. Ragnar felt like a member of a special needs group as he sat around the table with these losers, discussing what toys Larry LoveDeath should give the children.

Mood thrives best in acceleration, innovation, a stimulating environment, and bursts of growth, but LoveDeath was solid and stable. LoveDeath was like a Gdansk shipyard, customs office, or power plant, and this was where Ragnar was forced to kick his heels. All around him blinked old screens on a permanent loop showing repeats of the long-vanished mood of the golden years. Endlessly showing the first launches of long-forgotten stars. This was death mood, as it was known at iSTAR.

In spite of it all, Ragnar managed to keep face and looked humble the next time he and LoveStar met. Ragnar had been humiliated but didn't let it show.

"I understand, my lord," he said. "You're testing me. You're finding out what I'm made of before appointing me as your right hand. You're hemming in my ideas until they fuse into a nuclear core, which you can split and unleash when LoveGod comes into being."

LoveStar absented himself and watched Ragnar from a distance. He was pleased when he saw the increasing tics and twitches, the manic mood swings: sometimes Ragnar would sit as if numb, then explode in a rage, only to be euphoric half an hour later. It was as if the idea was going to drill its way out of his head, taking his wits with it. But finally, when Ragnar seemed at breaking point, when his head seemed about to explode, he managed to get himself together and sit straight up in his chair, staring as if in a trance at rocket after rocket launching into the air, but of course LoveStar couldn't see what was going on in his cordless head. He couldn't see the plan Ragnar was forming.

One day Ivanov called LoveStar and asked him to come over to LoveDeath on the double. LoveStar hurried over, hoping fervently that Ragnar had finally exploded, but far from it. He looked better than ever. He was waiting for LoveStar in the meeting room. Hammers thudded all round as carpenters tore out the old furnishings.

"Right, Ragnar, tell him about the plan," said Ivanov, gleefully, rubbing his hands together from pure excitement.

Ragnar stood and cleared his throat.

"It's hard to squeeze any more mood out of LoveDeath," said Ragnar. "I can't show any successes on the marketing side, nor would it be possible in the normal run of things. LoveDeath is not growing. You can't increase the production of death without harming the image."

"Ha, ha!" guffawed Ivanov, overexcited.

"Death produces at its own rate," Ragnar continued. "The only real challenges are reduction of costs and increasing efficiency, which are the preserve of economists and engineers. Not moodmen. But as I was sitting last week watching rocket after rocket launching into space, I began to think about all the unclaimed orders that have been orbiting aimlessly, getting in everyone's way, and then I had an idea."

Ragnar took a deep breath, flung out his arms, and thundered like a prophet:

"THE MILLION STAR FESTIVAL! WE'LL SHOOT UP A HUNDRED MILLION BODIES! A HUNDRED MILLION BODIES WILL FORM A SATURN RING AROUND THE EARTH! WE'LL CLEAN UP THE WORLD'S CEMETERIES! WE'LL ACQUIRE THE MOST VALUABLE REAL ESTATE IN MAJOR CITIES! WE'LL BUILD ON THE PLOTS AND MAKE A HUNDRED MILLION STARS RAIN DOWN ON EARTH!"

LoveStar heard no more. He absented his ears and eyes in a desperate search for a resting place, but his eyes couldn't find the forest pool anywhere. At the coordinates there was nothing but a reddish brown sea of mud, wheel ruts, and rotting vegetation as far as the eye could see. His ears encountered nothing but the din of traffic, human throngs, and screaming crowds at sports stadiums. He wandered further but either it was too dark or the sunlight was too harsh or the noise too great. He switched back to his own head from time to time, and when he saw that Ragnar had finally fallen silent he said to Ivanov:

"Do you agree to this?"

"I think it's stupendous!" said Ivanov.

A bald woman in a style-free lab coat and green glasses knocked on the meeting room door.

"Excuse me," said Ivanov, "it's the interior designer. It's agreed, isn't it?"

LoveStar nodded and Ivanov went off to fawn over the designer, leaving them alone in the meeting room. Ragnar the moodman had managed the impossible: to turn the situation to his advantage. The whole LoveDeath apparatus had begun to revolve around Ragnar and iSTAR.

"Keep up the good work," said LoveStar. "Confer with Ivanov. I won't be involved any further." He stood up and headed for the door but Ragnar whispered after him:

"The dead shall rise again!"

LoveStar spun round.

Ragnar smiled strangely, gazed radiantly into LoveStar's eyes and whispered:

"When you find the place, when you find God, when you become God, we'll let the bodies fall and burn up in the Million Star Festival. Then there will be no more death on earth. It will be clean from corruption and decay. As was prophesied at the coming of the Savior: 'There shall be a resurrection of the dead, both of the just and unjust.'"

LoveStar walked menacingly toward him, hissing between clenched teeth: "LEAVE ME IN PEACE! GO!!!"

"I get it," said Ragnar, "you need time to adjust . . ."

A new, unexpected spirit was created around LoveDeath. Ragnar was the brains behind the Million Star Festival as well as its spokesman. The magician Ragnar was everywhere, the mood-man who had changed tack and become an example to leaders and governors all over the world. "Worth the risk—lower your dignity and show what you're made of."

LoveStar opened *Newsweek*. The headline was: "Feast of Stars Ahead!"

The LoveDeath Million Star Festival will be the most spectacular display of all time!

Ragnar Ö. Karlsson (37), head of the LoveDeath Mood Division, got the idea for the festival several months ago and had himself transferred from his exalted position as head of iSTAR to LoveDeath, in pursuit of his idea. A hundred million bodies will form a Saturn ring around the earth and a hundred million stars will shoot simulta-neously to earth. It is expected to be the most spectacular display mankind has ever witnessed.

"Will the festival follow the course of the sun?"

"There'll be no need. The lights will be so brilliant that it will be as bright as day all over earth, especially since the dead will be dressed in thicker costumes than usual."

LoveStar threw aside the paper and turned on CNN [demo-graphic: women/BA+/45+]. A brunette newsreader was on screen, asking penetratingly:

"You mentioned thicker costumes in *Newsweek*. Won't they make people look too fat?"

"Far from it. We can let you try one on afterward. (laughter)

240

The design is stunning, and we're taking particular care to ensure that people won't look ridiculous during their final moments. We use special ceramic fibers, so instead of burning up in twenty seconds the million star bodies will take around four minutes."

He switched to BBC World [demographic: men/MBA/PhD+/35+].

"You were head of iSTAR and considered, in spite of your youth, one of the most influential moodmen of the century, with the exception of LoveStar himself, of course. Why were you demoted to LoveDeath?"

"Some people interpreted it as a demotion, but in fact Love-Death was in need of mood. I sought after this job. It's part of a bigger project," he said, looking straight at the camera. "It's part of a much bigger project."

"When can we expect the Million Star Festival?"

LoveStar switched off, turning over to a panel discussion on Swedish State Radio for a target group of arts and culture enthusiasts. "I've always had an artistic streak and I regard art and mood as an inseparable whole. The towers in the world's major cities could almost be called sculptures; the architecture is perfectly organic, as indeed the inspiration for them comes from nature. Many art critics have already come to regard the Million Star Festival as concept art. The mere act of creating the Saturn ring is the largest work of environmental art in the history of mankind. And of course we're bringing death closer to people."

"But you don't have a fixed date?"

"Understandably, we can't set a fixed date for the fall. There are a number of factors to take into consideration. The weather conditions must be favorable—no hurricanes, monsoons, or that sort of thing. But you can rest assured that no one will miss the Million Star Festival."

"How can you be sure?"

"For this once we will activate the speech centers of all cordless people. I know it's controversial, but our contracts allow it in exceptional circumstances and we're confident that no one on earth will want to miss this. Everyone will shout out in unison when the festival begins. In fact, the world won't need much warning. The sky is never far away."

HELL

MONTHS PASSED. RAGNAR'S STAR WAS IN THE ASCENDANT AND LoveStar couldn't avoid him. His face was everywhere. The towers rose, the dead were fired up to the Million Star Belt, and Ivanov did little but praise Ragnar. "One hell of a boy, that Ragnar! Damn it, you've got an heir in Ragnar!"

Ragnar summoned LoveStar and Yamaguchi down to Love-Death. They were greeted by Ivanov. He was unrecognizable, his old suit replaced with a ridiculous mish-mash of garments. Yamaguchi swore when she saw that the offices had been refurbished according to "style-free style." Wires and pipes protruded with the sole purpose of emphasising the undesigned rawness of the space. On the walls were photographs and drawings of the towers under construction: Buenos Aires, Hong Kong, St. Petersburg, Rome . . .

"Ragnar's going to unveil the new LoveDeath campaign," said Ivanov. "I warn you, it's cutting-edge stuff, but it's getting tougher out there, so we have to go further. Ragnar, over to you."

"Good morning," said Ragnar, bowing deferentially to Love-Star. "The Million Star Festival is ready to launch but, as you know, LoveDeath's customers have not all paid up on time. The department reported a mere seventeen percent profit for the last quarter. That's below the expected $9,980 billion figure, and there are various explanations for this. For example, we have not had widows turned out of their homes, and in my opinion this policy has caused us considerable damage. We've also had problems with smugglers. Vagrants and paupers have been abandoned outside our offices all over the world, and more often than not we've allowed them to tag along. Particularly since we began accumulating bodies for the Million Star Festival. I think it's time LoveDeath put the pressure on again. People take LoveDeath too much for granted."

LoveStar appeared not to be listening. He was doodling a pattern on a piece of paper.

"You're not going to have them buried, are you?" asked Yamaguchi in disgust.

"No," said Ragnar. "Here are some shots of the new campaign," he said, starting the advertisement.

The first film clip showed monstrous yellow trucks driving in a column across the barren wastes and rough tracks of the Odadahraun lava field. It looked autumnal; the surroundings were gray and icy. The picture quality was poor, as if viewed from a plague-fly. The trucks drove past barriers and dirt roads, splashed across a stream feeding a reservoir, and from there up a steep slope. Then for the first time the cargo became visible from the plague-fly. Yamaguchi paled when she saw what was on the back of the trucks.

"This is horrible! Please turn it off!" She closed her eyes and shrieked: "TURN IT OFF!"

"What's the matter?" asked Ragnar. "Dead is dead."

The plague-fly followed the trucks across the lava field through drizzle and sleet, but now the cargo was constantly in view and when the trucks drove over bumps the load bounced, sending hands and feet flapping limply in the air.

"Hey! Something fell off the back!"

It lay naked and corpse-white on the track, but the trucks carried on regardless, crushing it into the dirt road. Ravens perched on surrounding rocks, waiting to snatch a piece of carrion.

"Stop!" yelled Yamaguchi. "Are these real pictures? Were those real bodies?"

The column of vehicles carried on until it reached the rim of the crater, known as Hell, by Lake Oskjuvatn. There the trucks took turns reversing to the edge and tipping their loads down into the boiling, sulfurous mud.

"Where are the tourists? Where are the swimmers?"

The trucks tipped and tipped in a constant stream, their cargo either floating or lying half-submerged, though here and there legs, arms, and gaping heads stuck up out of the ooze.

Yamaguchi was white in the face.

"That's the vilest thing I've ever seen! Was it a real film, Ragnar? I demand to know. Were the pictures real?"

"I'm really pleased with this one," said Ragnar with a gleam in his eye.

Now there were trucks driving up a rugged, black mountain. A cutaway showed that it was the volcano, Mt. Hekla. A crater had been blasted in the summit and red lava surged and boiled in the wound. The same scenes were repeated. The trucks tipped lifeless loads down into the boiling morass and a caption appeared:

STOWAWAYS GO TO HELL!
LOVEDEATH!

"Do you mean to show this to people?" asked Yamaguchi. Ivanov laughed.

"I told you it was hard-hitting! You should have seen your face." Ragnar looked at Yamaguchi as if she was a fool. "This is not aimed at a general audience. It's to show the illiterate, poor, and stupid target groups that there's no point sneaking bodies here in the hope that they'll go to heaven. There's no point being dumped here without a dime and thinking that if people die in this country they'll automatically get launched. This is what happens to stowaways! They go straight to Hell! The fires of hell await them!"

"LoveStar! Aren't you going to do anything?" yelled Yamaguchi.

LoveStar said nothing. He just looked from Ivanov to Ragnar and knew that nothing could be done.

"What sentimental nonsense is this?" asked Ragnar. "LoveStar himself had the idea for the 'Rotting Mother' campaign. This is no cruder than that was in its time! I saw it when I was little. It had quite an impact. My grandmother had just been buried. We kids went sobbing to Mom and Dad, begging them to have the old woman fired up. Of course it didn't work. LoveDeath was so expensive then; it cost as much as a new Ferrari."

"Who made this advertisement?" asked LoveStar.

"As I said, the bodies were just abandoned outside and a plague-fly . . ."

"WERE THE PICTURES REAL?" asked LoveStar.

"It was just rubbish that had been left lying around, just a few days' worth of raw material. We didn't kill anyone. It would all have rotted anyway," said Ragnar with a shrug.

LoveStar got to his feet.

"Everybody out except Ragnar!" he growled.

Yamaguchi and Ivanov made themselves scarce.

Unflinching, Ragnar walked up to LoveStar with determined steps.

"You'd better get used to this!" he whispered. "It was prophesied: the dead shall rise again! You could perfect the world if only you wanted to. We could get a better grip on things; you need me. You're getting old and soft; you can't do it alone. What's love without death? What's heaven without hell? EH? What's God without the Devil, LoveStar? You can't have God without hell. You'll never get a proper grip on the people. If you don't create hell, the people will do it themselves. You have no choice. We're going to use this advertisement!"

"You're mad!"

LoveStar grabbed Ragnar's collar, but the other man reacted fast, seizing LoveStar's wrist so hard that his knuckles whitened. Ragnar was younger and stronger. He looked LoveStar straight in the eye.

"We've already got death fully under our control," he said, tightening his grip. "The old method is no longer on offer. We've got love too, but that's a problem; love is undermining us. We'll use LoveGod to calculate people a little less accurately, thereby preventing the decline of consumption. Those who divorce will be forever excluded from LoveDeath and sent to hell. The same applies to those who do not subscribe to LoveGod. Those who do not pray, those who do not confess to LoveGod and do not reveal their innermost desires will be excluded and cast into the pit of Hell or fires of Mt. Hekla. That way it'll all work out. People want answers; we can provide them. Get used to it. You've found the final solution. Love, Death, and God. You're God already."

Releasing his grip, Ragnar marched out and LoveStar collapsed into a chair, closed his eyes and sent up a prayer to goodness knows where. "You who are in the place, save yourself if you can. You who are in the place, take my life from me . . ."

CRY-TRAP

LOVEGOD WAS HURTLING AHEAD LIKE AN EXPRESS TRAIN AND THERE was no way of stopping it. Nothing stops an idea, and LoveStar felt as if he himself was standing on the tracks. If he called off the search, someone else would find the place; that was quite certain. The technology existed. The ring was closing. The leader of the search party seemed to think he could sense God himself:

"He seems to live at a different pace. He must be able to see light traveling. For him every day is like a thousand years. In his eyes we move slower than the grass that grows before our eyes. He seems to move like a wave. For him every second is like 4.2 days. He could be here now, in Africa now and back here now. Three seconds for us. Twelve days for him. He could be everywhere at once, according to our perception."

LoveStar locked himself away in the tower and whispered out of an open window:

"This wasn't my idea. I didn't want to be God." He watched the ravens soaring on an updraft by the floodlit rock.

He tried to doze but started up in a panic and looked around.

"WHO'S THERE?" He paced the floor. Looked under the bed. Turned on the bathroom light. There were mirrored walls on both sides, so he saw himself form two endless rows, receding into infinity. "I'm the first in the row and the last," he thought, getting gooseflesh. "I'm he who is and was and is to come." He peered harder to see where the reflection ended, but as far as the eye could see, in the deepest depths of the mirror, he felt someone was standing watching him. He ran into the bedroom and fetched a pair of bird-watching binoculars that he kept under the bed, raised them, and saw EYES STARING straight at him! He let out a shriek, flung away the binoculars, and saw himself again in thousandfold rows. He felt a cold draft behind him, turned to the other mirror, and yelled into the depths:

"HELLO! WHO IS IT? Who are you? What do you want of me? Why did I have to find you? Why did I have to find out your ways?"

No one answered his prayer. Announcements arrived daily:

"The ring is closing in!"

"The ring is a snare," thought LoveStar.

The leader of the search party called in the middle of the night. The line crackled and the sound was poor. As if the conversation was the photocopy of a photocopied photocopy.

"I THINK WE'VE FOUND THE PLACE!"

"Where does it end?" he whispered.

"YOU'LL NEVER BELIEVE IT, BUT IT'S HERE UNDER TABLE FOUR AT A BURGER JOINT IN TEXAS!!!"

Silence on the line, followed by a roar of laughter from the leader of the search party. He was losing his marbles, too.

"Are you drunk?"

"Just celebrating. We've ruled out Antarctica, North and South America, the Pacific, the North Atlantic, Scandinavia, Eastern Europe, the Himalayas, and the bulk of Asia. We're closing the ring. Get ready; it could happen any moment."

The search was a snare that was tightening around LoveStar's neck. Every time he received reports of success a chill passed through him. He ran into the bathroom and vomited bile. He had no appetite. He took refuge in honey, had the sun brought to him on a white plate. He chewed slowly, watching himself dreaming in the mirror, but he never slept.

In the middle of one night the author appeared in his room.

LoveStar regarded him with contempt. "What are you doing here?"

"The secretary gave me this appointment."

"In the middle of the night, without asking me?"

"She said she was taking the initiative."

The author was holding something behind his back. LoveStar paled and recoiled into a corner.

"What have you got there?"

"I talked to your daughter," said the author coldly. LoveStar got gooseflesh.

"What did you do to her, you bastard?"

The author looked pityingly at LoveStar. "I interviewed her before you fired me. I thought you might like to have the recording."

The author laid a small box on the table and left.

LoveStar opened the lid and a familiar woman's voice sounded in his head, with an accent acquired from years spent abroad: ". . . I think my brothers hated him. They blamed him for what happened to Mom. I don't remember her at all; I know she was beautiful, especially when she was young, but I was only a few months old when she died. I grew up mostly with my grandparents. They never spoke to him or about him much. I didn't see him often. I don't really know what life was like before she died. I'm sure he loved Mom in his own way; he talked about her as if he did, though he's never mentioned her in public. She was sick and I think it's unfair to blame him for her death; he probably wasn't perceptive enough to help her. I don't know whether he tried very hard to see me; my grandparents said he didn't, but I went to stay with him once a year, anyway. He lived in his office, which was kind of strange. He put me to bed in the evenings and sometimes told me stories. I don't know where they came from; I expect he made them up himself. There was one I must have listened to a thousand times. I recorded it secretly when I was six. I've looked after it carefully. You can have a copy if you want."

There was a rustling, the theme tune to a kids' TV show, then another rustling in the middle of the song, a short silence, then even poorer sound quality as LoveStar heard the echo and fragments of a distant conversation. He recognized his daughter's voice, twenty-three years younger, a clear child's voice.

"Do you know any stories?"

Then he heard his own voice:

"Once there was a king called Medias. He went on regular visits around his kingdom in all his finery with his horse and his hound, but it was the same wherever he went; no one recognized him. Medias went to the butcher, the baker, and the shopkeeper, but he always had to wait in line like everyone else, and no one ever bowed to him. He often had the greatest difficulty getting back into his palace because the guards would stop him and demand identification. One day Medias was sitting sadly in his palace when a dwarf appeared to him.

"'What troubles you, good sir?' asked the dwarf.

"'No one recognizes me,' said Medias.

"'I'll grant you one wish,' said the dwarf.

"'I wish everything I touch would become famous,' said Medias, 'I wish everything I touch would appear on the front pages of newspapers all over the world and that everyone would recognize me and bow and scrape before me and worship me and long to meet me. I want people to remember all their lives that they once saw or heard King Medias!'

"'You shall have your wish fulfilled,' said the dwarf and vanished.

"The next day Medias went to the butcher's to buy a sausage and two chickens, and before he knew it somebody had photographed him, an interview was taken with a woman who had touched Medias's hand in the shop, and the sausage he bought became world famous and was known as Medias Sausage. The farmer who raised the chickens became renowned all over the world as the farmer who raised the chickens that the king bought. Medias mounted his horse, and it became the most famous horse in the world. Medias touched the castle, and people came from all over the world to see it. He went to the barber and the shopkeeper and the baker and always the same story; they all became world famous and sought-after royal bakers, shopkeepers, and barbers. If he patted a dog, people at once wanted to name their children after it.

"One day he met in his palace the most beautiful maidservant in the world. She had blue eyes and thick blonde hair, infectious laughter, and snow-white teeth, and they had a secret tryst in the summerhouse. Medias touched her lightly and tentatively and she touched him, so that in the end they had touched so much that there wasn't a patch the size of a hand anywhere on their bodies that hadn't been touched, caressed, or kissed, and in due course they had two beautiful sons. The maidservant immediately appeared on the front pages of every newspaper in the world. Photographers snapped and snapped away at her until she was red-eyed and white-faced from all the flashes. She tried to flee in Medias's world-famous sports car, driving frantically away from the flashes, but the photographers had lined the road and they snapped and snapped until she was blinded, drove into a lamppost, and was killed.

"Medias grieved and wept, and this was reported in all the newspapers in the world. Their boys wept day and night, but this wasn't mentioned in the papers because the king had never touched them. Kings don't need to touch their children because they're so well cared for by their nurses. But now they were inconsolable. They wept when the day nurse came and sobbed when the night nurse came and quavered: 'I want Daddy! Daddy, comfort me. Daddy, cuddle me. I feel so bad, Daddy.' But Medias just stood at a distance, looking at them sadly. He couldn't face touching anyone ever again."

Silence on the tape.

"That's a sad story," said the child's voice forlornly.

"Yes," said LoveStar, "it's a sad story."

"Good night, Daddy."

The recording ended. LoveStar sat in his chair, but then something happened inside him. "The author has sent me a cry-trap," he thought, and even though he clamped his eyes shut, he couldn't stem the flood, and the tears poured and he shook and was filled with a strange fear. He sent up more prayers to the place, in the feeble hope that if there was someone listening to the messages, that someone would be able to get away in time: "You who are in the place, save yourself before it is too late!"

Yamaguchi entered the room. She took LoveStar's clasped hands and looked into his eyes. She had deep, dark, beautiful eyes.

"The waiting is over," she said gently. "We've had a final confirmation from the leader of the search party. We've found the place. We know where the prayers go."

"Where?"

"They end in the desert. Where we suspected."

"Is there anyone there? Is HE there?"

"We haven't seen anyone."

LoveStar looked around and whispered, "But where do the prayers end up?"

"In a hollow tree stump." Yamaguchi produced a picture of the stump.

"So? Have you examined the place?"

She hesitated a moment, then said, "No one dares go anywhere near it."

"What do you mean? No one dares go near a hollow tree stump?"

"The first people to reach the spot were going to peep into the stump, but the villagers warned them against it. They said if anyone went near the tree stump the world would end. Someone went near and . . ."

"What?" whispered LoveStar.

"He was struck by a bolt of lightning," she whispered back.

"Couldn't you send other people?"

"We did send someone else."

"And?"

"Another bolt of lightning."

LoveStar shuddered and felt as if a deathly cold draft was blowing on him. As if there was no rock wall behind him any longer, only a window open to the icy night.

Yamaguchi continued. "We couldn't find anyone else to go. Everyone said it was your idea, so you should go."

"That I should go?"

"It's your company."

"So? Do you think the world will end?" asked LoveStar.

Yamaguchi didn't answer.

LoveStar considered the choices. Two people had been struck by lightning. The villagers said the world would end. He had no other choice. He wasn't a free man. He was slave to an idea and came to the only possible conclusion that a starving, insomniac, and idea-infected mind can reach:

"If I don't go, someone else will."

Yamaguchi was waiting for LoveStar in the doorway.

"The plane's waiting," she said. "Are you ready?"

"How can one be ready?" muttered LoveStar, putting on his jacket. He looked over the Oxnadalur valley. Smoke curled from a turf farm; a mountain was reflected in the lake.

"It's beautiful, the valley, isn't it?" said LoveStar.

"Yes, it's beautiful."

"It wasn't as beautiful when I bought it."

"No," said Yamaguchi. "The plane's waiting. We'll meet there in five minutes."

LoveStar walked uneasily around his office, then took the elevator down and proceeded toward the launchpad, where he was ambushed by Ivanov. He was ashen-faced and shook his fist at LoveStar.

"YOU'VE BETRAYED ME! WHY DIDN'T YOU LET ME KNOW?" Ivanov was trembling with fury.

"I don't know what you're talking about. We'll discuss it later," said LoveStar curtly and hurried toward the plane.

"I'VE FOUND OUT WHAT THE TOWERS ARE SUPPOSED TO HOUSE!" Ivanov called after him. "THEY'RE HOLLOW INSIDE! THEY'RE YAWNING ABYSSES! THEY'RE VAULTS!! ON THE NORTH WALL OF EACH THERE'S A STAR!!!!!"

LoveStar shut his ears and hastened his stride. Ivanov was quickly left behind and yelled louder:

"ON THE NORTH WALL OF EACH TOWER THERE'S A STAR! IN THE MIDDLE OF THE FLOOR THERE'S A STAR! THERE'S A STAR HANGING FROM THE CEILING! THEY'RE A THOUSAND GIANT CHURCHES! RAISED TO WORSHIP LOVESTAR!!! THEY'RE RAISED IN YOUR HONOR, LOVESTAR! DID YOU KNOW ABOUT THIS? WORD HAS STARTED TO SPREAD. WHERE ARE YOU

GOING? WHERE'S RAGNAR? WHAT'S THE MILLION
STAR FESTIVAL FOR?!"

LoveStar boarded the plane. Yamaguchi was sitting at the
back, waiting for him. She rose, came up to him, seized his
hands, and kissed him on the brow.

"Good-bye," she said. "Take care."

"Aren't you coming?" asked LoveStar.

"The leader of the search party will meet you," said Yamaguchi. She looked into his eyes, handed him a folded note, and
glanced once more over her shoulder before vanishing out of
the door.

The plane soared into the air. LoveStar read the note:

> *You've never asked me about love.*
> *I've calculated the world,*
> *but you've never asked me about love.*
> *I calculated you long before inLOVE*
> *and long before LoveDeath.*
> *your other half is*
> *me*

DESERT

THE PLANE LANDED AT AN OLD MILITARY AIRBASE IN THE MOGA desert of northern Kenya. A search party with three helicopters was waiting to transport LoveStar over the endless sand dunes toward his goal. The helicopters landed some three miles from the tree stump, where jeeps were waiting to race the group over the inhospitable, windswept plains until they reached a small, rundown village. Armed guards kept watch over the villagers and the tree stump on the outskirts of the village. Beside the stump sat a child.

"The child was there this morning," said the leader of the search party. "No one in the village knows who it is. We haven't a clue where it came from."

The child was hiding something in its hand. According to the measurements, every prayer in the world was drawn precisely to the child's hand. LoveStar walked in a big circle around the child and the tree stump, measuring the waves. There was no mistaking it. He put the monitor down on the sand; no need for that any more. He looked up at the sky, which was blue with no hint of a thunderstorm. The child sat quietly by the stump, looking at what it was holding. LoveStar took a step toward the child but hesitated when it looked up. He felt a knot in his stomach; it was all happening too fast. He hadn't thought properly about the follow-up; the plane had been too quick. "Ships sail at the speed of the soul," he thought, looking at the ground, unable to spy his shadow anywhere, and suddenly he felt the need to wait for his soul to catch up. He glanced over his shoulder as if to look for it but found only the hard stares of the armed guards and the fear, or perhaps sorrow, in the eyes of the villagers. A gray-haired woman with a child in her arms met LoveStar's gaze. "DON'T," her eyes implored. "DON'T!"

LoveStar looked at the sweating leader of the search party. There was no turning back. Hesitantly he took a step, feeling the need to limit their number. He had been flown to the heart of the world at three times the speed of sound, then driven to the tree stump as if to a drive-in serving window. It wasn't quite appropriate. It was too easy. He was still stiff from the flight; it couldn't be this easy. Perhaps it wasn't allowed to be this easy. Like being driven to the top of a mountain. He felt he should turn back and walk all the way like a pilgrim, talk to old people, children, youths, whores, customs men, and beggars, sleep out under the stars with shepherds and grow deeper in wisdom and learning, but it was too late for that. The place had been found and the child was unlikely to wait there forever. He inched closer to the child, as if treading on thin ice. He was halfway there when suddenly he stopped as if he had changed his mind. He took off his jacket and removed his shoes. The sand was hot and the sun burned. Now he saw the child better; he felt like he knew it. He approached it warily, as people approach a savage dog.

"Hello," said LoveStar.

The child looked at him without answering.

"What have you got there?"

The child opened its hand. In it was a seed.

"May I see the seed?" asked LoveStar in a tremulous voice.

The child shook its head.

"Why not?" asked LoveStar.

"I'm supposed to guard it."

"From whom?"

"From you," said the child.

"No, no, that can't be right," said LoveStar.

"What would you do with it?"

"I would look after the seed and you can go and play."

"Is it a game?" asked the child, smiling, but the smile didn't reach its eyes. "You can be it."

"What?"

"Gotcha! You're it!"

The child touched him with the hand that was holding the seed.

LoveStar screamed as something like lightning blasted through his body, followed by a terrible sound, like the roar of a raging torrent, then the floodgates opened and countless voices poured through him, whispering crying praying a hundred thousand voices like hail pounding on a tin roof; a hundred million jarring voices burst their way through him, echoing in his head so he couldn't distinguish a word or understand the languages as they all talked at once, sometimes a voice pricked like a pin, sometimes one brushed across his heart like a burning jellyfish tendril and he writhed in agony as a thousand voices stung him like a swarm of bees, filling his heart with pain, loss, and grief, while the waterfall of words surged through him, making his heart revolve like a mill wheel driven by jarring weeping voices that he couldn't answer or comfort because they were inexorable and flowed on endlessly, old voices and broken voices and children's voices clear as a spring before mingling in one brown tide-race like a glacial torrent brown and in a flooding rush after the thaw, and sweat sprang out on his forehead like spray and his eyes leaked like a sieve and it seemed the waterfall would never cease its thundering because although the touch only lasted a second, every day was like a thousand years, and so the torrent poured through him for a hundred hours and all that time the ache in his chest was so indescribably painful that he would have died if he hadn't clutched on to the sentiment that all the voices seemed to contain: HOPE.

"Aren't you going to play?" asked the child.

LoveStar was bewildered, hardly able to breathe. His chest felt heavy as lead. Only a second had passed. People were standing nearby as if nothing had happened. The world was in its place. He wiped the sweat and tears from his face.

"Do you still want the seed?" asked the child.

Beads of sweat dripped into LoveStar's eyes; he blinked and looked at the sun. The Million Star Belt glittered on the horizon like blood red sparks.

The child looked in the other direction. The child pointed east.

"You can have the seed if you give me a star."

LoveStar looked to the east and recognized the star that was shining low over the sandblasted eastern mountains. It was LOVESTAR, the first star to twinkle in the evening sky. He looked at the seed in the child's outstretched hand and nodded. He said nothing, simply agreed, searched in his pockets and found the note from Yamaguchi. He sketched three lines on the back to form a mountain and desert. In the sky he drew a star. Under the picture he wrote: "The child owns the LOVESTAR that twinkles behind a cloud."

The child put the seed into LoveStar's hand, and with that the world warped before his eyes. The child ran off. The child was gone. No, the child was standing behind him, frozen in its footsteps, and LoveStar walked around it because it reminded him of a boy he had known when he was little, it reminded him of an old picture of his grandmother, it was just like his daughter and an old man . . . He didn't finish his thought because abruptly he lost control of time. To his right, time was standing still and a bird hung in the air, while under the bird a house rose and crumbled, another rose and crumbled, and around it people grew and declined, flowers sprouted and shriveled, trees rose and rotted, while the bird hung still in the sky. Clouds piled up and the sun raced across the sky again and again and again as if the earth was a blue fist and the sun a yellow stone in a sling, swinging in circles, and a glacier sailed forth from it like a white ship, clearing all before it, cities and cars, mountains and planes, all out to sea. Icebergs broke off into the sea and filled the world to the horizon and ice covered the earth, which became as white as the clenched fist that was swinging the sun around it, making daylight flash like a strobe at a disco, until the glacier receded and waves washed the rocks, washed the rocks, washed the rocks, but there was nothing left, not a car, not a house, until the hand released the sling and the sun was hurled into space, dwindling small and pale as a star until all was dark.

LoveStar stood in the middle of the desert. The child stared at him with eyes that seemed variously blue or brown or green, but it was only a moment since it had placed the seed in his hands. He felt he had seen this child before but couldn't place it.

"Great-grandfather," thought LoveStar. "The child is just like me."

The child walked barefoot out into the sea of sand and over a dune until its head vanished behind it.

Black as the sun.

TRUE LOVE

SIGRID AND PER HAD A DATE AT EIGHT IN THE EVENING IN A little restaurant high up in the rock face with a view over the lake. It would supposedly change her life once and for all. She put on a white dress, took the elevator upstairs and sat down at a table overlooking a falcon's nest on a rocky ledge. The young birds screeched and their mother flew up with a ptarmigan in her beak. The chicks tore it greedily apart.

Sigrid waited and eight o'clock drew near. She had eaten nothing on the way north and was famished. The waiter brought her a message from Per: he was running a bit late so she should get herself something to eat from the buffet. She was surrounded by couples who chattered like a colony of seabirds and had strangely similar tics.

"What would you like?" the waiter asked a young man and older woman at the next table. The woman was on the plump side with black hair and unusually bright, beautiful eyes. Obviously newly calculated. Sigrid amused herself by trying to guess their nationality. "She's probably from Greece or Turkey; he could well be Belgian." They discussed photosynthesis in broken English and the young man was clearly so funny that the woman kept shrieking with infectious laughter, making him shriek as well. Sigrid couldn't see what was so funny; it was clear that only half the joke lay in the words.

The waiter coughed. "What can I get you?"

"Do you have any more like that?" asked the woman, pointing at the man with a giggle. "I'd like one of those for starter, another for main course, and the third for dessert!"

"Shouldn't we eat something?" asked the man, wiping the tears from his eyes.

"Maybe," she said, sticking out her tongue, and they proceeded to tongue-synthesize until the waiter interrupted them again.

"If you're not going to order anything, I'll have to ask you to return to your room."

"Is there anything you want?" asked the young man, gazing into her eyes.

"Yes, there is," she whispered, taking a deep breath. The next minute they had disappeared down the corridor.

Indridi squirmed in his seat the whole way north. He checked the speedometer, cursing buses and puffins on the road: the latter had obviously been freshly distributed. Fat and flightless, they waddled singing over the heathland. Indridi writhed as if to make the car go faster. Simon stamped on the accelerator and overtook a long line of buses. A thick forest of iron appeared; they were nearing the intersection where the country's power lines met, two hundred dead-straight rows of pylons converging on the hydrogen plant, like a spider in its web.

The forest of iron was behind them and now the peaks of LavaRock appeared ahead, followed by the entire mountain range. Swans flew toward the sun. They turned down a valley and drove over a stone bridge across a river until finally they saw the glass wall. It reflected the mountain opposite, making the valley seem perfectly symmetrical. Clouds and sky were reflected in the glass so the peaks appeared to perch on clouds. The letters forming LOVESTAR seemed to hang in thin air. An empire built on clouds? An empire hewn in stone.

The whole place was still teeming with puffins. Tourists had no need to set foot outside in the open air unless they wanted to: most arrived by underground trains from the towns of Keflavik, Akureyri, or Egilsstadir, which delivered them to a station below the theme park entrance lobby. From there escalators took them straight up to the sky-high reception hall with a sloping rock face on the one hand and a bright glass wall on the other.

Simon stopped the car at the main entrance and they got out. Drizzle from a recent LoveDeath launch fell on their faces and an airship marked LoveDeath passed before the sun, casting a dark shadow over them. Indridi peered despairingly around him in the feeble hope of spying Sigrid. Simon connected himself to reception.

"Hello, I'm looking for Sigrid Gudmundsdottir."

"One moment," answered a voice. "Unfortunately there's no Sigrid Gudmundsdottir registered."

Simon thought for a moment:

"Sigrid Møller," he ventured hesitantly, seeing how the name Møller pierced Indridi's eardrums like a needle.

"She's due to be calculated in half an hour," came the answer.

"I need to talk to her," said Simon. "It's urgent."

"According to our information, you're in close proximity to the man she was calculated away from. For security reasons we can't give you any further information."

Indridi set off at a run toward the immense glass wall and entered the vault. He stood there among the crowd in the middle of the floor, turning in circles.

"SIGRID! ANSWER ME, SIGRID!" he yelled. "SIGRID! WHERE ARE YOU, SIGRID?"

Escalators delivered thousands of people upstairs and thousands more descended to the underground station. The world spun around Indridi as he wandered despairingly among the hopeful thousands who had come to find love. He bumped into old people sitting expressionless in wheelchairs while their excited grandchildren ran laughing after Larry LoveDeath. He was ambushed by traps and harangued by howlers:

"Shop! Drink! Eat!"

"Take a stroll round the vaults!"

"Who knows, you may find your one and only!"

"I'M LOOKING FOR HER!" growled Indridi.

He accosted passersby, pulling out a picture of Sigrid, but received only smiles: "She's cute!" or a surly "No, thank you!" He was led astray by secret hosts who tried to direct him to nightclubs, fast-food chains, casinos, shops, and fairground rides: "I think I saw her at the StarDeath café." It was like looking for a drop in the ocean. He was carried by the flow and stranded at a table onto which he climbed, calling again and again over the crowd: "SIGRID!" until he could call no more and turned his eyes up to the vault where fulmars soared like angels, in and out of the giant air-conditioning vents. He turned in a circle and the vault spun around him until he fell dizzily to the floor. Simon marched up, dragged him out and back to the car.

"Indridi. Calm down. We must be methodical. Tell me about Sigrid."

"She's gorgeous," said Indridi.

"Indridi, be serious. What's Sigrid like? She doesn't like crowds or big cities, does she? She's more into suburbs, the seaside, grass, and trees, isn't she?"

Simon didn't need to ask. It stood clearly written in her dossier.

"How do you know that?" asked Indridi.

"I know more than you think. She's not here," said Simon, starting the car. He raced back down the valley to where green slopes replaced the glass wall. He turned off the road and drove along a tarmac footpath up the mountainside until they reached a viewing platform. The untouched Oxnadalur valley met their eyes. On the platform was a sign:

NO ADMITTANCE BEYOND THIS POINT
The valley is protected.
Don't bother the shepherd.

"Sigrid's happiest in peaceful surroundings, isn't she?"

"Yes," said Indridi.

"She's bound to have a view of the untouched Oxnadalur valley! She's bound to steer clear of the crush at the glass wall! It's our only chance. That she's sitting at a window, looking out over the valley. Run, Indridi! Run to higher ground. Run around the valley and she's bound to see you!"

"The valley's protected," said Indridi, dithering.

"Run!" screamed Simon.

Indridi opened the gate and ran down the stony slope with Simon on his heels. They slid down screes, clambered over rocky places, ran down heathery slopes, and followed narrow sheep-paths along the lake. Here and there windows opened in the rocks and angry employees or security guards bellowed at them.

"Get out!"

They ran up a low incline at the northern end of the lake and waved at the black rock face. They shouted and called but nowhere could they see Sigrid. Indridi looked at his watch and broke down.

"NO!" he yelled until the valley echoed.

It was twenty-five past eight.

"A MAN WALKED INTO A BAR"

SIGRID SAT IN THE RESTAURANT, CHEWING DEEP-FRIED PTARMIGAN.
She tried to remember a joke to have up her sleeve in case she
needed to break the ice and make Per laugh. "A man walked
into a bar . . ."

She looked at her watch; it was ten past eight and dusk was
falling over the valley. Suddenly she saw a man walk into the
room. There was no mistaking. It was Per Møller! Wearing a
blue suit and yellow short-sleeved shirt on which was printed:
Per Møller. He was better looking than she had expected and
wandered nervously around the restaurant, scanning the din-
ers, obviously in search of his one and only. Sigrid stood up,
smoothed down her dress and tried to smile. Per smiled and
apologized for being so late.

"Have you eaten?"

"Yes," she said, "I was so hungry."

Per sat down opposite her. He wore reflective sunglasses so all she could see were her own eyes in the silver lenses.

"Good," he said, looking around nervously.

"Is everything all right?" she asked.

Per stuck a fried potato in his mouth and licked the grease off his finger.

"Everything's great," he said, but he still seemed rather tense. "Everything's excellent. The biggest day of my life. It's just weird to meet you at last," he said, drumming his fingers. "All we need now is better music."

Per darted over to the bar and soon Sigrid's favorite song boomed from the speakers. The Cones' cover of a Beatles song that Boyz had made famous in their time. Sigrid was amazed when Per returned.

"That's my favorite song!" she said smiling.

Per smiled and wriggled. "Mine, too," he said. "I first heard it in Sicily."

"I've been to Sicily, too!" said Sigrid. "Where did you stay?"

"Sicily, fantastic place," said Per.

There was an awkward silence for a few seconds. Per cleared his throat several times. Sigrid wondered what to say, then remembered her joke. "A man walked into a bar . . ."

Per looked at her blankly.

Sigrid blushed. She tried to explain the punchline.

Per drummed his fingers. "Perhaps I'll have a beer to loosen up." He went to the bar and downed two bottles of beer, then came back, a fraction calmer. He sat down opposite her and held out his hand.

"Can I see your hand, Sigrid?"

Sigrid held out her hand shyly.

Per extended his middle finger and rubbed it against hers. All his attention was focused on this activity, so he didn't notice Sigrid looking at him strangely.

"What are you doing?" she asked.

He came to, whipped back his hand, and said awkwardly, "I just love rubbing fingers." He sweated. "Perhaps I'll have another beer."

A cordless iSTAR group manager was lying in pink swimming trunks under a palm tree on the Playa Azul beach in Costa Rica. The group manager oversaw around 120 service reps who were each in turn responsible for a 120-strong target group. The group manager resembled a stranded tortoise; his head seemed too small for his huge belly. His skin was as brown and shriveled as a medieval manuscript. He was sweating like a pig and scarlet in the face as he turned the air blue with curses, shouting at an absent computer operator.

"What the hell has he been up to? His monthly report is absurd. What's come over him?"

"We don't know yet; he's put an additional lock on his home zone," said the computer operator. "I'm going to try and break in by the back door."

"How can the turnover in his group have fallen by 90 percent in one month?" wailed the group manager.

"Don't ask me. You're supposed to pick up on these things," said the operator. "This service rep has obviously gone without surveillance for months; the lock was added four months ago."

The group manager didn't answer, just smothered himself in sun-tan oil.

"I'm in," said the operator. "Oh my God!" he burst out.

"What?"

"This is unbelievable."

"Connect me too, man!"

The operator connected the group manager to the service rep's home zone. The group manager was flabbergasted.

"I've never seen anything like it! Disconnect him this minute!"

Per swayed in time to the song that was booming around the room.

"I'm looking forward to going home and making something," he said. "How I do love handicrafts, and I'm really into old people, too."

"I work at an old people's home," said Sigrid, now astonished. She smiled her brightest smile for the first time.

"Oh, really?" said Per, humming along to the cover version of the cover version of the Beatles song. "Incredible, these old people's homes. My grandmother wanted to go to an old people's home, but we told her she might as well go straight to LoveDeath. She didn't listen, and then of course she got bored at the home."

"Not enough is done for the old," said Sigrid.

"No, but we couldn't amuse her! By the time she finally went to LoveDeath she had wasted millions on paying for the home, quite unnecessarily. Lots of homes seem to hang on to old people forever, just to make money . . ."

Sigrid couldn't think of anything to say. "Why don't you take off your sunglasses?" she said at last.

"My shades, yes," he said, smiling. "I'd forgotten about them."

Sigrid reached out for the glasses. "I want to see your eyes."

Per took her hands. "No, not yet." He glanced around furtively.

"What's the matter? Are you sure everything's okay?" she asked. "Are you looking for someone?"

"You're so cute I can hardly believe I'm at the right table," said Per, gazing at her. Sigrid looked around, smiling in embarrassment.

"Perhaps I'll have another beer," said Per and returned to the bar.

"He's seriously lost it," said the operator, rummaging through the service rep's files and scanning his visual report.

"Look at this! He's got this blonde on the brain!"

The group manager received the visual report.

"Twenty-four hours spent gawping at the same woman?"

"Twenty-four hours? Here's a whole week in her life. From morning to night! Her getting dressed, her in the shower . . . Hey! Look at this! She's getting down to it with her boyfriend. Incredibly imaginative, the young people nowadays!"

"Get on with it, please!"

"She slept for eight hours with him watching her the whole time. He's completely obsessed!"

The group manager was silent. He ran through the visual reports, fast-forwarding through endless hours of footage of the same girl.

"Ugh," said the operator as he opened a file. There were thousands of pictures of a man with text across his face:

KILL KILL KILL KILL KILL KILL KILL KILL KILL KILL
KILL KILL KILL KILL KILL KILL KILL KILL KILL KILL
KILL KILL KILL KILL KILL KILL KILL KILL KILL KILL
KILL KILL KILL KILL KILL KILL KILL KILL KILL KILL
KILL KILL KILL KILL KILL KILL KILL KILL!

There were digitally altered pictures of him with a bullet hole in his forehead, pictures of him with a bleeding wound on his neck. Pictures of him lying in a forest clearing with limbs amputated. "God, he's gone crazy, man!" said the operator. "You're in deep shit, Mr. Group Manager."

Per Møller staggered over from the bar. Full of self-confidence after the fifth beer, he went straight up to Sigrid, coughed, and said:

"Shall we go to your room? I've waited so long for my one and only that I'm feeling a bit . . ." He formed a ring with the thumb and forefinger of his left hand and poked the middle finger of his right hand into the hole, moving it in and out.

Sigrid looked at him and giggled, thinking he was joking, but apparently he wasn't. The sunglasses slipped down his nose and she looked into a pair of watery, slightly protuberant gray-blue eyes. She gazed deep into those eyes, waiting for the current that she had so often felt between herself and Indridi. She expected an indefinable feeling, a flash, sense of pleasure, shortness of breath. But his eyes were dull. She tried to work him out; he had a big mouth and long, bony fingers.

"I thought you wanted to talk," said Sigrid, seeking some way out.

"Maybe I'll bring along a beer," Per interrupted her. "I'll die if I don't have a Tuborg after sex."

"Maybe I should have a beer, too," said Sigrid. She had a great knot in her stomach and looked around for a butterfly. She saw one and latched on to the hope that it was a concealed camera. This could be one of inLOVE's candid camera shows, in which she had been calculated away from her love merely in order to create suspense before her true match was revealed. Then everyone would laugh and joke and all would be well. Of course, she mustn't judge Per from their first half hour together, but this couldn't be scientifically proven love.

"You're not having a beer. Go into the bedroom and get yourself warm and wet for me."

He took out a package and gave it to her.

"Thanks," said Sigrid, blushing. She meant to take his hand politely, but Per lunged at her and stuck his tongue down her throat.

"There's more," said the computer operator. "He's fiddled with their connections. He's made himself a complete middleman. All their business and communications have been going via his home zone, no wonder he's been neglecting his target group . . ."

The group manager was speechless and the operator sent him a bunch of texts.

"Here are more than one hundred hostings that he's bought on his own tab, look here: [FREE YOURSELF, SIGRID]. He's employed a secret host as a subcontractor to work on them. Did you really not notice this? Don't you have a surveillance program?"

"Open the text files!"

The operator opened the text files. [Victim of freedom . . . Cool competition for secret hosts! Project: Indridi Haraldsson. Mercy trip with LoveDeath. Seventy-five percent commission!]

"Open hunting license and 75 percent commission!" said the operator.

"What nonsense is this?" said the group manager. "LoveDeath doesn't pay anyone 75 percent commission. He's paid for the trip out of his own pocket!"

"Open hunting license," said the operator heavily. "That's totally prohibited except in exceptional circumstances."

"He certainly didn't get permission from me," said the group manger.

"Dear, oh dear, is there no end to this?"

"What?"

"Look! Here are some wave images that were supposed to go to inLOVE. Compare the images!"

"What?" asked the group manager.

"Can't you see that he's falsified the woman's inLOVE assessment? He's sent inLOVE an image of his own wave and registered it under her name! He's had himself fraudulently calculated, the son of a bitch!"

"What the fuck?" said the group manager.

"You should have picked up on this," said the operator sternly. "I'll have to let the inspection department know!"

"Just a second," said the group manager.

"What?"

"This is a bit embarrassing for me. You must see that. I'll take care of Per; he won't get any more assignments. I'll find a new service rep. I'll pay you well for your help. This won't go any further . . ."

"You're a beautiful girl," said Per, taking a slurp from a bottle of Tuborg. He put it down and grabbed Sigrid's ass in full view of the restaurant. "You're a hot chick," he said, holding it tight with his left hand and groping up her skirt with the right. Nimbly he slid her underwear aside and stroked a finger from her pubic hair up her crack as if skimming cream off a cake. He licked his finger and said: "You're my one and only; you're a warm, beautiful, gorgeous girl."

DISENGAGE:
BURN BODIES

DUSK WAS FALLING AND THERE WAS LITTLE CHANCE OF INDRIDI'S finding Sigrid now. It was almost half past eight; it was too late. Puffins sang in the late summer calm, cows lowed, a shepherd called in the distance, and Indridi lost heart. Somewhere deep inside the lofty rock apartments the fair Sigrid had been matched with Per Møller. LOVESTAR twinkled behind a cloud. From time to time flashes from LoveDeath lit up LavaRock, etching its outline sharp as the knife that was turning in Indridi's heart. Booms followed the flashes, echoing in the valley like heavy sobs. A mist crept down the valley and a cool drizzle from LoveDeath dampened his face. He descended from the knoll and headed toward the mountain, down a small gully where a stream skipped between rocks and grassy banks into a small pond, and there he walked with bowed shoulders to the rock wall. He probably hadn't cried this much since the day he was reborn. Now, grievously wounded, sorrow gushed from his heart.

When Per licked his stubby finger, Sigrid could hardly grasp what was going on; she had nearly thrown up when he stuck his tongue right down to her tonsils. His mouth was full of beer and potato chips. She stared at him with disgust and horror, clamped her thighs together, and tried to loosen his grip as Per reached for his Tuborg. He was fairly drunk by now.

"Take your present. I'll be along shortly."

Sigrid ran out of the restaurant, leaving Per waiting calmly by the bar. Sigrid took the elevator down and opened Per's gift. It was an Anthon Berg chocolate and a video cover with a picture of Per on the front. He was standing bare-chested in unzipped jeans behind a bare-breasted woman in a nurse's uniform who was bending over, the letter "M" of "Møller" obscuring what exactly they were up to. Sigrid's head had been stuck onto the nurse's body and Per's head was two sizes too big for the man's torso. The gift was accompanied by a yellow note:

"I'm famous. You can warm up with the film."

Sigrid shuddered, threw away the package, and rushed out of the elevator. She ran as fast as her legs would carry her, searching for a way out. The ceiling was made of glass with trout swimming to and fro across it. She ran past a door opening into a large conference room. A small waterfall fell into a pond outside and a gray horse was grazing on the bank. She ran down another corridor until she got to her room, locked the door, and flung her belongings into a suitcase while looking around for something sharp to defend herself with. Taking care not to turn her back to the door, she found a nail file and aimed it at the entrance.

She got gooseflesh, felt as if someone was standing behind her, looked slowly over her shoulder, and screamed. A dark figure was lurking in the dusk outside the stone bay window.

It was a weeping man. She peered at the silhouette.

"Indridi?" she whispered. "INDRIDI!"

He didn't hear her. He stood bowed down by the rock. Sigrid fumbled for a button or emergency exit and finally found a lever that opened the rock like a sliding door. She stepped barefoot from the rock in her white dress, out on to the dewy grass, and gently touched his hand.

"Indridi dear, don't cry. It's all right. I'm with you."

Indridi looked at her and they embraced as if they were embracing for the first time, and they embraced as if they were embracing for the last time, and they embraced the embrace of those who wish to embrace forever until death does them part, and they wept, kissed, and gazed into one another's eyes until Sigrid said:

"I'm sorry, my darling. I'll never leave you again."

Sigrid looked up at the sky; dusk had fallen. LavaRock towered above them. LOVESTAR twinkled behind a cloud and there was a shooting star.

"Someone just died," whispered Sigrid.

High up on LavaRock in a small lighting tower Ragnar Ö. Karlsson, moodman for death, kept track of the global position of LoveStar's private jet on his eye-lens. He had already organized the Million Star Festival in his head: as the jet descended and came in to land, a hundred million stars would fall from heaven.

When LoveStar stepped out of the plane, he would set foot on an earth that was finally purified of death and decay.

Ragnar connected himself to the iSTAR mother base and with the old password obtained access to speech-center orders. There he entered another password that opened access to cordless mankind. He weighed up a few possible sentences but decided to keep the message plain and simple:

WORD: [THE MILLION STAR FESTIVAL!] :WORD

He contemplated the message for a few seconds while CON-FIRM flashed before his eyes. He confirmed and was tempted to add a sentence to greet LoveStar as he stepped from the plane:

WORD: [HAIL TO LOVESTAR!] :WORD

He connected himself to the LoveDeath mother base. There he registered using yet another password, and an image of the earth viewed from space appeared before him. He gazed entranced at his creation: the Million Star Belt coiling round the earth like a silver serpent. A menu flashed before Ragnar:

[DISENGAGE? : BURN BODIES?]

LoveStar's jet began its descent, from forty thousand feet to thirty thousand, then down to twenty thousand feet. Ragnar raised his hands like the conductor of an orchestra. He touched the menu:

[DISENGAGE : BURN BODIES]

Back on the hill, Simon hesitated in disappointment, sighing as he watched Indridi walk away with bowed head and eventually lean, hunched over, against the rock face. Although he was worried about leaving the car on the mountain ridge and keeping an eye out for security guards, he decided to sit down among the hillocks, keep a low profile, and give Indridi time to recover. Suddenly a bright opening appeared in the wall beside Indridi and a white-clad woman stepped barefoot from the rock. She embraced Indridi and Simon was amazed at the sight; it was Sigrid. She embraced Indridi and he envied . . . NO! He was HAPPY for Indridi. Deep in his heart he was happy for Indridi and Sigrid, and his eyes filled with tears. He gave a sigh of relief, filling his lungs with air fragrant with cinquefoil and forget-me-nots. He wanted to shout for joy but controlled himself because he didn't want to spoil this beautiful image in the half-darkness: a man embracing a barefoot woman on the dewy grass. He watched them smiling and fumbled at his own chest in surprise as he felt a tickling above his midriff: "I think I know where happiness lies," he thought, breathing deeply, like a parched man slaking his thirst in a mountain stream. "Happiness lies here," he thought, trying to hold his breath and see how long he could hold on to the feeling. As he held his breath, he heard heavy panting behind him. He looked over his shoulder and saw, to his terror, the most fearsome beast he had ever set eyes on.

"WOLF!" he whispered. "WOLF!!!" he yelled. "WOLF, WOLF!!!"

The Big Bad Wolf leapt over Simon, showing him its pale belly. He watched the beast run puffing and blowing down the grassy gully, straight to the rock where Indridi was clasping Sigrid with eyes shut in an intimate, unsuspecting embrace. The wolf swallowed them both in one mouthful, darted in through the rock opening and flopped down on Sigrid's soft bed. There it lay snoring when Per staggered in wearing a red dressing gown, a beer bottle in his hand. His gown hung open and his erect penis was smeared in Anthon Berg chocolate.

"They say you like marzipan . . ." Per came to an abrupt halt when he saw the wolf in the bed. "Sigrid, are you sick?"

He stared rigidly at the monster, which lay snoring under the blanket with eyes the size of saucers and teeth as sharp as the spikes around the palace at Amalienborg. He went warily over to the wolf and lifted the blanket.

"Hey, Sigrid! Why have you got eight breasts?" he moaned before recoiling in terror and running screaming from the rock, straight into Simon, who croaked when he saw Per with his flopping penis and flapping dressing gown.

A momentary silence. Their eyes met and they both shouted simultaneously:

"THE MILLION STAR FESTIVAL!"

A strange hush descended on the world and they looked up at the sky.

Bright dots appeared in heaven like a hundred thousand red-glowing mouse eyes in the darkness.

DISTRESS FLARE

GRIM STOOD ON THE GLASS BRIDGE AND SAW THAT MT. ESJA WAS wearing a black cloud cap. He had never seen the mountain wearing a black cap before. A white cap is called a cirrus cloud, his grandmother had said, and forms in a northerly wind. But what wind forms a black cap?

He received a message from the security firm:

[wolf still not found]

Sigrun from the Mickey department rang in a panic. "Send your eyes over here THIS MINUTE!"

Grim went cold when he saw the scene. The walls were all splattered with blood, and Sigrun was standing cursing in front of a cage full of lumps of meat and bloodied fur.

"What happened?" asked Grim. "Are you all right?"

"The new generation is even worse," said Sigrun. "Mickey 8.04 seemed gentler on the surface, but he repressed his rage until he burst. See for yourself." She sent him a film clip: Mickey was sitting in a cage. He growled, baring his teeth, and tried to bite a member of staff, but, when he was prevented, his head turned as red as a toadstool and burst with a bang.

"I don't understand this," said Sigrun.

"Didn't you put more rabbit into him?"

"I had to remove it again; their eyes got bigger and softer, but there were problematic side effects. They became so horny."

"What about the tortoise addition?"

"That didn't work either. It had a calming effect, of course, but they'd live forever."

"Destroy that generation, then," said Grim heavily. "We'll start on Mickey 9.01 first thing tomorrow morning. I'll let iSTAR know. I warned them about possible delays."

Grim was filled with trepidation as he watched the black cap crawling over the mountain. iSTAR's patience was wearing thin, and for a moment he felt as if something dreadful was brewing. Grim tried to distract his thoughts by watching the news. A report from Paris: when the citizens woke up in the morning, the Arctic terns had vanished; no one knew where they had gone, but they had left the city strangely silent and empty. Next came another item about animals. All around the world, sea creatures had started coming ashore. He watched clip after clip of beaches covered in a seething mass of capelin, dolphins, minke whales, cod, jellyfish, and sea scorpions. The animals thronged ashore, tumbling in the surf and rotting on the sand while gulls and ravens tore at the carcasses.

Grim was about to turn off the news when an advertisement appeared on his lens.

A picture appeared of an ordinary middle-class Chinese home (the largest target group). A tomcat sprayed the carpet and a woman made a sour face, but then her child came in with its Mickey, made it spray over the cat pee and then rubbed it off. They walked around the apartment with the Mickey, making it pee, and, lo and behold, everything was shining clean. The cat was kicked out and the child hugged its Mickey lovingly. The advertisement was computer animated. The child wouldn't have survived two seconds with a real Mickey in its arms. Then came the slogan.

NOW EVERYONE CAN OWN A MICKEY!
MICKEYS! BETTER THAN DOGS OR CATS!

Grim blanched. This wasn't an attachment intended solely for him but a real ad for the Chinese family market. For a billion people. He called iSTAR immediately.

"Was that intended for my eyes only?"

"No," said the man. "Everyone's in the Mickey target group."

"But they're not ready! How many times do I have to tell you?"

"We've done surveys. People find them irresistible."

"Mickeys are extremely dangerous!"

"Mickeys are what the people want. It's too late to stop the campaign."

"NO! It's impossible!"

"It's out of your hands."

"I'm not delivering a single Mickey until they're ready. They have to be good-natured and neutered, with a short lifespan. That was the plan and I'm sticking to it!"

"The Mickeys are already being distributed to the Chinese market. Production is going ahead at full speed. Don't worry. Their temperament, fertility, and lifespan will be controlled by drugs."

"You don't know what you're doing! Where did you get the formula?"

"The formula for Mickey 8.04 was sent to the factories in Brazil and China. The initial production capacity is a million Mickeys per month. The campaign has been launched. There's no way of stopping a campaign once it's off the ground."

"My superiors at the Science Council will stop you!"

"We spoke to our subordinates at the Science Council. They deemed it possible with appropriate countermeasures. We'll take the greatest care. The breeding units are designed to withstand a nuclear attack."

The Mood Division was completely out of touch with reality.

"The campaign is supposed to follow us, not vice versa!" yelled Grim and hung up.

Suddenly Grim realized that the fault did not lie with the Mood Division. It lay with human nature. The Mickeys were soft and white as seal cubs with huge, innocent eyes, tailor-made and rigorously tested to make people like them. Even though they were utterly savage, humans were incapable of fearing them. Nature itself couldn't have come up with a more cunning predator in a hundred million years.

Grim was filled with a terrible regret. He regretted having let himself be tricked into the Mickey research. He didn't believe in anything under iSTAR control that went by the name of science, but now he needed some form of mental solace. Confirmation that he had made the right decision in spite of everything. For the first time in his life he was tempted to check out REGRET. He connected himself and asked:

"What would have happened if I had turned down the Mickey project?"

He ticked the ten-thousand-point answer. REGRET responded five minutes later:

"iSTAR would have made you develop a drug that would enable mammals to evolve from day to day instead of over millions of years. iSTAR would have added the drug to the drinking-water supply with the result that in the morning people would have developed huge legs to run to work but once there, their legs would have shrunk and dangled from their bodies like two warts while their brains became grotesquely enlarged, their eyes bulged, and hearts swelled in order to make their hands type at high speed on the computer, while at lunchtime people evolved back into their old forms, though slightly better-looking, more muscular and firmer with a straighter nose, a curl in their hair, a handsome set of pecs, and pert buttocks and piercing great eyes for the girls in the grocery store, whose breasts grew in competition over the customers' compliments and whose lips plumped and arms multiplied until there were two to pack the shopping, one to operate the cash register, one to reach for a packet of chewing gum, one to fiddle with their hair and adjust their bras, and a seventh to receive a note saying: How about this evening? Answer: Yes. Then hormones flooded their bodies, their breasts continued to grow, the man's penis grew like bamboo (which can grow up to three feet a day) and they met up looking glamorous at a bar and pumped the scent of pheromones into the air while at home the sex glands upped their production until the man turned into one giant python-like penis and the woman was nothing more than mouth, breasts, vagina, and clitoris, and their two tongues writhed like uncontrollable fire hoses and their hearts pumped pure endorphin and orgasm and happiness through their bodies until nourishment was required, at which point mouth-tentacles darted into the kitchen and sucked dry the fridge, cans, and jars in order to build up more energy and produce more endorphin, while other tentacles wriggled into the water supply in search of water to cool them and drive their growth, and in the end hunger drove all the tentacles from all the houses out into the street where they met and felt the stimulation along with the hunger and need for more energy and nourishment to satisfy their growing bodies and everywhere there were mouths in search of flesh or vegetable matter to feed on until the bodies had eaten every last bird, every last child, and every last cat in the neighborhood before uniting to form tubes that sucked water up from springs, and a huge colon which delivered feces to the sea, and a giant jaw that raced around the oceans like a sea monster, devouring plankton and whales, seals, and shoals of capelin to satisfy its insatiable body, and the flesh spread over the world, growing thick hair at the Arctic but further south breasts grew to the sky in vain competition over sunlight and suntan, milk leaked from the breast mountains and down into valleys while penises grew like mushrooms on the flesh, titillated by hailstorms, gushing sperm like shoals of herring which spattered, drying out in the sun, onto the browning skin which dried out and split until it spurted blood like a volcano until the flesh couldn't find any more life to suck up to itself and rotted and became maggot-ridden while on the flesh flowers and trees eventually grew, and the layer of flesh became buried deep in the earth where it compressed into thick, black oil. This could have been pumped out millions of years later and fed into cars and you could have felt the lust flowing up into your body when you put your foot down on the gas pedal."

Grim shook his head and read REGRET one more time. He had paid 10,000 points for this but didn't understand a word.

"Bullshit," he muttered, "this REGRET is total bullshit." He spat, then abruptly shouted:

"THE MILLION STAR FESTIVAL!"

He became one voice in a choir of billions.

He looked up at the sky and saw red dots appearing in heaven like distress flares sent up by a thousand million drowning sailors.

DON'T DISTURB
THE WORLD

A WOMAN SAT IN LAEKJARTORG SQUARE, WAITING FOR A BUS. The time was 11:20 PM. She had been waiting a long time for the right bus, probably two weeks. She checked REGRET.

"What would have happened if I'd taken the Number 113 at 8:56 PM?"

"You'd have been killed."

"How?"

"The world would have ended."

The woman was overwhelmed with an indescribably comforting feeling. She breathed easier. "That was a good thing," she thought. "It was a good thing I didn't take the bus at 8:56 PM. I've saved the world," she thought happily as she watched people going about their daily business. "The world would have ended if I'd taken the 113, yet no one bothers to thank me," she thought, looking around in the hope of finding a half-eaten hot

295

dog. She had just crawled under the bench and was reaching for a drink can when she looked up and saw a man in a dark suit looming over her. He was accompanied by a lanky teenager.

"You're coming with us. That's enough of this. You're coming with us now."

The woman was crazed with terror. She shook her head. "No!" she cried, locking her fingers on the bench. "No, I'm not coming."

"Mom, come with us. It's all right. We'll look after you."

"NO! The world might end."

"There, there. You need rest. You need a bath and clean clothes; we'll be very gentle."

The woman closed her eyes and shook her head, sobbing. "No, you don't understand. I mustn't disturb the world! I MUSTN'T DISTURB THE WORLD!!!"

The man nodded to the younger one and they each took one of the woman's arms and led her between them into bus number 113. She struggled against them, screaming and kicking, but they managed to drag her onto the bus. They sat on the back seat with her between them, holding her tight until the bus set off. The woman stopped fighting.

"We're going home now, Mom," said the man as the bus raced down the highway.

"You don't know what you're doing," sobbed the woman. "You mustn't disturb the world! You mustn't disturb . . ."

"THE MILLION STAR FESTIVAL!" yelled every single passenger on the bus.

Everyone looked enchanted at the red spots in the sky as they headed for earth, but the woman closed her eyes.

"I told you the world would end! I told you!"

LICHEN

LOVESTAR SAT IN THE PLANE WITH THE SEED IN HIS HAND.
The scheduled landing was in twenty minutes, and he had lost
control over time. He felt the plane was either cleaving the air
at seven times the speed of sound or else hanging dead still. At
those moments everything went quiet and the air was filled with
a thick, muted silence and the engines turned like a windmill
in a gentle breeze. He looked out; there was ice in the air and
the frost grew like lichen on the wings of the plane, settling
on the windows as though someone had breathed on them.
LoveStar tried to say something aloud to himself, but nothing
could be heard except a long-drawn-out moan [m]. LoveStar
spied a small hole in the frost. He peered down to earth at a
moon-gray desert while the lichen grew on the wings, but then
time suddenly jerked into motion again, the frost melted in an
instant, and LoveStar screeched:

"THE MILLION STAR FESTIVAL!"

He nearly jumped out of his skin and the seed fell to the floor.

He flung himself on all fours, searching for it in desperation. "How dare he make ME howl?" he choked, stretching under a table, sighing with relief when he saw the seed and picking it up with infinite care. He examined the seed in his hand; it was gray and there was no vibration. "Perhaps it's dead," he thought, horror-struck. He would step out of the plane before the whole world with a DEAD seed in his hand. He had to be sure that it was alive, so he decided to send it a prayer. He clasped his hands around the seed and prayed to God: "Dear God, don't let the seed die," but the seed did not vibrate. He clenched his teeth and looked around. He had to have confirmation. "Perhaps you have to say: You who are in the place," he thought and shuddered at the thought, but he had to try. He had to see what would happen, so he closed his eyes, clasped his hands, and directed the prayer ardently and sincerely to the man who held the seed: "Dear LoveStar, don't let the seed die." The prayer boomed as if in a hollow space, echoing in his head, then a short circuit shot an arrow into his heart and stopped its beating for an instant. LoveStar gasped and fumbled at his chest. "Strange," he thought, "you're not aware of your heart until it stops beating."

When he opened his eyes the plane was bathed in red rays. He squinted out of the window and saw that the sky was studded all over with red dots, making the land below no longer moon-gray but fiery red. The plane began its descent.

Time stood still, turning a split second into an hour. He heard a heavy sound like drawn-out thunder, like a bottomless bass. The lights were sucked out of the windows, and the plane slowly rolled belly up. It happened so slowly that he could easily follow the movement. He listened harder and heard the sound as a very slow noise. When the plane was upside down he made his way calmly to the front and opened the flight cabin door, but there was nothing there. He was confronted with a yawning black sky, studded all over with glowing bodies that hung as if in a sling, all at the same height. One of them had just shorn the flight cabin off the plane. He looked down at the reddish-white glacier and knew that this was where he was headed, so he tightened his fist about the seed and stepped out into the night.

He fell to earth like a snowflake in a blizzard, and though the air friction was enough to rip off his clothes, he did not feel the cold because every split second was like an hour, and for ten hours his life played through his head like a developing film. When he smashed into the glacier he felt nothing. The pain signals could not pass up his broken spine to his brain. He looked up and wondered how far he had fallen. He saw LOVESTAR twinkling behind the bodies, unaware that his leg was missing, his liver had burst, and his heart was shattered. LOVESTAR twinkled faintly and went out. Someone just died, thought LoveStar, clenching his hand tighter round the seed.

THE MILLION
STAR FESTIVAL

"THE MILLION STAR FESTIVAL!" THE WORLD HOWLED WITH ONE VOICE. In every house, in every town, in every city people howled these same words. They echoed through the corridors of mental hospitals; they were heard from the nurseries of maternity wards; they resounded in parliament chambers and the managerial offices of multinationals, exposing burglars and hired assassins. "THE MILLION STAR FESTIVAL!" burst from the mouths of newsreaders, chat-show hosts, secret hosts, howlers, sportsmen, and buskers. Women moaned it at the height of orgasm, men shrieked it as they begged for mercy and gasped it in place of dying words. "THE MILLION STAR FESTIVAL!" people said in their sleep and woke to dead silence. Everyone in the world rushed to windows and out into streets or up onto roofs, where they stood, gazing up at the sky, whether it was day or night, clear or cloudy, rain or storm. The world stood silent, waiting for the Million Star Festival. There was not a sound, not a whisper, nothing at all, not a whistle or a song when a million red dots appeared in the sky.

Instead of burning up with a flash or glitter, the bodies fell in a red glow, and the world had never seen such beauty. All went according to plan for the LoveDeath Mood Division, and the bodies fell faster and grew hotter, turned as yellow as candle flames and left trails in heaven like golden rain, giving rise to exclamations of wonder all over the world.

After four minutes, the bodies blazed green, then rapidly turned bluish-white like welding flames, and finally glowed white, clearer and brighter than the sun. Over every human being on earth appeared a thousand suns that spanned the vault of heaven from east to west and north to south, bathing the children of earth in a pure white light so that no one cast a shadow. The suns were brilliant and all heading to earth at twenty thousand miles an hour.

Simon closed his eyes, Per closed his eyes, Yamaguchi closed her eyes, and so did Grim at the Puffin Factory. All over earth people closed their eyes; many fell on their faces, looking away from the glare and turning to the earth. Just as their eyes closed, the first booms sounded. Heavy, dreadful, menacing booms, but no one could see what was happening because the brightness had blinded them even through their eyelids.

Now something happened that the moodmen hadn't bargained for. The costumes were so thick that instead of burning up entirely, they heated up like hotplates and inside the costumes human flesh boiled, simmered, and bubbled. When 180-pound bodies fell from a height of six thousand miles, hitting the earth at twenty thousand miles an hour, the energy released was equivalent to a medium-sized nuclear reaction.

There was an immense crack as a hundred million bodies crashed simultaneously to earth. The ensuing earthquake was greater than any experienced since man first walked the planet. Harmless old women thundered through seventy-story skyscrapers before blasting the foundations from under them, and thus the glowing bodies rained down over the world. Thus houses crumbled and cities exploded, and fires were ignited that burnt up forests and harvests all over the earth. The bodies smashed the glass wall and shell of Oxnadalur. They smashed the Statue of Liberty, and they smashed the LoveStar temples in major cities. The bodies brought down airships and airplanes and crashed into the ocean, raising waves that sank ships and washed coastal cities out to sea. The bodies broke up the iSTAR headquarters, burned out the howler center, and turned the whole cordless world into howlers one last time.

"Hail to LoveStar!"

Every mouth howled these words as cities burned, fields went up in flames, the oceans boiled, and mountains were razed to the ground.

In the depths of Oxnadalur in an out-of-the-way corner of the theme park, there was a room quarried in the rock of a narrow gully. There Indridi and Sigrid were aware of nothing but the heartbeat and snores of the wolf. They lay pressed together inside the wolf, as if sewn into a haggis, and the world may have shaken from the human rain, but it was nothing compared to the booming of a snoring wolf. Indridi caressed Sigrid's breasts, while she took a firm hold of his penis with sensitive fingers and directed him to the right place to prolong their embrace. Thus they made love in the wolf's stomach while the world crumbled outside.

JOURNEY'S END

ALL WAS QUIET WHEN INDRIDI UNZIPPED THE SNORING WOLF THE following morning. He crawled out and saw that the animal was covered in gray dust. He held his nose: the air was thick with a stench of death. He peered around and saw that the room was also covered in dust, making the daylight so gray that he hardly had to squint to accustom his eyes to the light. Outside nothing could be heard but the desolate moaning of the wind and the crackling of fires. Sigrid poked her head out through the opening and made a face.

"It smells of 'money,'" she said, holding her nose. "I've never known it so strong."

The wolf woke up when Indridi zipped up its stomach and straightaway began to wash Indridi and Sigrid, licking them high and low as they stared anxiously around, trying to work out what had happened to the world. A great rock blocked the door to the passage and the stone bay window facing the gully was broken. Sigrid slipped on her shoes and they stepped outside.

The valley was pitch black, the ground so hot that it smoked, and all the grass and heather had been scorched away. Melted fat mingled with blood poured down the stream bed. They picked their way carefully, as if the earth was a thin crust over geothermal springs. Above them towered the peak of LavaRock, broken and sharp as an arrow stabbing the gray clouds. Neither speaking a word, they held hands and tried to send their eyes around the world but saw only interference, burned-out ruins, and scorched earth.

The wolf sniffed the air and followed some scent until she found a burst heart below a blackened human head. She pushed at the head with her gray paw, causing it to fall with a splash into the stream of blood. Beneath the head, tatters of red dressing gown were revealed.

Sigrid covered her eyes.

"Let's get out of here, Indridi!" she said.

Indridi stared stiffly at the man's head as it rolled down the gully, but Sigrid burst into noisy tears and screamed until the silence echoed:

"LET'S GET OUT OF HERE, INDRIDI!!!"

Indridi put his arms around the wolf's great head and whispered in her ear, "Save us, dear wolf! Carry us away from here!"

The wolf lay down. Indridi leapt on her back and Sigrid mounted behind him. The wolf clambered over rocks and screes and up slippery slopes until they reached the mountain ridge. On the peaks facing them, flames rose from the hydrogen spouts of the launchpads; through the smoke and haze they saw that the glacier had melted and the bodies from the cold stores had been washed away by the flood and lay among the scorched remains of the LoveDeath airships, buckled containers, and toasted buses. A blackened star hung on the remnants of the glass wall.

They headed up on to the moors and raced over gullies and past ravines, around craters and over rocks. Everywhere they saw the same blackness and from all over the land rose the choking stench of death. The wolf panted, her tongue hung out, but she didn't slow her pace.

The wolf ran along the highland freeway, and Indridi and Sigrid closed their eyes to avoid seeing the people who sat at the scorched steering wheels of their cars. Planes circled in the sky. They tried to wave to them, send them a signal, but in the end the planes' fuel ran out and they plummeted to earth. The wolf ran through the buckled forest of iron where the electricity pylons met, jumping over buzzing power lines, which coiled like poisonous snakes shooting sparks.

Ribbons of smoke rose and formed dark clouds that swam across the sky like sharp-toothed whales. When they mounted a low hill it appeared as if one of the clouds had fallen to earth. A glacier lay before them, dirty and sandy as a black sperm whale, its tail burst to reveal its white blubber, the river bleeding from it, rusty red and steaming.

"Now it's up to you, dear wolf," said Indridi, patting the wolf's grimy coat. "Now it's up to you."

They dismounted and the wolf preceded them on to the glacier. It was growing cooler, and though they were stiff from tiredness and hunger they could not stop. They made detours around crevasses, their feet soaked and their clothes offering little protection. On the highest point of the glacier the wolf lay down and refused to go any further. Indridi lay down beside her.

"There's no point, Sigrid," said Indridi. "We might as well die here."

Instead of lying down beside him, Sigrid stood shivering in the chill wind, peering around, and spotted a small bump. She stared harder and saw a hand emerging from the glacier. Sigrid went closer and found an old man lying frozen in the ice, his body apparently shattered, his skull all out of shape, his eyes wide open.

"I've found a man," said Sigrid.

"Let him be," said Indridi, weeping. "Everything's dead. There's no point, Sigrid."

Sigrid bent down and opened the white hand. A small seed was revealed. It was green.

"Indridi. I've found a seed!"

Sigrid took the seed carefully from the man's hand. When she looked up she saw a gleam of light at the edge of the glacier. Her heart was filled with pure hope.

"Come on, Indridi!"

Sigrid dragged Indridi away and the wolf followed at a snail's pace. Sigrid led the group with the seed in her hand, and in this way they walked over the white desert, heading for the ray of light. As they drew nearer the glacier became sandier and dirtier, and at last they saw that the sunbeam ended in a grassy valley surrounded by white glaciers on every side. Clouds hid the peaks, but above the valley the sky was clear. Sigrid took a deep breath.

"There's no smell of death here," she said.

They walked down into the valley and found a fallen helicopter. In it lay two lifeless pilots like abandoned chicks in a nest. An iron cable ran from the helicopter and they followed it to a grassy hump and in the hump they found a door. They opened the door and looked around; light shone in through a torn window screen. There was no one to be seen in the house but the beds were made. Indridi was hungry; he searched everywhere for something edible but in vain. One room was full of boxes, marked National Museum. They opened one; it was full of swords.

The wolf howled with hunger and Sigrid stroked its pelt. Indridi went out with a sword and an old cauldron. He dismembered the pilots, boiled down their flesh, minced it, and made little bundles that he put in the wolf's stomach. That evening milk began to leak from her teats.

"Mmmm, honey . . ." came their murmurs from the darkness.

The following morning Sigrid went out into the yard with a pot, which she filled with soil. With gentle fingers she pushed the seed into the soil and patted the earth lightly over it. Then she heard a bird screech.

"An Arctic tern?" she thought.

Sigrid called Indridi out of the house and together they watched a white cloud passing like a ribbon of fog down the valley until it was full of terns.

"Terns," said Indridi. "So the world hasn't ended."

Sigrid held the pot and looked at the marks her fingers had made in the soil.

"A seed becomes a forest."

About the Author

Andri Snær Magnason is one of Iceland's most celebrated young writers. He has written poetry, plays, fiction, and non-fiction, and in 2009 he co-directed the documentary *Dreamland*, which was based on his book *Dreamland: A Self-Help Manual for a Frightened Nation*. In 2002 *LoveStar* was named "Novel of the Year" by Icelandic booksellers and received the DV Literary Award and a nomination for the Icelandic Literary Prize. His children's book, *The Story of the Blue Planet*—now published or performed in twenty-six countries—was the first children's book to receive the Icelandic Literary Prize, and was also the recipient of the Janusz Korczak Honorary Award and the West Nordic Children's Book Prize. Andri is the winner of the 2010 Kairos Award.

About the Translator

Victoria Cribb was born in England but spent a number of years traveling, studying, and working in Iceland, as a translator, journalist, and publisher. She has degrees from the University of Cambridge, University College London, and the University of Iceland. Her translations from Icelandic include *The Blue Fox*, *From the Mouth of the Whale*, and *The Whispering Muse* by Sjón (all published in the UK by Telegram); *Stone Tree* by Gyrðir Elíasson (Comma Press); and *Arctic Chill* (with Bernard Scudder), *Hypothermia*, and *Operation Napoleon* by Arnaldur Indriðason (all published in the UK by Harvill Secker). Her translation of *The Blue Fox* was long-listed for the Independent Foreign Fiction Prize in 2009, and her translations of *Arctic Chill* and *Hypothermia* were short-listed for the CWA International Dagger in 2007 and 2010, respectively. She is currently studying for a PhD in Old Icelandic literature at Cambridge, where she lives with her partner.

About Seven Stories Press

Seven Stories Press is an independent book publisher based in New York City. We publish works of the imagination by such writers as Nelson Algren, Russell Banks, Octavia E. Butler, Ani DiFranco, Assia Djebar, Ariel Dorfman, Coco Fusco, Barry Gifford, Martha Long, Luis Negron, Hwang Sok-yong, Lee Stringer, and Kurt Vonnegut, to name a few, together with political titles by voices of conscience, including Subhankar Banerjee, the Boston Women's Health Collective, Noam Chomsky, Angela Y. Davis, Human Rights Watch, Derrick Jensen, Ralph Nader, Loretta Napoleoni, Gary Null, Greg Palast, Project Censored, Barbara Seaman, Alice Walker, Gary Webb, and Howard Zinn, among many others. Seven Stories Press believes publishers have a special responsibility to defend free speech and human rights, and to celebrate the gifts of the human imagination, wherever we can. In 2012 we launched Triangle Square *books for young readers* with strong social justice and narrative components, telling personal stories of courage and commitment. For additional information, visit www.sevenstories.com